HOMEWRECKER
INCORPORATED

S. Simone Chavous

Without love, marriage is just business. At least that's what Claudia Mason tells the women who seek her firm's unique services. With wealthy husbands who see their wedding rings as meaningless pieces of jewelry, they trust Claudia to do whatever is necessary to gather the hard evidence needed to shatter an ironclad prenup.

She is the best in the business and has yet to meet a mark she couldn't get the goods on, solidifying her belief no man can be trusted. After landing a client who is her ticket to retirement, she is on top of the world. Until a chance encounter with Greyston Michaels turns her carefully controlled world upside down.

Greyston shows Claudia a part of herself she thinks she's lost, making her question everything she believes about men--and love. But in Claudia's world, following her heart is bad for business. And business is everything.

Homewrecker Incorporated is an 85,000 word standalone novel best suited for mature readers

For Mom, I miss you everyday.

Table of Contents

Prologue - 1
Chapter 1 - 5
Chapter 2 - 18
Chapter 3 - 34
Chapter 4 - 51
Chapter 5 - 60
Chapter 6 - 67
Chapter 7 - 73
Chapter 8 - 110
Chapter 9 - 121
Chapter 10 - 134
Chapter 11 - 155
Chapter 12 - 173
Chapter 13 - 191
Chapter 14 - 202
Chapter 15 - 221
Chapter 16 - 238
Chapter 17 - 252
Chapter 18 - 257
Chapter 19 - 263
Chapter 20 - 275
Chapter 21 - 281
Chapter 22 - 287
Chapter 23 - 292
Chapter 24 - 300
Chapter 25 - 308
Epilogue - 312

Prologue

"What the hell, Claudia?"

I looked up from my theory of architecture textbook. Grace Dawson, my new roommate, glared at me from the doorway of our dorm room with her hand on her hip.

"You were supposed to get dressed while I was gone. The party started almost two hours ago!"

I glanced down. "What's wrong with yoga pants and a T-shirt?" I smirked with a wink.

"More than I have time to explain to you right now," she quipped back with a slight Southern accent.

I looked at the time on my phone. "It's late. I have practice early tomorrow."

"Oh, hell no! You swore if I gave you an hour to study you'd come with me, bitch. So let's go." She stomped into the closet. I sighed and closed my book to the sound of hangers scraping the rod as Grace continued to chastise me.

"We've lived together over a month, and you haven't done anything but go to volleyball practice and do your homework. I really don't know how I got stuck with such a nerd for a roommate."

She leaned out from the closet and flashed one of her bright smiles, letting me know she was teasing.

"All of us can't be freaks of nature who don't need to study to get straight As. Some of us have to, you know, try a little."

I studied more than I needed to because, as my mom put it, I was persnickety in my need to be the best. I smiled, thinking about her. Our family had been through some hard times the past couple years, especially my mom. So much so I'd wanted to stay home another year before going to Cornell, but she wouldn't let me put my life on hold. Coming to the University of Illinois was a reasonable compromise since home was about an hour away. Not to mention they'd offered me a full ride athletic scholarship.

"I don't want to hear it! I have three jobs and a full schedule. I just know how to relax and have a good time once in a while." She danced her way over to my chair. "I swear it's the secret to my success, so you have to give it a try. You know, for scientific purposes," she drawled with a grin in perfect mocking of my Midwestern accent.

If that was true, it explained how she scored As on tests without cracking a book. She hadn't missed an opportunity to socialize in between work and class since school started. I don't know how she managed to find the time.

"Yeah, well, you don't have to drag your ass out of bed at six in the morning just to have Coach ride it about your run time being too slow," I replied in one last-ditch effort to avoid fulfilling my promise.

"No, I have to get my ass up even earlier to cover the morning shift at the athletic center." She crossed her arms over her chest.

Shit, she had me. I scowled, glancing at the stack of study cards on my desk.

"Just come out for an hour. You'll be tucked into bed before midnight. I saw Lance coming in when I left." She wagged her eyebrows, no doubt hoping his presence would entice me.

As much as I was against relationships and hanging out socially with men in general, I had to admit Lance was ridiculously hot. I'd made the mistake of mentioning that to Grace after he started as the TA in my Intro to Architecture class. After watching what my mom went through with my dad, a boyfriend was out of the question, but the occasional hookup with a guy who was incredibly sexy and, based on the work I'd seen, extremely good with his hands sounded good. Meaningless sex seemed to be the only thing that kept my mind off of all of the other shit in my life, and it'd been a while since I'd had any.

"Fine, one hour."

The following squealing and hand clapping made Grace look a bit like a seal before she darted back to the closet.

"I have the perfect dress for you!" she said, rummaging through the packed space.

When she pulled out the cute little designer knit dress I'd admired on the first day of school, I felt genuinely excited to go out. She loved to tell the story of how she picked it up for ten dollars at a secondhand store, like most of her rather stylish wardrobe. She liked to say, "You don't have to spend a million to look like a million."

Having grown up with money, I wouldn't have batted an eye at paying full price for designer brands, but when my father left, all of that left with him as far as I was concerned.

I'd just pulled the dress over my head when my phone vibrated on the desk. Grace frowned at me.

Jess's cell number flashed across the screen and I smiled. "It's just Jessica. I'll make it quick." I crossed my fingers over my heart as I picked up the phone.

"Hey, Jess," I answered, my tone cheerful.

My little sister calling meant she was at home with Mom since Dad banned her from having a cell phone at his house, which always made me feel better about being gone. Mom hated being alone, and she'd been crushed when Jess chose Dad in the divorce. I understood. She'd always been a daddy's girl, and Mom could be intense when she got into one of her moods.

Instead of hearing Jess's sweet, happy voice, all I heard were her wailing sobs and indecipherable rambling. The only words I could make out were *Mom* and *wake*. I looked at Grace. Her face mirrored what I was sure was panic in mine.

"Jess, what is it?" My voice rose with fear. "I can't understand you. Where's Mom?"

I pressed the phone hard against my ear as if it would help me to understand her better. Somehow Jess managed to calm down enough to say four words that changed my life forever.

"Mom won't wake up."

Chapter 1

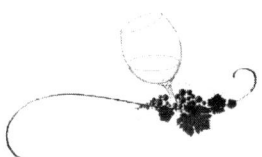

Fourteen years later

"Oh fuck yes! That's it!" I screamed as Ty Harris pounded into me.

My screams were 85 percent faked and 15 percent ecstatic anticipation from my imagining the new pair of red-soled heels I was going to buy with my commission.

As I lay on my back, staring up at the reflection of this hulking linebacker's impressive physique in the mirror on the ceiling, I thought idly of a funny video I'd seen featuring an enthusiastic Pomeranian and an unlucky teddy bear. I bit my lip to stifle a laugh.

"Aahhhh!" He groaned against my ear as his orgasm pulsated through his body.

At least it was over quickly.

"Damn, baby." He rolled off me. "That was fantastic. Just what I needed. Tonight's game was brutal."

Fantastic, really?

We lay in awkward silence for a few moments. Ty chewed his lip, no doubt trying to come up with an excuse to kick me out.

"So, um, you want me to autograph something for you before you go?"

Smooth, dude.

"Really? That would be so great!" I feigned excitement in the saccharine tone I'd adopted for the job. It was a little trick I'd learned from Lydia who handled most of our professional athletes. I'd only gotten stuck with *Mr. Fantastic* because she was busy tailing a golfer on the PGA tour in North Carolina that week.

"Can you sign my ticket stub from the game?" I got up from the bed and crossed the room to dig the Dolphins ticket stub out of my purse.

Athletes, particularly football players, were easy targets. Like shooting fish in a barrel. All wives had to do was slip their lawyers a couple of hundreds and ironclad infidelity clauses magically appeared in their prenups. Jocks like Ty were either too self-involved to notice or too arrogant to think they could get caught cheating. That was where I came along.

"For sure." He took off the condom, got up, and walked past the trash can to flush the evidence down the toilet.

At least he'd learned that much, although I had no intention of stealing his little swimmers. I had everything I needed thanks to the camera hidden in my purse. The time-stamped and dated ticket he signed--on tape, I might add--was a bonus. He was going to have a hard time pulling out the pathetic "it wasn't me" defense in the divorce proceedings thanks to that extra tidbit.

I shimmied into my panties and then into my skintight tube of teal spandex Lydia claimed was a dress, taking care to retie the halter neck as my breasts stretched the fabric of the neckline, before I slipped on a pair of black stilettos. I fluffed my hair in the dresser mirror until I looked like a slutty hot mess. The corporate men I usually worked tended to prefer a more sophisticated look, but this was a job and when in Rome...

He passed me the signed ticket and leaned in to kiss my cheek.

"Thank you so much!" I tossed my long blonde hair over my shoulder.

"So, um, maybe we can hook up again next time I'm in town," he suggested.

Not likely because we'd met at a yacht party that night and he didn't have my number. He probably didn't even remember my name, which was as fake as my screams.

"Sure." I smiled as I tucked the ticket into my purse.

"You need me to call you a cab or something?" He opened the door.

Mr. Fantastic's sad attempt at being a gentleman, I see.

"No, I'm good. Thanks again, this was fun."

"All right, good night, then."

When the door closed, I pulled out my phone and started walking toward the elevators.

"I got everything we need and more," I said as soon as Patty picked up. "I'm sending it to you now."

"How was your flight?" I smiled up at Grace as she stepped into my office.

It was good to finally see her in the flesh after playing phone tag and travel roulette for the past few weeks.

"Long." She pulled me in for a quick hug before crumpling into the chair on the other side of my desk.

I knew all too well how taxing the two hour time difference between L.A. and Chicago was on a late-night flight. I'd made the journey several times over the years for various engagements, including the one right before Mr. Fantastic. Coming back from Florida was definitely easier because I gained an hour.

"I'm glad to be home. Mr. Jackson was a tough nut to crack, but once I got him to open up"--Grace paused to let the drama grow thicker--"he was a complete freak!"

"Really?" I grimaced at the thought.

"Uh-huh. I'm telling you the old white dudes love a little brown sugar." She turned in her chair and slapped her ass for emphasis.

"I'll take your word for it." We both laughed, and I went back to work answering an e-mail when Grace started fidgeting with her hair. "What?"

"So I talked to Patty on the ride over." She gave me a look. "According to her, that video of you and Eric Bennett was something else."

She smirked.

Fucking Patty. She was supposed to set us up with clients, walk them and their attorneys through the evidence we gathered, and cut us our checks. Gossiping about what we did to get that evidence wasn't in her job description. Too bad all the contracts and nondisclosure agreements we signed for our clients didn't apply when she was talking to us; us being me, Grace, Lydia and Bridget, the co-owners of Homewrecker Incorporated. Yes, the name was right on the nose, a sort of joke amongst us girls since we didn't exactly pass out business cards or have a storefront. Our work was by referral only but for official purposes, like our tax returns, we were Mason, Dawson, & Associates, LLP Private Investigators.

"Well?" Grace fished some more for details about my time with Alaina Bennett's husband.

It wasn't as though we weren't constantly talking about what we saw and did with our marks. The topic was standard when we got together, but the Bennett case was one I preferred to forget.

"It wasn't that bad, just some handcuffs and a leather strap or two." I hoped it would be enough to sate her curiosity.

"Oh shit! Eric Bennett is even kinkier than old Mr. Jackson!"

Kinky wasn't the word I would have used to describe it. He was something much, much darker.

"Welcome back, Grace," Bridget Hall said, popping her head in the open doorway. Grace and I jolted at the unexpected interruption.

"Damn it, Bridget! Are you trying to give us heart attacks?" I half-teased, glad for the distraction from the conversation about Eric Bennett.

She was quick on her feet and replied, "I thought stealth was a job requirement around here, boss lady."

"Touché," I said. Bridget was right, after all. "I hate it when you call me boss lady. You own just as much of this place as I do."

I shifted my stern stare from her to Grace, who was just as guilty of treating me as if I was in a position of power over her and the rest of the girls.

"That's only because you're too nice for your own good." The petite redhead shrugged as she looked to Grace for any sign of solidarity.

Grace obliged with a nod. Sure, I'd put up my inheritance money to start the venture, but Grace was the one who'd ultimately talked me into getting into the home-wrecking business in the first place.

"I can think of a few men who would disagree with that statement." I smirked.

One thing was certain: I was very good at my job. Not to say the other girls weren't good. Lydia and Grace were both great, and they were willing to do whatever it took to get the job done, but they favored an investigative approach. Investigation took time. I was more hands on, so to speak. I closed most cases in record time and just happened to satisfy some of my own needs in the process.

"Hey, Bridge, while you're here, can you take a look at my laptop?" Grace grabbed her bag from the floor.

"Not a problem."

Bridget took the computer and set it down on my desk to start working her IT magic. The girl was a technology genius and drop-dead gorgeous to boot. It was impossible to understand how she'd made it to the ripe age of twenty-six with her virginity intact. Granted, she was cripplingly shy around strangers and dressed to hide what I happened to know was a stellar body, but she'd been a computer science major in college for God's sake. A self-conscious hot girl in that field was like an injured seal swimming in a cove of killer, albeit nerdy, whales.

Being technologically illiterate, I zoned out when Bridget started talking about firewalls and virus scans. I intended to catch up on e-mails while I waited, but instead only stared at the screen as, despite my best efforts, my thoughts turned back to Eric Bennett.

The hair on the back of my neck stood, and I shifted uncomfortably in my chair. As hard as I tried to forget about him, Grace bringing up that video made my former mark an unwelcome presence in the front of my mind. When I'd bumped into him under the alias of Cynthia Matthews in the lobby of his firm's newest L.A. hotel, he'd been polite and charming. A facade he maintained for several weeks before his true colors bled through. It was fitting I'd posed as an aspiring actress. I'd put on a great show for him and the camera despite the warning bells blaring in my head--the ones I should have listened to.

"Well, that should take care of the problem," Bridget said, pulling me from my thoughts. "I'm going to head out. I just stopped by to get the burners from your last jobs."

Grace rifled through her bag while I retrieved two phones from the desk drawer. I glanced down at the older one, internally cringing as I recalled the last conversation I'd had on it. I felt lighter the instant Bridget took the only connection Eric Bennett had to me from my hand.

"Farewell, Cynthia Matthews and Gloria Drake," I said, wiping my hands clean of my bogus identity.

We liked to keep our real initials in our aliases, C.M. for Claudia Mason, G.D. for Grace Dawson, and L.D. for Lydia Davis. The consistency made them easier to remember out in the field.

Bridget didn't work marks because she was ridiculously shy, and a virgin, so no fake names were necessary for her. Not that the rest of us had sex with all of our marks, at least Grace and

Lydia didn't, but it was always a possibility if we couldn't get the evidence otherwise.

"So are you going to give me the details on that hunky football player or what?" Grace leaned forward and placed her elbows on my desk.

"Not without a few drinks in me." I smiled as I pulled a bottle of our favorite brandy from the cabinet at the back of my office.

Grace shook her head in disapproval, tapping her finger on the nonexistent watch on her wrist.

"None of that; it's five o'clock somewhere. Besides, this is a tradition." I poured two glasses of brandy and passed one to her. "You and I have shared a glass of this after every one of our Homewrecker Incorporated engagements, and since we both just finished jobs, that means two glasses each. You wouldn't want to jinx our 100 percent success rate after all these years, now would you?"

She let out a dramatic sigh as I raised my glass.

"To Homewrecker Incorporated: conquering the world one cheating asshole at a time."

She lifted her glass to mine with the other hand perched on her hip. "And getting paid in the process!"

We shot the brown liquid as though we were back in college.

"Do you remember when Elizabeth gave us our first bottle of this stuff?" Grace grabbed the bottle to pour our second glasses. "I nearly shit when I looked up how much it cost!"

"Yes, but I think the check she slipped in the card was far more shocking," I said, recalling the large commission she'd paid us after her divorce settlement was finalized.

When we'd agreed to help our friend get proof her abusive husband was cheating, we had no intention of getting paid for the favor. Nor did I intend to go as far as I did to get it, but after weeks of following Joseph Perry and seeing him in countless compromising positions with more than one woman, we could never get the definitive proof of intercourse Elizabeth's lawyer insisted she needed to trigger the infidelity clause in their prenuptial agreement. Under normal circumstances, sleeping with a friend's husband wasn't something I would have ever considered, but Elizabeth was desperate for a way out.

Earning that much money for just a few weeks of work right out of college was far better than the lousy salaries we were making, so Grace did some research and found Patty's firm, which specialized in placing women with our newly discovered skill set with clients.

"Speaking of getting paid, Patty wants a call with us this afternoon," Grace said, picking up her bag.

"That was fast." I turned off the lights as we stepped out of my office. We'd both been home less than twenty-four hours, and we typically had at least a few weeks off between cases, if not more. The home-wrecking business wasn't exactly predictable.

"She wouldn't give any details, but she made it sound as if this job was a pretty big deal, like great-white-whale big."

I raised my eyebrows at her use of the phrase. An engagement that big meant financial security; it was the one we all dreamed of. The one that could send us on our way to retirement.

For me that was the little vineyard I'd been dreaming of buying since my mom took us on a spontaneous trip to Tuscany the summer before my seventeenth birthday. That trip was the last great memory I had of my mom. It was also the spark that ignited my rather intense passion for wine. My thirty-second birthday was right around the corner, and while I might still have a few good years left in my current business, by its nature, it was a young woman's game.

Sure, I could continue running Homewrecker Incorporated, recruit young new talent and serve as more of an agent like Patty. After all, she'd started out just like me who knows how long ago, but that wasn't for me. I liked my work with our marks. It gave me an escape I'd come to crave, but I recognized there were less complicated ways for me to scratch that itch. When my time out in the field was over, I intended to live a much simpler life.

"There was *one* detail she shared I know you're not going to like, but I told her we'd hear her out," Grace continued cautiously as we stepped onto the elevator.

I turned to face her, crossing my arms over my chest.

"The client is local," she blurted out, stepping back out of the elevator just as the doors closed me in alone.

"That was a bit dramatic." I tapped my foot on the marble floor of the foyer. I'd waited for her outside our apartment.

Grace shrugged, stepping past me into the penthouse we shared. Our makeshift offices were a floor below us. Given the work we did, which often strayed precariously into the gray area of what was considered legal, we decided it was best to keep all aspects of our business low-key, eliminating the need for a traditional office space.

"I figured you could use the ride up alone to think before you dug in those stubborn heels of yours." Grace walked across the hardwood to the glass wall overlooking Lake Michigan and the Chicago skyline.

She knew me too well. "It's our number one rule; don't fuck where we live."

"You know, you don't always have to fuck the marks, Claud." Grace stared at me pointedly. "All I'm saying is we listen first, and then decide if it's worth it to make this one exception. We've always known this gig couldn't be a long-term venture. Besides, don't you want more? I know I do. I want a real relationship with a man who isn't married, and this could be the money I need to make a real difference for kids like my brother."

Sure I wanted more, but my goals weren't as lofty or as noble as Grace's. I'd had some tough times when I was younger, but nothing quite as hard as what she'd gone through.

When she was only fourteen, her nine-year-old brother was diagnosed with muscular dystrophy. His disease was aggressive and ruthless. By age twelve he'd lost the ability to walk. Her mother, instead of stepping up to take care of her son, turned to drugs, leaving Grace to care for and raise her brother. With no other family to take them in, Grace covered for her mom time and again, knowing if she didn't the state would likely take her brother away. By the time she finished high school, Adam required full-time medical care. To pay for a long-term care facility, Grace worked three jobs while going to college on an academic scholarship. That first facility he was in wasn't ideal, but it was far better than anywhere the state would have sent him, and it was what she could afford at the time.

Adam was the reason she'd wanted to start Homewrecker Incorporated in the first place. With the money from our first year in business, she moved him to one of the best facilities in the country, which happened to be just outside of the city making it easy for her to visit him often.

As much as she did for her brother, Grace wanted to do more. She'd dreamed of starting a foundation to help families like hers for years. That's why she was so keen on considering the Chicago job. Thinking about all she'd been through and how strong and caring she was made my eyes sting.

"Okay, I'll listen to what she has to say, but no promises."

Taking on the kind of work we did as Homewrecker Incorporated at home was risky. There were nearly three million people living in the city, but even a big place gets small when you're pretending to be someone else. Not working where we lived was a helpful piece of advice from a former colleague who'd had the misfortune of running into a mark in her real life. Her new husband was less than understanding. That was definitely not a situation any of us wanted to find ourselves in. Not that I was worried about ever having a husband, but I definitely didn't want to have to explain my work to my family.

"Thanks, doll," Grace said with a wink as she pulled leftover Chinese food out of the fridge. My stomach growled loud enough for her to hear.

Grace tipped a takeout container in my direction. "You want?"

"No thanks. I think I'm going to head up to North Avenue Beach for a run." I needed to work off all the shit about the Bennett case still plaguing my thoughts. A few laps around the peninsula was one of the best ways for me to clear my head.

"Just make sure you get your ass back here in time for the call at three." Grace said in between bites of lo mein straight out of the white cardboard container.

"Sir, yes, sir!" I said with a smirk, waving backward over my head as I walked down the hall to my room to get changed.

Chapter 2

I paced in front of my desk as we prepared to break our most important rule in running Homewrecker Incorporated. When Patty revealed the new client was willing to pay quadruple our standard commission--in advance, plus a hefty bonus upon completion of the job, regardless of the outcome--there was no argument or debate from me. Grace and I called Lydia and Bridget as soon as we hung up with Patty. They agreed even faster than I did. We had to go for it.

"Patty just messaged. She's received the signed agreements and she's going to call us in five," Grace said, rushing in. The look on her face was somewhere between elated and terrified.

"Someone should get Bridget so we can get started." I fidgeted with the phone, double-checking the cords were plugged in tightly.

Bridget appeared in the doorway as if she'd heard me talking about her. She looked as nervous as I felt.

Grace bounced around as if she'd drunk about ten energy drinks.

"Jesus, can you sit the hell down? You're making me even more nervous," I said.

Grace pursed her full lips, obviously not appreciating my tone. "Sorry, I'm just freaking out."

"I know!"

She returned to the bouncing. "I just want to know who it is already!" Her Southern accent was much more noticeable when she was anxious.

"It's the right move," I said, my eyes following Grace's athletic frame around my office. "It's the smart move," I continued, unsure if I was trying to convince her or myself.

"Do we know who it is yet?" Lydia said, picking up the line. She wouldn't be back from North Carolina until late that night.

"No, we're waiting for Patty to dial in," Grace said, finally sitting down next to Bridget in the other seat in front of my desk.

"Are you all there?" Patty asked, sounding every bit the New Yorker she was.

"We're here," I replied, leaning closer to be sure she could hear me.

"So, first things first, Claudia, the client has requested you for the job."

"What, why?"

In the past, the wives didn't play any part in determining which of us were assigned to their case. Once Patty sent an engagement our way, we always made the call based on research and observation of the mark.

"She asked me who was the best. You've closed nearly twice as many cases as anyone else I have, and I don't think there's a man on the planet who can resist your charms, so I felt confident saying that's you. She wants you and for what she's paying us, we're going to give her whatever the hell she asks for. Which brings me to my next point. She wants the meeting first thing tomorrow and she wants to come to you."

"Here in our offices?" Grace cut her wide eyes to Bridget and then me.

I rubbed the pendant on my necklace between my fingers so hard I worried I would damage the delicate filigree design.

"Yes, she's concerned about being seen in a more public venue. Given who she is, it's understandable."

"Jesus, Patty, it's not bad enough we actually have to meet her? We have to let her come here?"

None of us had ever actually met a client before. We didn't meet them, we didn't talk to them, and they didn't know who we were beyond our aliases. In our business, anonymity was priceless.

"Trust me when I say she's got a hell of a lot more to lose than you do."

"For fuck's sake, Patty. Can you cut the shit and just tell us who it is already!" Lydia demanded after having remained silent since Patty got on the line.

You wouldn't know it to look at her, or talk to her with that sailor's mouth of hers, but the girl was a genius, literally. Her IQ tested at 165 when she graduated high school at fifteen. Einstein's IQ was 160. As such, in addition to fieldwork and helping our other resident smarty pants, Bridget, with computer shit, she handled all of our personal finances. The million-plus dollar penthouse Grace and I shared was courtesy of her investment savvy, the property value having nearly doubled in the five years we'd lived there.

"Open the e-mail I just sent all of you," Patty replied.

"Holy shit." I scanned the first attachment she'd sent.

It was an article from the business section of the Chicago Tribune. The story featured an announcement of G&G Components' impending acquisition of a foreign subsidiary. They were a well-known Chicago-based manufacturer of high-tech electrical vehicle components. While the company had become a wild financial success in recent years, the source of its notoriety amongst most Chicagoans was due largely to the philanthropic work of its CEO's wife. She was pictured in the article, looking as beautiful as ever standing with her husband at some event.

"No fucking way!" Lydia said through the speaker. "Are you saying Elsa Michaels is the new client?"

If you lived in Chicago, you knew of Elsa Michaels. She was a local icon, practically a saint, who ran a children's charity she founded. Not to forget her stunning beauty was just as renowned.

"That's exactly what I'm saying." Patty laughed with excitement. I stood and started walking around.

"The Michaelses always seemed like such a happy couple," Bridget said sadly.

She was definitely the hopeless romantic of the group. I blamed it on her lack of experience with men. The rest of us knew better than to believe in such fairytales. Well, Lydia and I did, at least. I'd questioned Grace's judgment when it came to men on more than one occasion over the years. Back in college, bad boys and jerks were her drugs of choice, and she always started out believing she could change them.

"Claudia, you lucky bitch," Lydia said with a groan. "Gregory Michaels can install his components in me anytime."

Lydia was always the perv of the group, which was saying something. I couldn't argue with her assessment, though. Gregory Michaels, no matter what his marital crimes might have been, was one of the most attractive men I'd ever laid eyes on. If he didn't have such a mind for business, a career as a model wouldn't have been much of a stretch. I had to admit I didn't hate the idea of being the one who would potentially get to fuck him.

"So you really think he's cheating? The way they were together, I wouldn't have guessed. They always seemed so in love," Bridget said quietly as she stood.

I looked at Bridget, my eyebrows raised in question. "Wait a minute, Bridge. Are you saying you know them?"

"I interned in G&G's IT department the last semester of my senior year. I never actually met Mr. and Mrs. Michaels, but I saw them meeting in the lobby sometimes." She shrugged.

I vaguely remembered seeing the internship on her résumé. It hadn't stood out amongst the vast array of other academic and professional achievements listed. I'd known Bridget was perfect for the job almost immediately. With her talent she could have gotten a job in IT at any big corporation she wanted, but Bridget was a hacker at heart. The world of clandestine investigation and surveillance at Homewrecker Incorporated allowed her to feed that passion. It didn't hurt she gained a full partnership when she joined us either.

"That's right, I'd nearly forgotten." I put an arm around her shoulder. At five foot nine, I felt positively Amazonian next to Bridget's small five-foot frame. "It's one hell of a fortuitous coincidence you having that connection," I said, looking to Grace who was smiling widely, clearly thinking the same thing.

"I wonder if they're hiring."

The anticipation in the office the next morning was palpable. Bridget rushed around organizing refreshments in the conference room we'd set up and on the table in the entryway. The whole office smelled of coffee and cinnamon with a hint of chocolate. She scooted past me, a chocolate glazed donut on a napkin in her hand as she tugged awkwardly at her black skirt, which fell past her mid-thigh.

"You look nice, Bridget," I said. She twirled in the doorway of her office. Her long red locks, pinned up elegantly on one side, gave her a soft, dreamy look.

"I figured it was a pretty important day, so I should dress up." She fiddled with her skirt as if she thought it would fly up spontaneously at any moment. "Is this too short? I bought the outfit last night after work, and the sales girl said it was just right on me and very professional."

I smiled, proud of her for making the effort. She usually wore baggy jeans and a nerdy T-shirt in the office. "She was right, it is perfect and not short at all. In fact, I think it would be perfect for your interview." It hadn't been much of a surprise when Bridget's old boss at G&G jumped at the chance to get her back on his team. He insisted she come in for an interview as soon as possible, which was really only a formality with human resources. He would have hired her right there on the phone if he could.

Her inquiry also led to an interesting tidbit about the upcoming retirement of Gregory Michaels' assistant, Janet, whom he'd inherited from his father's tenure at the helm of the company.

She wasn't leaving for at least a couple of months, but there'd been talk of getting her replacement trained before her exit.

I kept moving toward my office, hoping to look over my notes and the profile on Gregory Michaels one last time before Elsa arrived. It was just a way to distract myself from the nervous energy buzzing over my skin. I memorized every detail of the background information Bridget, and Lydia, who'd flown back late the night before, pulled together on our new target. It never ceased to amaze me how much you could learn about a person from the Internet.

I flipped past the first pages containing press releases and financial information on G&G Components. I stopped when something caught my eye: a photograph in one of the releases from several years ago. It was an unusual shot for a business piece, featuring Gregory and his twin brother Greyston Michaels hugging by the steps of the company's private jet, and their younger brother Chad standing a little to the side with his hand on Greyston's shoulder. Although Greyston's face wasn't visible in the shot, I knew he had to be as hot as Gregory. They were identical after all.

"Michaels Brothers Taking on Tokyo" sat on top of the picture. The article explained a joint venture with a Tokyo based electronics company being led by Greyston, G&G's chief operating officer. He was moving to Japan to oversee the project, where he was remaining for another year. Having his twin in the mix would have made my job far more complicated. If I remembered correctly, it'd been just a few weeks before the date of the article G&G started hitting the news in a big way as a leader in vehicle component technology.

It was hard to not be impressed by Gregory and his brothers, another article calling the company's front man a "visionary taking the reins from his father to lead G&G Components into the future." The next page featured a shot of Gregory and Elsa taken just a few weeks ago. The couple held one of those ridiculously large pairs of scissors at the opening of G&Gs new corporate offices.

"I know this case is good for us, but the whole thing makes me sad." Bridget looked down at the photo, her unheard appearance in front of my desk scaring the shit out of me. "Sorry," she said, noticing me jump. "I just wanted to let you know the private elevator was accessed."

She smiled apologetically. Because that elevator only serviced the top two floors of the building, the penthouse where Grace and I lived, and our offices the floor below, it had to be Elsa using the temporary access code Patty sent her.

"I guess this is it, then." I stood to smooth my black pleated tulle skirt and matching blazer. "How do I look?"

"Perfect. Hot, but still professional," she replied with an approving nod as she tugged at her own skirt.

"Thanks." I took a deep breath and walked to the entrance to greet Mrs. Michaels.

As I walked past my partners, I couldn't help but appreciate how beautiful and professional they all looked.

"I think it's best if you all sit down until I escort her in. It would seem less, um, anxious," I suggested.

"I'm so fucking nervous," Lydia said in a loud whisper as she tucked a lock of shoulder-length chestnut hair behind her ear.

We were all nervous. The commission and bonus we were looking at was more than the seven figures we'd made on all our jobs combined for the last eighteen months or so. Not to mention the connections a woman like Elsa Michaels had to an array of equally wealthy potential clients in questionable marriages.

The sound of clicking heels on the hardwood floor of the hallway just outside the door signaled Elsa Michaels' arrival. I pulled open the door, smiling brightly as I extended my hand in greeting. Wearing a lovely pantsuit from one of the premier designer's spring lines, she was even more beautiful in person than in any of the photographs I'd seen.

"I'm so sorry I'm late," she blurted, reaching for my hand as she crossed the threshold. "This is extremely difficult and I just needed a few minutes to get myself together before I came up."

I admired her honesty and her strength but was surprised by her humility. She was always so composed in public. Clearly those few minutes helped because she looked amazing. Strong and ready for anything. If I'd been crying, I would have broken out in hives and red blotches. One of several reasons I never let myself cry in front of anyone.

"No need to apologize, Mrs. Michaels. You're actually right on time. Can I just say it's such a pleasure to meet you? We're all big fans of the amazing work you do," I said, leading her around the corner to where everyone else was waiting.

"Please, call me Elsa. I think we're going to be far past any need for formality before this is over," she replied with a bright smile, attempting to make light of her situation, but despite her impeccable exterior, the pain in her eyes was evident.

"Here, let me take your coat, and please have a seat. Would you like something to eat or drink?" I gestured toward the table filled with various pastries, juices, and coffee while she set her bag on an empty chair and shrugged out of her blazer.

"Just some water. I haven't had much of an appetite lately."

"Of course." I hung Elsa's coat on the rack in the corner while Grace passed her a bottle of water. She opened it and took a long drink. Finally, she sighed and took a few moments to look me up and down.

"I can see why Patty recommended you," she said, finally sitting. "You're absolutely breathtaking, magnetic even."

I was accustomed to receiving compliments, mainly from men who were trying to get in my pants, but having a woman like Elsa Michaels speak about me that way put a flush of color on my cheeks. I respected her, admired her even, so her words had an impact.

"Allow me to present my associates, Lydia, Grace, and Bridget." I stuck to first names, although all hopes of anonymity were already lost considering we were standing in the building Grace and I lived in and Elsa's attorney's had nondisclosure agreements with all of our signatures on them. On a typical case, Patty served as a buffer and was the only one who signed the agreements our clients saw.

"It's a pleasure to meet all of you" Elsa said with a small smile. "Despite the unfortunate circumstances."

Each of my partners greeted her in turn before sitting again.

"So, Elsa, where would you like to begin?" I asked, taking my seat.

"I know that meeting me like this goes against your standard policies, but I'm sure you all understand the delicate nature of the situation, for myself and my foundation. Many of our large donors are affiliated with notable religious organizations; that kind of scandal could impact their desire to support the foundation, at least so long as I remained at the helm. The foundation is my life's work. It's my legacy. I couldn't imagine giving that up."

She looked to each of us and, seemingly satisfied we understood, dropped a stack of photographs on the table in front of me. They were the explanation to the mystery of her sudden suspicion in what, from the outside, appeared to be the most enviable marriage in Chicago. They also seemed to suggest I was an ideal choice for the assignment.

"It's a miracle whoever took these hasn't sold them to the highest bidder already."

There were approximately fifteen shots of Gregory Michaels with a woman who could have been my twin. Most of the shots seemed fairly harmless, featuring Gregory Michaels with this woman in a variety of places: restaurants, bars, standing by his car. Then there were the final two. The first was of Gregory leaving the Drake Hotel, the woman trailing a few feet behind him. Not particularly incriminating until I saw the accompanying photograph of her completely naked and straddling a man who may or may not have been him in what was definitely a room in the same hotel. I'd been there enough times to recognize it.

"I would guess they haven't been sold because they are holding out for a bigger payout from you to keep them concealed. Especially since you can't even see his face in the only shot that's really worth anything," Grace said, examining the pictures.

I wanted to add how shocked I was her husband would be so careless to be photographed at a hotel with his mistress, but that was a comment best left unsaid at the moment.

"Yes, I think you're right. Someone slipped them under the door of the bathroom stall when we were out to dinner several weeks ago. I wondered if it was just some paparazzi ploy to bait me into creating a bigger story--make a public scene between Gregory and me. So I tucked them into my bag and walked out as though nothing happened. I didn't know why I didn't ask him about them when we got home. It wouldn't be the first time the media has resorted to such desperate tactics for a juicy headline."

She took a sip of water.

"I'm embarrassed to admit it, but I let the pictures get into my head even though Gregory has never given me cause to doubt him before. It's just he's been distant for the past few months." She looked down at her hands. "He's under a lot of pressure with the company, and I've been swamped with the new children's education program the foundation is rolling out in South America. I've been traveling a lot and when I'm home, I've been so focused on--" Elsa fought back tears.

Grace retrieved a box of tissues from a side table and placed them beside Elsa. "Those photos would get to any reasonable person, Elsa."

Elsa pulled a tissue from the box and dabbed her eyes. "We've been trying to have a baby for nearly two years now. Obviously, things haven't moved along as easily as we hoped. We've had some, difficulties, but I thought we were getting through it. There are still options we haven't explored. Then these pictures showed up and a week later he suggested we hold off on trying to get pregnant for a while. Suddenly what the photos allude to seemed like the only reasonable explanation for his sudden change of heart. Having a family was the most important thing in the world to him, and now I wonder if his feelings have changed because we couldn't, because I couldn't get--"

The tears Elsa was fighting broke through. I placed a reassuring hand on her shoulder as she wiped them away and took a deep breath. "I'm sorry. I was certain I'd run out of tears by now."

"Please don't apologize, Elsa. I can't begin to imagine how hard all of this is for you." I squeezed her shoulder with a sympathetic smile.

"So here I am," Elsa said, clasping her hands together on her lap.

"One thing I'm confused about, Elsa," I sat back in my chair, "why do you need our help? You inherited a small fortune from your grandparents. Most of our clients come to us because they married into the money and would leave their marriages with nothing because of their prenups."

"It's almost funny." She wiped her nose with a tissue. "Gregory didn't even want us to have a prenup, but his family's lawyers insisted despite the fact I had my own money--more than him actually. But they claimed it was because of the company. I understood, especially with him in line to take over someday. The infidelity clause was his idea. I was young and in love, so I never bothered to read the fine print of the contract." She sniffled and rolled her eyes. "It's sad considering I was a law student at the time. So all I understood was if either of us cheated and we divorced, the other would be paid a hefty penalty. As you can imagine, that gave me a great sense of security in his fidelity. However, the standard of proof required to trigger the clause is incredibly specific."

She pulled a copy of the agreement from her bag and slid it over.

I flipped through the pages to the infidelity clause. "Shit." It was the only appropriate response. I passed the contract to Grace. "You need visual proof of more than one breach defined as sexual intercourse and sworn testimony from the other woman."

She nodded while Grace skimmed the contract.

"The thing is, I wouldn't even care about making him pay me the penalty, except his lawyers pulled a fast one with another section of the agreement. If we divorce without evidence of infidelity, the net worth acquired during our marriage will be split between us. Gregory's stock in G&G was transferred to him before we were married, but I didn't receive my inheritance--it was kept in trust--until I was twenty-five. Essentially he would keep all of his money and get half of mine. That's why I'm here."

"Jesus, that's fucked up," Lydia said and then clasped her hand over her mouth.

Grace gave Lydia a wide-eyed look of disapproval for using vulgar language with Elsa, while Bridget squirmed in the chair next to her. I, on the other hand, covered my mouth to keep from laughing at Lydia's outburst.

Lydia's gaze shot to Elsa.

"Mrs. Michaels, I'm so--"

Elsa burst out laughing, tossing her head back, her hand over her chest. Her infectious laugh spread to all of us. Every time the laughter started to die down, one of us would lose it again, keeping the shenanigans going for several minutes before we finally regained our composure.

"God, I needed that!" Elsa finally said, dabbing at the corners of her eyes. Tears of laughter suited her far better than the ones we'd seen earlier.

"So your husband has no idea about the photos or that you suspect anything?" I asked, getting back to the business at hand.

"No, I don't think so. I was discreet when I started looking into our prenup, which oddly enough, was what really made me start to question his faithfulness. What if he knew he would get to keep all of his money and half of mine? It's hard for me to imagine the man I've known all these years could do such a thing, but I have other people to consider as I move forward. It's not just my marriage on the line. It's my foundation, all the children we help, and all the children who still need our help."

Elsa Michaels was resilient. Even though I wasn't comfortable with the idea of meeting and actually working with my mark's wife, I already liked her. She was someone I could easily be friends with under different circumstances.

"We have a saying here, Elsa. *Without love, marriage is just business*," I said. "Like you mentioned, you have other people to consider. There's nothing wrong with protecting what's rightfully yours."

"So you are certain divorce is your goal at this point?" Grace asked cautiously.

"No, I'm not sure. But it will be the goal if he has been cheating on me, or if he would. I know myself; I could never forgive him for that. Now that this seed of doubt has been planted, I need to know the truth. He witnessed firsthand what my father did to my family. I was sixteen the night my dad left to be with his other family. Gregory snuck into my room and held me for hours while I cried myself to sleep. He swore he would never hurt me like that. He's my best friend. We've always shared everything, been true partners, at least I've always thought we were. I need to know if he's still the man who held me that night all those years ago," Elsa said, looking toward me.

The history with her father hit unfortunately close to home.

Her current predicament was exactly why I'd vowed never to let a man get too close. Clearly she was holding out some hope her husband was, in fact, faithful. Wishing despite whatever charms I threw his way, he would resist and prove his loyalty. I guessed there was a first time for everything, but I wasn't holding my breath.

"I have to ask this, Elsa. Are you certain you want to go down this path? Even with all the doubts you're having, it's obvious you're still in love with your husband. There's a very good chance you're not prepared to see where all this leads. Because of your infidelity clause, even if we confirm he's having an affair with this other woman, we'll need to go further than that. You understand what that means?"

"I'm not the kind of woman who can bury her head in the sand and pretend everything is fine when it's not." Elsa sat up straight. "This is what I need right now. I need to know if he's cheating on me and if he is, I want him to pay."

Despite my well-founded belief every man is capable of cheating, a part of me hoped Gregory Michaels would be the exception to the rule.

"Okay, then," I finally said.

She sighed, looking relieved and terrified all at once.

"So what happens now?"

I glanced at each of the other girls. "Now we do whatever it takes to get you some answers."

Chapter 3

I'd been nervous when I met Elsa Michaels for the first time the week before. Those feelings were nothing compared to the tempest of anxiety swirling through my mind and body as the cab pulled up to G&G Components. No amount of research or preparation could have equipped me for the rapid beat of my heart or the sheen of sweat covering my skin. I was usually calm, completely in control on jobs, but something about this one had me off my game.

Get it together, Claudia, I thought when the cab came to a stop. It wasn't my first rodeo, so to speak. There was no reason to get myself so worked up for a meeting with Gregory Michaels' assistant, set up courtesy of Bridget's old real boss, new fake boss, Ben. It was unlikely I would even see Mr. Michaels during the visit. A busy CEO would rarely be found sitting around the office. Although there was at least a chance I might bump into him, so I'd pulled out more than a few of the stops when I got dressed in a sexy gray sheath dress and matching jacket.

Thanks to Elsa, I knew everything from how Gregory Michaels took his coffee in the morning to which nineties ballads he sang in the shower. Perhaps meeting with, or at least talking to, the wives before a job wasn't such a bad thing after all. However, talking to them after would be another story entirely.

I tugged at the hem of my dress. Looking into the rearview mirror at my reflection, I ignored the obvious stare of the driver. He'd been fixated on me for the bulk of the short ride from my building. Glancing at the meter, I passed him a fifty dollar bill.

"Keep the change."

He turned and gave an appreciative nod for the large tip, but with the way his eyes moved up and down my body as I slid closer to the door, he was appreciating a lot more than the money. I pulled in a steadying breath and clutched the portfolio containing my falsified résumé to my chest as I reached for the handle.

"I could wait until you're finished?" the driver said. "My shift ends in a couple of hours," he added hopefully.

Clearly the outfit I'd chosen had the desired effect.

"Thanks, but my boyfriend is picking me up after my meeting. Have a nice afternoon." I smiled, looking in his direction but avoiding eye contact, not wanting to encourage his attentions.

I'd found the mention of a fake boyfriend wasn't usually enough to dissuade most men, and given the boldness of his stare and his repeated attempts at conversation during the ride, it was likely he was one of them.

"What about--"

I closed the door a little harder than I intended to avoid hearing more of what the driver had to say. On another day, I might have politely indulged his attentions, maybe even flirted a bit, but my stress level made his advances a complete annoyance instead of harmless flattery.

The delicious aroma of a nearby Chicago hotdog stand tickled my senses. My stomach rumbled. My nerves told me I wasn't hungry for breakfast that morning. I inhaled deeply as if the scent alone would sustain me. Lunch would have to wait until after the meeting. With a loud growl, my stomach made its disapproval of that decision known.

I made a beeline to an empty bench I spied a few yards from the entrance of the building and sat to gather myself. Punctuality being one of my finer traits, I had twenty-five minutes before I was due up on the executive floor.

My phone buzzed in the bag beside me. It was my sister, Jessica, her third call of the day, all of which I'd ignored. We'd had our regular weekly call a few days before, so I knew what she wanted. The anniversary of Mom's death was approaching, and she was calling to check on me.

We'd stayed somewhat close over the years despite a fundamental difference of opinion about our father, whom I'd refused to see or talk to for nearly fifteen years. Early on, she'd attempted to persuade me to give him a chance to explain his side of things, insisting there was more to what happened between my mom and him than I knew. What I knew was my mother was dead and he'd moved on and married his mistress before she was cold in her grave. Jessica finally stopped pleading for him when I made it clear if she didn't let it go, she would join him in the ranks of estranged family. The threat was empty, I loved my sister, but she heeded it nonetheless.

Trying to steady my nerves, I took in the sleek, modern lines of G&G Components' new headquarters. My knowledge of architecture was limited, having only taken one class on the subject before changing my major. It was hard not to appreciate the beauty and ingenuity of the building. Taking deep breaths and focusing on the small details of its construction and the sounds of the city moving around me lessened my anxiety. I chalked my uncharacteristic nerves up to doing a job at home for the first time.

Ten minutes passed by the time I looked at my phone again. Pretending to take a selfie, I used the camera as a mirror, happy to find my little city sidewalk meditation smoothed the worry lines. I once again looked like my normal, confident self as I tucked a stray strand of hair behind my ear and strode toward the door.

I looked up and all of the composure I'd worked so hard to regain melted away. A few yards behind me, staring at me in the reflective glass, was a man who made my heart stop. My breath hitched and I was paralyzed as my mind raced for the appropriate response to Gregory Michaels' unexpected appearance. Whatever mutiny my body staged against my mind wasn't the response I was hoping for. By some miracle, the door opened in front of me, breaking the spell.

An average-looking man in a nondescript business suit held the door, waiting politely for me to pass through. In a daze, I shuffled in and spun around to find Mr. Michaels standing in the same spot, still looking at me. I knew he couldn't see me through the dark glass, but that didn't lessen the impact of his gaze. He walked toward the door, his expression intent, purposeful. I struggled to take a step back, as if some invisible force pulled me toward him. I'd never felt anything like it before, so I did the only reasonable thing I could think of.

I ran.

The ladies restroom was just a few yards away so I ducked inside.

What. The. Fuck? I leaned against the door of the woman's bathroom. That wasn't me out there. Men didn't have that effect on me; I had it on them. I was always in control. Every step I'd taken regarding men for as long as I could remember was part of a well laid out plan. Until that moment.

I pulled the door just enough to peer through the crack. My pulse thudded in my ears. Looking at him, completely uninhibited by the risk of discovery, it was impossible to deny my attraction to him. The flush of my skin and the fluttering in my stomach gave it away all too well.

Gregory Michaels scanned the lobby, looking for something, or someone. Knowing in my bones what he was looking for was me pleased me far more than it should have. Ignoring the temptation to exit and let him find me, I kept watching. He approached the desk manned by two security officers.

"Oh! Excuse me!" the woman entering the bathroom nearly shouted.

I jumped back, my hand over my chest. The surprise flooded me with an extra dose of adrenaline as if my senses weren't already on high alert. Still holding the door open, she studied me for a moment before looking over her shoulder back into the lobby. Turning back to me, she giggled with a knowing expression and stepped through the doorway.

"He has that effect," she said, moving past me as the door closed.

Thank God the door blocked me from view. I smiled at her unashamed. Under different circumstances I would have openly appreciated Gregory Michaels with any nearby woman, or man for that matter, who had the use of their eyes. Blindness was surely the only defense against that kind of appeal.

"Is that Mr. Michaels?" I played dumb. There was no doubt who he was. I'd spent more time than was necessary looking at pictures of him for my *research*. None of that research prepared me for my body's reaction to him

She raised her eyebrows.

"Oh, this is your first time seeing him in person. I would tell you it gets easier, but I've worked here for over a year and still get nervous around him."

I could understand why.

I shrugged, smiling at her in the mirror.

"Thanks for the heads-up. I'm interviewing to replace his administrative assistant."

"Lucky you! I thought they were looking to fill that position internally." She extended her hand. "I'm Stacy, accounting department. You better watch out. More than one of your new coworkers will be pissed if you get the job."

It sounded like a joke, but the look in her eyes told me she was serious.

"Claudia, *Claudia Winston*," I replied as we shook hands. The last name from my childhood felt strange on my lips.

I'd decided to use my real first name for the job, considering I was working at home and there was always the possibility of running into someone who knew me. People don't typically shout out last names when they bump into acquaintances on the street, and even if they did, a new last name was much easier to explain away.

Winston was my father's last name. I legally changed my last name to my mother's maiden name after she died. It was another way to cut my father, Robert, out of my life.

Apart from my name, the rest of my identity was entirely fake. Bridget created a false work history, school transcripts, and credit report under a recycled social security number, which I then used to rent a small one-bedroom apartment a few blocks from my real one. Bridget ensured everything was in place for me to pass the intense background check G&G's human resources department would run if I was considered for the position.

"Unfortunately, the yummy Mr. Michaels is only for looking at. He's happily married to a gorgeous saint of a woman," Stacy said before reapplying her lipstick in the mirror.

I contained my sarcastic laugh. Forget that his wife hired me to seduce him and was considering divorce, the way he'd looked at me told me in no uncertain terms his marriage was far from happy. Poor Elsa. Guilt tugged at the corners of my mind. Another odd feeling for me. Clearly meeting my mark's wife had more of an impact than I'd anticipated.

"Good to know."

I glanced at the door, wondering if the coast was clear. Of course the goal was for me to meet him, and his initial reaction to me was far better than I could have hoped for. The problem was *my* initial reaction to him. I needed to be in control. It had to be on my terms. After all, he was just another job. He was just another job. It didn't hurt to remind myself a second time.

"Well, I guess I'll see you around." Stacy headed for the door.

I held my breath, waiting for a glimpse into the lobby from my safe vantage point.

With no sign of Mr. Michaels, I moved closer to the exit to get a better look before the door closed. He was gone as far as I could tell. I only had a few minutes before my meeting with Janet, so it was now or never. Inhaling deeply, I slung my bag over my shoulder and stood tall.

I strode over to the security desk, using every ounce of the acting skills I possessed to maintain a facade of self-assurance.

"Hi." I smiled at the Mack truck of a security guard. "I'm Claudia Winston here to see Mrs. Janet Peterson."

He flashed a cocky grin, reminding me of Mr. Fantastic from Florida.

"Go on through, um, *Ms.* Winston," he said, taking an obvious peek at my left hand.

Stepping through the gate, I consciously told my feet to take each step toward the elevator. How the hell was I supposed to sit through an interview, knowing a man who'd evoked such a tempest of emotion in me was somewhere close by? I whispered prayers as I walked, unsure if they were to keep him away or bring him to me.

When the elevator doors parted, it seemed they must have been the latter.

"Going up?" Mr. Michaels said, a half smile smug on his face as he leaned against the wall. His head tilted forward and his warm honey-colored eyes glinted through long lashes.

Fuck. Me.

Fuck. Me. It bore repeating.

After a brief moment of stunned gawking, I managed a smile and tore my gaze from those sexy, full lips. I didn't know how I forced my legs to move me onto that elevator. Once I was on, I turned my back in an attempt to guard myself from him.

"What floor?" His tone sounded amused, although the alluring timbre of his voice sent a shiver down my spine.

The one we were standing on would have sufficed for what I had in mine.

"Um, seven," I replied over my shoulder. My voice caught slightly in my throat.

God, he smelled divine, like leather and fresh spring rain. He reached forward around me. I could feel his eyes on me while he pressed the button to take us up. It was hard to breathe so near him, as if all the oxygen burned away by the sizzling attraction between us. I'd known he was gorgeous before, I'd met plenty of attractive men in my life, but this was different. I tried again to remind myself he was just another job. I couldn't afford to lose control.

Still, standing so close to him, I realized what I'd seen of him before was like gazing at a distant star. You recognized its light, its beauty, but it wasn't until you were sucked into its orbit you could fully appreciate its power. That's how I felt being alone in his presence. As if some invisible yet undeniable force was drawing me in. Gravity.

"This must be my lucky day." I chanced a glance over my shoulder as he resumed his relaxed position against the wall, seemingly unaffected.

My stomach tightened and I pulled the portfolio closer to my chest. I was certain he could hear my heart pounding in the relative silence.

No, fuck that. I had to get it together. It was just a simple case of instant chemistry, and he was just another man--a job, nothing more, nothing less. Sure, I'd never felt anything like it before, but that didn't matter. So what if he'd caught me off guard, and I'd wanted to fuck him the instant I laid eyes on him. It might not have been exactly what I'd planned for, but this was an opportunity, not only to get the job done, but also to have one hell of a good time doing it. I could roll with it.

"It just might be," I said, my tone bordering on sultry as I turned slightly toward him.

Jesus, those eyes. Flecks of gold around his irises danced in the light, his amusement apparent. My confidence waned.

"Claudia Winston." I offered my hand. "I'm here interviewing to be your new assistant, Mr. Michaels."

"Then it's definitely my lucky day, Ms. Winston. It's a pleasure to meet you." He gripped my hand with both of his. Butterflies fluttered in my stomach.

The word *pleasure* coming out of those full, pouty lips made me think of just that. I saw visions of him kissing paths across my naked body and fought the urge to moan. He raised my hand toward his face. God help me, those lips. He paused, looking at me with a ridiculously sexy smirk before pressing his lips to my skin. My breath hitched and I found myself wishing I'd brought a change of panties. I couldn't believe how brazen he was. I expected more of a challenge, considering the image Gregory Michaels portrayed to the public, but I wasn't about to look a gift horse in the mouth.

He held my fingers, staring into my eyes for far longer than I should have been comfortable with. The last thing I wanted was for him to stop touching me. My mouth parted as my mind raced for some of the witty flirtatious banter that always poured from my mouth so easily in the past.

The chime of elevator's arrival on the executive floor broke the sexually charged silence. He stood up straight, reluctantly releasing my hand.

"Oh, Gregory! I didn't expect you back for another thirty minutes or so," an attractive woman who looked to be in her late fifties said when the doors parted. "You must be Ms. Winston. Bruce called up to let me know you were on your way up, so I thought I'd come greet you. I'm Janet Peterson."

"It's nice to meet you." I stepped out the elevator.

"Well, Gregory, do you need anything before I get started with Ms. Winston? You have a call with Maxwell United in forty-five minutes. I already printed the reports Joshua prepared and put them in the folder on your desk."

"No, Janet, thanks," he said, the back of his fist over his mouth as though he was stifling a laugh.

"All right, then. This way Ms. Winston." Janet walked past the receptionist desk.

I glanced over at the brunette sitting behind it who was staring past me with the look of a starstruck teenager at some boy band concert. When her gaze shifted to me, those doe eyes turned to daggers. Stacy from accounting wasn't lying. Getting the job was going to make me some enemies.

Mr. Michaels didn't pass us to go into his office. I could feel his presence behind me, watching me.

"Ms. Winston, can I get you something to drink? Coffee? Water?" Janet asked when we arrived at her office that was located just outside of Mr. Michaels'.

"No, I'm fine, thank you."

"All right, then. Have a seat and we can get started."

"Actually, Janet, since I have some time, I'll interview Ms. Winston." Mr. Michaels placed his hand on the small of my back and guided me toward his office door.

My body hummed with excitement, and I tried not to let it show in my expression. Janet's mouth hung open. I gave her an apologetic smile; it was the only thing I could come up with.

"But, Gregory, we discussed--"

The frosted glass of his office door closed on her words.

I stood silent while he looked around the room for a moment and held my breath in anticipation as I willed him to turn around and grab me. Of course, that wouldn't be beneficial to my case. Since I was supposed to be meeting with Janet only, we hadn't bothered with any surveillance equipment. For a moment, I didn't care. I wanted him with every cell in my body, but I couldn't give in to that desire so easily.

I'd had good chemistry with marks before, but what was going on between Mr. Michaels and me was like the discovery of the atom bomb.

He strode over to a cabinet by the desk and flipped over two glasses.

"Would you like a drink, Ms. Winston?" he asked in a low voice.

"I'll have one if you are," I replied, my tone as seductive as his.

He'd caught me off guard in the elevator, had me playing defense. It was time to go on the offensive. I pulled my gaze from the rather enticing view of his broad back draped in a bespoke suit and laid my résumé on his desk while he poured. He turned to me with the two drinks in hand, holding one out to me. I looked up into his golden hazel eyes with a sly smile, letting my fingers drift softly over his as I took it. No wedding ring, I noted. So far, he wasn't anything like I expected. The job was definitely going to be easier than I'd anticipated.

Taking a sip of an excellent scotch, I held his gaze as I eased down into the chair behind me. I crossed my legs, letting my beige pump dangle off my foot as I licked the drink off my lips. He sucked in a breath.

I placed the glass on the desk and turned the chair toward it.

"So, are you ready to begin?" I looked up at him over my shoulder; my words open to interpretation.

"I'd rather go over plans for you to have dinner with me tonight," he said matter-of-factly.

"I'm sorry, I thought you were married, Mr. Michaels?" I ran my tongue over my teeth.

"That didn't seem to matter a moment ago, or did I imagine you were flirting with me?" He smirked.

I turned back to him, feigning offense.

"Maybe I'm just friendly," I replied with a mischievous grin.

"Maybe I was talking about a business dinner," he retorted before taking a sip of his drink.

I laughed. He was definitely charming.

"So just a business dinner, then? To discuss my potential as your assistant?" I uncrossed my legs suggestively, giving him a glimpse of the tops of my lacy pantyhose and garter. He cringed almost, but not quite imperceptibly at the action. My confidence surged.

"It can be whatever you want." He stepped forward to set his glass next to mine. The fabric of his pants brushed my leg. I was tempted to spread my legs further and pull him to me right there. Shit, I needed to rein it until I had my surveillance equipment ready to capture the action.

"Don't you even want to take a look at my résumé before you invest any more time on me?" I pointed to the paper on his desk.

"I don't need to see it to know it would take a lifetime to fully absorb all of your talents, Ms. Winston," he responded, his eyes darkened.

Holy fuck. I crossed my legs again to relieve a tiny bit of the tension building between them as my panties dampened further. Who was I kidding? They were completely soaked at that point.

"Such flattery, Mr. Michaels." I shifted in the chair. I took a big gulp of whiskey. "Okay, dinner, then. What time?"

"How about I pick you up at your place at eight?"

"How about I meet you at Remy's Steakhouse at eight?" I countered. "I love a good piece of beef." It was a cheesy line, but based on the look he gave me, it served its intended purpose.

"It's a date."

"No, it's a business meeting." I smirked before tossing back the last of my drink.

We continued flirting as he halfheartedly perused several lines of my manufactured résumé. He made a good effort, but it wasn't long before he was pouring us another drink.

"How is it a woman like you isn't married?" he asked suddenly.

"What makes you think I'm not?"

"No wedding ring." He nodded toward my hand on the fresh glass of whiskey.

"You're not wearing yours," I shot back.

"Are you married?" The flirtatious smile he'd maintained for most of our encounter disappeared.

I looked at him, trying to decide if it would be better for him to think I was married. We'd used that strategy before. Some men felt safer having an affair with someone who had something to lose as well. I suddenly felt a little sick to my stomach. That was all I would ever be to him or anyone--an affair. Although I had no idea why I cared. I never had before.

"No, I'm not married," I responded honestly.

He looked relieved and opened his mouth to say something but stopped at hearing a male voice just outside the door. A woman, presumably Janet, laughed rather loudly. The man followed suit.

"I think our time is almost up," I said.

"I believe you're right," he replied, giving me a strange look.

He stood quickly as the door swung open, and his mouth broke into a devastating smile. He practically ran around the desk and to the door, grabbing the other man in a tight embrace. Confusion, surprise, shock, those words don't really touch the feeling I had when they finally separated.

"What the hell, Grey, you trying to steal my job? Why didn't you tell me you were coming home?" the other man said, finally looking at me. "Ms. Winston, I presume? I see you've met my jokester of a little brother."

"Calm down, you're three minutes older," the man, who I'd been shamelessly flirting with for the past thirty minutes, responded.

He looked at me, flashing that gorgeous smile, and shrugged.

Fuck me. Again.

Chapter 4

Janet was still chuckling when she pulled me out of Gregory Michaels' office to finish my interrupted interview. The brothers, the fucking identical twin brothers, remained inside catching up or some shit that was beyond my comprehension at the moment. My mind was reeling. No, fuck that. I was pissed! What just happened? I got played. That's what happened. I schooled my features to hide the panic brewing inside me, considering I'd just agreed to dinner with the wrong man.

What was worse was the disappointment of knowing the man with whom I'd just had the most insane chemistry of my life was off limits. It was too much to hope Gregory Michaels and I would have the same kind of spark, even though they were twins.

"Greyston wasn't due to come back from Japan for another year," she said when we sat down. "But I still should have noticed it was him. When they were little, it was impossible to tell them apart, but their personalities started shining through later on. I guess I was too preoccupied when he showed up to really look at him." She shuffled a pile of papers in front of her. "It's just like him to surprise everyone. His parents will be thrilled. I don't think he's been home once in the last five years." She lowered her voice. "Messy breakup. Probably why he was so eager to move away for so long instead of sending someone else."

"So he's not married?" What the fuck was I doing? The last thing I needed was to show any more interest in the wrong Mr. Michaels.

"No, Gregory is the only one of the three brothers who's settled down. Of course, Chad is a lot younger and has quite a reputation with the ladies. No real surprise considering how handsome they all are," she said, sounding proud like a mother would. "Greyston certainly seemed to take an interest in you."

She watched me closely, eyebrows raised, waiting for a response.

I laughed.

"I think he was just playing a prank on us. I have to admit I was a bit shocked when he offered to interview me himself before you'd even talked to me. Especially since I'll be working with you so much over the next few weeks if I get the job." A thought hit me like a bolt of lightning. Could it have been Greyston Michaels in the pictures with the mystery woman? How long had he been back in town? I fought the urge to excuse myself to call the girls. The smart move was to proceed as planned until I knew for sure.

She smiled at me.

"Well, let's get to it, then."

We talked briefly about my work history, but Janet spent most of the time talking about her years working for Gregory and his father before him. I listened obligingly, needing her approval if

I was going to have a prayer of taking over for her as Gregory's assistant.

Janet looked at the clock on the wall beside us. "Oh my, listen to me. I've been talking your ear off this whole time and it's well past lunch! Do you have any questions for me, Claudia?"

We'd been on a first name basis since fairly early on in the conversation.

"It was all good information if I'm going to be working or Mr. M...I mean, Gregory," I said, correcting myself. According to Janet, Gregory kept things fairly informal with the employees who closely worked with him. It was a promising revelation. "Do you know when you'll make a decision about the position?"

"I was supposed to meet with a couple of girls from downstairs tomorrow, but between you and me"--she whispered behind her hand--"I've never cared for either of them." Janet gave me a wink. "Not to mention, I just love that little friend of yours, Bridget. She's about the cutest thing I've ever seen. Had nothing but great things to say about you. You should expect to hear from me by tomorrow afternoon. I'm sure Gregory, the real Gregory, will want a chance to chat with you before making it final." She laughed. At least she thought the situation was funny. I was not amused. "I bet you're starving, so I won't keep you any longer. We should be able to get you started by the end of the week."

"Thank you so much, Janet. I look forward to hearing from you." I smiled. I needed to get out of there before that door opened if I was going to have any prayer of getting out of dinner with Greyston Michaels.

We shook hands and I slipped out of her office. Two pairs of legs were visible at the bottom of Gregory's office wall where the glass was clear. I turned and took a step just as the door opened. Shit. I squeezed my eyes shut.

"Ms. Winston, can I walk you out?" Damn, his voice was sexy.

"That's not necessary. I can see myself out, but thank you," I replied, turning but trying to avoid looking directly into those gorgeous eyes again.

"Please, I insist." He moved closer and put his hand out. "I suppose we haven't been properly introduced. Greyston Michaels, at your service."

There was a hint of promise in that last statement.

Despite myself, I laughed at his feigned formality. I was still pissed. At least I should have still been pissed at him for fooling me.

"Nice to meet you, Mr. Michaels. I really do need to get going," I replied, taking his hand.

The contact sent a tingle up my arm. I pulled my hand away and gripped my portfolio, moving it in front of me. As if on cue my stomach growled loudly. The corner of his mouth turned up as his gaze drifted down to the source of the noise. Why did I look at his lips? My stomach tightened again, definitely not due to hunger, at least not for food.

"Please, call me Grey. All my friends do." He looked back up. "Let me take you to lunch."

"I can't. I have plans."

It was true, I was supposed to meet with the girls back at Homewrecker Incorporated to debrief. Not to mention I felt the need to make him pay for his little identity switching stunt and regain my control over the situation.

"So, Grey, do you always lie to your friends about who you are?"

There was no point in small talk.

"When did I lie?" he asked as we rounded the corner, a cocky grin smeared over his delicious face.

"When we first met, you knew I thought you were your brother. Then when Janet called you Gregory, you didn't say otherwise before you took me into *your* office," I said, lowering my voice when I caught sight of the starstruck receptionist watching us curiously.

"I believe you called me Mr. Michaels when we met. That is, in fact, my name, isn't it?" he said with one eyebrow cocked. "And you said you were here to interview to be my new assistant. I will be needing a new assistant now that I'm home."

"But no one knew you were even coming, so you knew I wasn't here for you," I whispered over my shoulder, pressing the button for the elevator repeatedly as if that would somehow force it to arrive sooner. "You lied by omission."

"Exactly. You weren't here for me, but I wasn't ready to let you go and telling you would have meant doing exactly that. Besides, I think I'm the one who should be upset here. Janet has known me my whole life, and she can't tell me from my brother? And you? The woman of my dreams steps out of a cab right in front of me my first day home, and she's only interested in me when she thinks I'm my very married brother."

He moved closer. The heat of his body warmed my back even though we were inches apart.

"Perhaps we should be discussing that, Ms. Winston," he whispered against my hair.

He made some valid points, but the only thing sticking in my mind at the moment was the bit about me being the woman of his dreams and the feel of his hot breath on my neck.

"I-I--" I stammered and then stopped, took a deep breath, and turned to face him head-on.

Big mistake. Even with me standing nearly six foot tall in heels, he was several inches taller. I found my eyes lined up with those gorgeous, ultra kissable lips. All rational thought left me as I contemplated saying fuck it all and sliding my tongue over them. By some miracle, I managed to get ahold of myself. I took a step back and looked him in the eye. If it was possible, they were even sexier than his lips.

"I'm not interested in your brother." His eyes lit up. "Or anyone else," I added, an obvious fabrication considering the way my gaze slipped back down to his mouth. I even bit my lip, as if in invitation. He stepped closer and God help me, I didn't attempt to get away.

The elevator door opened behind me, but I couldn't move. I barely noticed another woman join the receptionist behind her desk. I was sure they were both watching us, but I couldn't have cared less who was around in that moment.

"So I'll see you tonight, then," Grey said with no question in his voice as he moved closer. His breath smelled of the scotch we'd been drinking. I imagined he'd had another with his brother after we'd separated.

"I don't think that's a good idea." I tore my gaze from his mouth. I looked back up into the deep amber-colored pools and found myself drowning in the desire I saw in them.

"Oh my God! Mr. Michaels, Mr. Greyston Michaels?" the receptionist's companion squealed, rushing over to us. "I'm so sorry, sir. I had no idea you were coming home, or I would have had your office prepared. I'm Rebecca Turner, the new office manager." The rather attractive brunette shoved her hand into Greyston's chest, completely ignoring my presence.

Greyston looked annoyed but turned away from me to take it. "My apologies Ms. Turner, I just arrived in town last night and I wanted to surprise my brother."

My body yearned for his closeness, which was just the wake-up call I needed. I had to get away from him and get my head back in the game. The elevator had closed already but hadn't left the floor. A quick touch of the button, an open door, a step backward, and I was inside.

His head whipped toward me while the office manager continued talking as if she hadn't interrupted us. She put her hand on his forearm. I felt an unfamiliar twinge in my stomach and glared at her and then at him. He grinned at me, a knowing look in his eyes.

"Eight o'clock, Ms. Winston," he said, watching me as the doors closed.

Hidden safely in the elevator I sagged against the side. So it was definitely Gregory in the pictures, but what the fuck was wrong with me? I couldn't even begin to process what happened. It was a bad dream--a nightmare. Or maybe it was the best dream I'd ever had. I really couldn't decide. I needed to leave before I did anything stupid, like go back upstairs and drag that flirty little office manager down the stairs by her hair.

Shit, I was fucking jealous. I didn't get jealous. I also didn't do insane chemistry with strange men who weren't my marks. I needed to get my shit together and refocus on why I was there in the first place.

I thought of Gregory Michaels. Was he wearing his wedding ring? Did he even look at me? I couldn't remember anything except he looked exactly like the man whose mere presence rendered me virtually senseless.

The elevator stopped, and I quickly straightened up so as not to appear like an insane person using the wall to hold her up. I moved forward, assuming I'd arrived back down at the lobby.

The doors opened and I stepped forward, nearly running into someone attempting to board the elevator.

"Oh," a familiar voice said in surprise.

"I'm sorry." I stepped back. "I thought this was the lobby."

Bridget joined me in the elevator. I'd completely forgotten she would be somewhere in the building. Her old boss hired her back on the spot the week before, which was no surprise considering how talented she was.

"Nope, one more floor to go," she said casually as the doors closed. "It's so weird seeing you here," she whispered once we were alone. "How did it go with Janet?"

"Fine." I wasn't ready to tell her the truth.

After my encounter with Greyston Michaels, it was clear I was in trouble. I should have been thinking about how to get Lydia to replace me on the job. Our types were similar, and I hadn't made any sort of impression or connection with the man I was intended to meet. A reasonable excuse would be easy to manufacture, and Lydia was a great investigator and she'd made it abundantly clear she was willing to do a lot more than investigate Gregory Michaels.

Still, I convinced myself stepping away wasn't an option. I worried I may have compromised the mission, but I could recover from the setback who was Greyston Michaels. Patty said it herself: I was the best and there was too much on the line for me to step aside because of a few minutes of harmless flirtation with the wrong man. I'd made a commitment to Elsa, and I refused to admit failure to the most important client we'd ever had.

That was why I kept my little mishap to myself. It had nothing to do with the fact giving the job up meant I would likely never see Greyston again. Everything was going to be fine. I just had to figure out my next move, and what I was going to wear to dinner.

Chapter 5

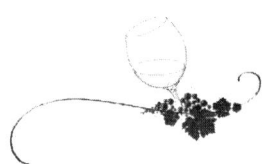

"I've tapped into all the cameras on G&G's premises, so we can at least see who's coming and going. They cover the main entrance inside and out, the entire lobby, the elevators and the hallways on each floor." Bridget pulled up the camera feeds on her laptop. She'd slipped away for lunch only, so she would have to head back to G&G shortly.

I leaned forward to get a better view, secretly wishing for a glimpse of Greyston. Grey. God, I loved his name.

"Gregory would have to be an idiot to do anything obvious there anyway," I added.

"So you're on a first name basis already?" Grace elbowed me. "Did you meet him today?"

"Only for a moment in passing. We weren't even introduced. He seemed to have a lot going on at the time, so I couldn't really get a read on him."

That was definitely true; I'd barely even looked at him.

I'd been racking my brain on the ride back about whether or not I should mention anything about Grey, ultimately deciding it would be impossible to hide. Based on that slutty office manager's reaction, the news of Grey's return would be buzzing around the office by the time Bridget returned from lunch.

"I did meet his brother," I said, which didn't get much of a reaction as Bridget and Lydia hovered over the computer engrossed in technical speak about the security at G&G. We all knew the three brothers owned and ran the company. They assumed I meant the younger brother, Chad. "His twin, he's back from Japan."

It took them all a moment to realize what I'd said.

"No fucking way!" Lydia responded. "There are two of that sexy ass man running around in this city as we speak?"

"I thought he wasn't coming back for at least a year?" Grace asked, obviously concerned. "Why would Elsa not mention this?"

"She didn't know." I rubbed the pendant of my necklace nervously between my thumb and forefinger. "It seems his return was a complete surprise to everyone, including his family."

"So exactly how identical are we talking?" Lydia asked. "Say if one had you bent over fucking your brains out and the other tagged in, would you notice the switch?"

I laughed. She was always so fucking crass and I loved her for it.

"I'm not sure. I only saw them for a few seconds." It wasn't a total lie. I really did only see them together briefly, and I didn't exactly get a chance to do a full comparison.

"Shit, this could be a huge problem. If you did manage to get evidence of Gregory Michaels cheating, any decent lawyer will try to argue it could be his brother," Grace said. She was always good at looking at each case from the perspective of our mark's lawyers.

"Guess you're just going to have to say his name!" Lydia swatted my ass as I passed by on my way to the cabinet at the back of my office. I needed a drink.

My stomach tightened as I imagined being bent over the desk in Gregory's office. Unfortunately, it was the wrong twin standing behind me in my fantasy; at least the wrong one for the job. As far as fantasies go, Grey was definitely the right twin.

"You'll need to figure out how to tell them apart. Your testimony will have to be tight, and you'll need to be able to prove you're certain which man is which," Grace said as I poured myself a drink.

"Anyone else want?" I held the bottle up. "You seem pretty hell-bent on believing Gregory Michaels is a cheater, Grace. Aren't you supposed to be the more optimistic one?" I bumped her shoulder.

"I'm just being realistic. I wasn't convinced until she told us about the prenup. He had to know Elsa was getting screwed over in the deal; his lawyers wouldn't keep that from him. If he's capable of that, cheating wouldn't be much of a stretch."

"No drink for me," Bridget replied, her shoulders sagged. "I have to get back to work."

She gave a quick wave and headed out.

Grace and Lydia had no such objections to a lunchtime adult beverage.

Grace's comment about my testimony popped into my mind again. I felt ill as I envisioned myself in a room with the twins and a bunch of lawyers as I played a game of name that twin and recounted my sexual exploits with Gregory. I imagined Grey standing there, his expression full of hurt and disappointment.

Jesus. I'd really gone off the deep end thinking about a guy I barely knew being hurt by me doing my job. He wouldn't be hurt; he would be fucking pissed, for his brother and his company. If I got evidence of cheating and Elsa went through with a divorce, Gregory would have to sell a good chunk of his stock in G&G to pay the infidelity penalty. I found the small part of myself, which had been wishing earlier Gregory would be the first man to prove me wrong, had grown exponentially larger.

"We'll have to put surveillance on both of them." Lydia interrupted my train of thought. "If we can document where the twin is when you get the evidence, it will make our case stronger."

It seemed she was finally getting serious about the work. When she did, she was a force to be reckoned with. That was my moment. I should have confessed right then and there about my attraction to Grey and more importantly, his attraction to me. I could have easily made up some excuse to pass on the assistant's job, but there was no guarantee Lydia could step in and get it. What if Janet ended up giving it to one of the girls internally? It was too much of a risk; I had to stay the course.

"She's right. We'll need to keep tabs on both of their movements," Grace said. "I'll get in touch with Patty to hook us up with a couple of investigators she trusts." While Lydia and Grace were more than qualified to handle the simple tail jobs, we'd decided because we were working locally it would be better to outsource.

"I think we should hold off on the surveillance. At least for a few days until I get back in, actually meet Gregory Michaels officially, and secure the job." Or at least until I'd managed to straighten things out with Grey. Being spotted with him could be hard to explain.

Grace eyed me questioningly. "Why would we wait? For all we know he might actually be fucking that girl from the pictures or any number of other girls. Any evidence of cheating, even if it's not enough to break the infidelity clause, will make our case that much stronger once we do have the evidence we need."

"Except we don't know who took those photos. Someone else has been tailing Gregory Michaels and we don't know why. They don't work for Elsa, so what's the angle?"

"I thought we agreed it was a paparazzi ploy, like Elsa said," Lydia replied.

"I've just been thinking. What if it's not about that? What if it really is about money and they're planning to shake Elsa down. Whoever sent them is probably betting she will pay a lot of money to avoid even the appearance of a scandal." I was grasping at straws.

"Then why haven't they made any attempts to contact her with a price?"

"Maybe they're waiting for a juicier story, something she'd pay more to cover up," Bridget added. I could have kissed her.

"Exactly. The first round of photos were probably just to put Elsa on edge, to make her question Gregory. If they're waiting for more marketable photos, they'll still be watching Gregory and Elsa every chance they get."

It was actually a really good point.

"That's why we need to wait on surveillance. Risking the paparazzi thinking Elsa hired an investigator to follow her husband is like throwing chum out to sharks. There's too much on the line for us to rush into anything and risk feeding some tabloid scandal, which is exactly what Elsa is trying to avoid. Let me get in a room with Gregory and secure the assistant's job, see how he responds to me. Once I'm working with him, I'll be able to watch him closely and figure out what's really going on."

My motivations might have been all wrong, but my ideas were right. The Michaels job was different from any job we'd ever done and not just because of the rules we were breaking. There were other, unpredictable players involved, so we needed to take a different approach with the case. It had nothing to do with Grey. At least that was what I was telling myself. He was just a minor hiccup in our plan. The others, especially Grace, were already stressing out enough. I didn't need add to it. I could handle Grey.

"Okay, we'll wait until we hear back from you," Grace said, ending her call with Patty. "She's going to call Elsa to discuss the implications of the twin being in town."

"Is she concerned?" I asked.

"She didn't seem as worried as I would have expected. I'm guessing the fact we get paid no matter what has something to do with it. How about you? Are you doing okay? You've seemed off since you got back. Are you having doubts about taking a job at home?"

"I'm fine, just worrying about covering our asses." I smiled. I should have known Grace would be able to tell I was holding something back.

"Listen, Claud." Grace took my hand. I knew she meant business when she called me that. "I know this time of year is hard on you. If you're not up to this, it's not too late to try to get Lydia to interview in your place. Her approach might be different, but we both know she could handle it."

If I hadn't already felt like shit for lying to my partners and friends, I definitely did then. I'd gotten so caught up in what had happened earlier, I'd nearly forgotten about my mom's anniversary, which was coming up. Fourteen years had passed since I lost her.

"I'm fine, Grace, really. The distraction is good for me, you know that."

"Okay, but you let me know if that changes or if you need to talk." She put her arm around my shoulders. "You want to head upstairs and order some takeout?"

I still hadn't eaten lunch, but I found I no longer had much of an appetite. I was too anxious about dinner with Grey.

"Actually, I was thinking about going for a run and then taking a drive down to see Jessica. She's been calling today, and it's been a while since I've seen my niece."

It had been way too long since I'd seen little Izzy and my sister. They also provided an excellent excuse for me to be out for dinner. I almost never went out without Grace or one of the other girls when I was home, so she'd definitely be curious about me leaving. With the drive, I could spend a couple of hours with them and still make it to the restaurant by eight.

It would be a short meal and by the time it was over, Grey would no longer be a problem and everything would be back on track.

Chapter 6

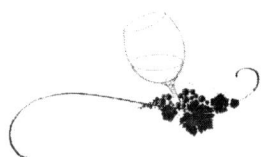

"Auntie Claudia!" Izzy squealed as she raced toward me across the lawn.

I swore my niece grew cuter every time I saw her. I closed the door of my cherry-red RS7 and I jogged to meet her.

"Hi, pumpkin." I scooped her up into my arms. At five years old she was barely the size of the average four-year-old. "Who's this little guy?" I pointed to the stuffed bunny in her hand.

"Bobby the bunny." She proudly pushed him up to my face to give me a closer look. "Grandpa Robert gave me him."

I fought the frown that pulled the corners of my mouth at the mention of my father. While Jessica respected my wishes to not talk about him, I could hardly expect my niece to understand, so I just smiled.

"Well, what a lovely little bunny he is."

The screen door squeaked and snapped shut as my sister walked out onto the wraparound porch of her classic country ranch. It was exactly what I pictured when I thought of the perfect family home, complete with a picket fence and an inviting porch swing. Around back there was an inground pool and a charming tree house Izzy was too small to climb into by herself. Behind it was a rather extensive playset with three swings, two slides, monkey bars, and rings. The house was fairly modest, considering the money my sister had courtesy of an inheritance from our mother but more so from our father who'd put a sizable amount of money in trust for Jessica after mom died. He'd attempted to do the same for me, but I wouldn't take a penny from that man.

For the most part, Jessica's trust remained untouched because Shawn was adamant about them making it on their own. I really admired that about my sister's husband. The only extravagances he compromised on were for Izzy's benefit.

Jessica walked over to us, her expression worried as she pulled us into a hug.

"I'm so glad to see you, Claudia, but I wish you'd called or at least answered when I did."

The door opened and closed again.

"If I'd known you were coming I would have asked him to leave." She placed her hand on my forearm, her expression apologetic.

My heart sunk.

"Hello, Claudia."

It'd been years since I'd heard that voice, but I remembered it as clearly as if it was yesterday.

My first instinct was to run to my car and peel out of there as fast as possible. My second was to walk straight up to him and slap him across the face. That was what I'd done the last time I saw him. Instead I gave Izzy a kiss on the cheek and passed her to Jessica before turning around.

I lifted my chin and said, "Robert."

"It's good to see you, honey." His blue eyes searched my face.

My stomach turned at his use of the endearment he'd assigned to me when I was just a naive little girl stupid enough to think her father was the greatest man in the world. He made his way down the steps toward us. He'd barely aged in fifteen years. Apart from a bit more gray hair, he was still the same handsome piece of shit I remembered. "You look so much like Teresa now."

I gasped and stepped back as though he'd punched me in the gut.

"Don't you dare say her name," I spat.

"Claudia," Jessica said softly. I glared at her and she lifted her hand in surrender.

"I shouldn't have come." I spun around to head back to my car. I was certain my face was probably as red as my car by that point. I hated I couldn't control myself around him but after what he'd done, I just couldn't handle it. My blood boiled and I needed to get out of there. Fast.

"Auntie Claudia, you have to play with me," Izzy demanded as I walked away.

"Sorry, pumpkin pie. Auntie Claudia has to go do some work, but we'll play next time. I promise," I said, turning briefly to give her a reassuring smile and a wink. "Maybe we can go see a movie soon?" She smiled brightly, nodding like any child would.

"It's a date." Satisfied she wiggled out of Jessica's arms and ran up to the porch where Shawn just stepped out.

"Claudia, please, just talk to me. Don't you think this has gone on long enough?" Robert strode toward me. Jessica wisely joined her family well out of the line of fire.

"Long enough? How long is long enough to hate the person who killed your mother?" I sneered, keeping my voice low enough that Izzy wouldn't hear.

He reached for my arm.

"Don't you dare fucking touch me!" I yanked my arm away and jumped into the driver's seat. He started to say something else, and I slammed the door. Something I would have yelled at anyone else for. That car was my baby, but I was too pissed to care. I revved up the engine, and after a brief moment of seriously contemplating running him over, I peeled out, spraying gravel at his feet.

I sped over the countryside, making my way back to the city. The speedometer approached one hundred miles per hour. Times like that I wished for a manual transmission, the ability to shift, to leave my problems behind one gear at a time.

My phone chimed in the seat beside me. I didn't have to look to know it was Jessica, a fact confirmed by the screen in the dash a second later. I ignored the call and slowed just enough to make my next turn without going off the road. My gym bag slid across the black leather and red stitching of the backseat. Thank God I'd grabbed it before I left. I needed the run I'd told Grace I was going to take before I went to my sister's. I had a lot of time to kill before eight, and I couldn't risk going back to the penthouse and being spotted by Grace with no excuse to go out again without her. I could have gone to the temporary apartment, but there was hardly anything in there and I needed a distraction.

As I took another turn, I hoped my dress wasn't getting wrinkled in the trunk. I regretted not hanging it in the car, but with the way I was driving, it probably would have ended up on the floor anyway. Thankfully, my gym had complimentary irons and steamers I could use when I stopped there to shower.

I should have canceled my date. Shit, not date, business dinner, but I told myself I didn't have Grey's number. Of course I could have called the office or Janet directly to get it or at least leave him a message, but that didn't cross my mind. Or if it did, I ignored it.

I was too busy stewing over that son of a bitch my sister still called Dad. I was determined to never refer to him as anything but Robert.

I managed to make it to North Avenue Beach in one piece and without getting a ticket for reckless driving. At one point I think my speed topped out at around 120.

I grabbed my bag from the back and kicked off my heels before I pulled my dress up around my waist and slipped into a pair of running shorts. I didn't bother to look around before I unzipped and pulled the dress over my head, which elicited an enthusiastic tap on my window and thumbs-up from a couple of college-age meatheads jogging by. I flipped them off. One, who was rather cute, pantomimed being stabbed in the heart as he jogged backward behind his two friends who were heading for the running path. He mouthed, "I love you," before turning around. I laughed to myself and slid my sports bra on over the black lacy number before I unclasped it and pulled it free.

A few minutes later, with shoes on and earbuds in, I was running through all my frustrations and repeatedly past the pack of frat boys I continuously ignored despite their best efforts. The playlist blaring in my ears wasn't one I listened to often, but the anger in the voice of the metal band's lead singer matched what I was feeling as my feet pounded the trail and I pictured my father's face below them.

Chapter 7

"Do you have a reservation?" The host asked when I entered the restaurant. I inhaled the aroma of steak and butter filling the elegant space.

"No, at least I don't think so. I'm meeting someone, but we only made the plans a few hours ago so I doubt he called ahead." I nervously played with the few golden strands of hair hanging loose from my French twist at the base of my neck.

"What's the name?"

"Michaels, Greyston Michaels."

"Oh yes, here it is. Mr. Michaels made a reservation for eight. You're rather early, so it will be a few minutes before your table is ready. Would you like to wait at the bar?"

"God yes," I replied.

I definitely needed a drink. My run, shower at the gym, and subsequent trip to the Art Institute of Chicago took my mind off things for a time. I always felt close to my mother when I walked amongst the beautiful paintings and sculptures of the Institute. She loved art and would take Jess and I on spontaneous trips to museums and galleries around the country a few times a year. It was a passion that had rubbed off on me. Unfortunately, the instant I stopped and let my thoughts drift, I was right back there staring into the face of the man who walked away and ruined everything so many years ago.

The host helped me out of my cream peacoat, revealing the open back of my black and cream dress with red lacing across the low-cut chest. I might have been there for a business dinner, but my dress sent an entirely different message.

"Vodka and soda," I said to the bartender when he approached. I definitely didn't nurse it and was ordering another just a few minutes later.

"A woman after my own heart," a very sexy voice said against my ear.

Much like the vodka, his presence got into my bloodstream and completely threw my body off balance. As much as I tried not to, I smiled when he stepped up right beside me, so close I could feel his warmth against the bare skin of my thigh. The familiar tension I felt low in my belly whenever he was around took on a whole new life. I longed for the touch of his hands on my bare skin.

He glanced down at his watch. "I see you were even more anxious for our date than I was."

"Business meeting," I corrected with a sly grin. "And I always say if you're on time, you're late."

Despite the protest of my body, which clearly wanted to get as close to Grey as possible, I was here to end our harmless flirtation, or whatever the hell it was between us. A task which would have better served with a sober, not fucked up by seeing my dad, mind. Who was I kidding? I'd known when I chose my dress for the evening that the night, very much like the day that preceded it, was not going to go to plan. At least not any plan I was willing to admit having.

Grey looked even better than I remembered and his lips even more kissable in the dim light of the bar. Seeing him again, I realized how different he was from his brother, at least from the photos I'd seen of Gregory. Grey's hair was just a bit longer and more disheveled. Gregory was the picture of a disciplined businessman--everything in just the right place. Grey had a more carefree vibe about him.

"So, Mr. Michaels--"

"Grey," he interrupted.

"So, *Grey,* what exactly is the purpose of the business meeting? Are you going to give me pointers on how best to serve your brother?" His jaw clenched and a fire lit in his eyes. "As his new assistant," I added, turning my body toward him. His face relaxed as I took a sip of my drink.

"To the contrary, like I told you, I need a new assistant. I believe your talents will be better utilized serving me."

He placed his hand over mine around the glass and pulled it toward him. His unexpected touch sent goose bumps over my skin. Keeping his eyes trained on me, he took a drink from my glass. His tongue flicked out over his bottom lip to catch a stray drop of the clear liquid.

"My need for you is far more urgent than my brother's," he continued, his eyes burning into me as he took the lime from the rim of my glass and sucked it between his lips. "I'll have one of these, as well," he told the bartender without looking at him.

I pulled my lip between my teeth and bit down to temper the urge to kiss him right there in the middle of the crowded restaurant.

Between the drinks and the stress of the day, I was far past worrying about my responsibility to Elsa Michaels. The only thing I was worried about was getting some release and from what I could tell, Greyston Michaels could give me that and more.

"You are the most stunning woman I have ever seen," he whispered, inching closer. "Those eyes, I've never seen anything like them."

"Oh yeah." I smirked. "What color are they?" I closed my eyes before finishing the question. No one ever really noticed their true colors, so I expected an educated guess at best.

"Well"--he leaned over and whispered in my left ear--"the left is sea green with hints of blue, like the ocean when you're far out looking down into the depths. The right"--he moved around, letting his lips brush ever so slightly over my forehead, to whisper in my right ear--"is blue like the sky on a perfect summer day."

I opened my eyes, surprised at his accurate response. My heterochromia typically eluded most people, even those close to me would say my eyes were either green or blue, never one of each, a trait inherited from my mother.

Whatever was left of my instinct to fight the attraction between us dissipated as I leaned forward until our lips were mere centimeters apart. "You're going to regret me," I whispered against his mouth.

"The only thing I would regret is not kissing you right now," he breathed, closing the gap between us. He gripped my hips, sliding me forward on the stool. My lips parted instinctually. His tongue slid along the seam of my mouth and then against my tongue. The essence of lime teased my taste buds. He pulled back, breaking the contact as quickly as it began. I groaned as my body revolted against the loss of his touch.

"We have plenty of time." He gave me a sexy smile as he picked up the drink the bartender must have dropped off while I was too distracted to notice.

I'm pretty sure I pouted a little, but I didn't audibly protest, instead choosing to join him in a drink. He was working me. Smooth. I imagined he'd left a long line of brokenhearted women in his wake over the years. I considered knocking his confidence down a peg or two and telling him we didn't have as much time as he thought. Right then, that night was it. It had to be. No matter what happened with Elsa's case, there was no chance of anything else with me for him, or any man really. Seeing my father further enforced my determination to stay permanently unattached.

"Pardon me, Mr. Michaels, your table is ready," the host said from behind us.

Grey flashed me a sexy smile before he stood and waited for me to pass. Following the host to the main floor, he escorted us to a private table against the back wall. Watching Grey sit, I got the chance to appreciate all six-foot-something of his chiseled frame. He'd changed out of his business attire and wore a pair of jeans that hung low on his trim hips with a fitted button-down black shirt that clung slightly to his well-muscled chest.

"So what do you think about my proposal?" he said after the waiter took our orders for another drink and appetizers. My heart fluttered at his choice of words. Jesus, I needed to get a grip.

"Excuse me?" I replied before taking a gulp of vodka and soda.

"To be my assistant." One side of his mouth turned up in a devilish grin. "I can guarantee working under me would be much more *fulfilling* than working for my brother."

God, he was cocky.

"I doubt I would get much work done if I was your assistant," I said, looking up at him as I ran my fingertip around the rim of my glass. "Besides, doesn't your company have some sort of antifraternization policy? I'm guessing kissing your subordinates is against the rules."

"You'd be my subordinate if you worked for my brother," he stated. That was true.

"That's why I'd prefer it if we could keep this *business meeting* between us." I inhaled the bouquet of the Harlan Estate Cabernet the waiter sat in front of me, noting the hints of licorice, blackberry, and vanilla. I took a sip and then nodded for a full pour.

"Leave the bottle, please," Grey said after the waiter filled his glass as well.

The young man set the bottle down with an appreciative nod before walking away, clearly pleased with the anticipated tip on a meal which included a $500 bottle of wine.

"I never kiss and tell," Grey said with a sly smile as he watched me enjoy my wine. "You know, you don't really strike me as the administrative assistant type, Ms. Winston."

"Exactly what type *do* I strike you as, then?"

"You strike me as the type of woman who knows what she wants and knows exactly how to get it. The job seems beneath you."

"I'm not sure Janet would appreciate hearing you say that."

He was right of course. It surprised me he was so perceptive about who I was after such a short acquaintance. The only depth the men I typically dealt with cared about was that of my neckline.

"I didn't mean it like that. Janet's great. There's just a different fire in your eyes. You actually remind me of someone."

"If you say it's an ex-girlfriend I'm leaving." I took my napkin off my lap to back up the feigned threat. He reached for my arm even though it was clear I was joking.

"It's going to sound weird now." He ran his hand through his hair. "It's my mom."

"You're right. That's fucking weird." I laughed.

"I thought women liked men who love their mothers," he said with a half grin.

"Maybe, but I don't know any woman who wants a man to say she reminds him of his mother." I laughed a little harder.

"Jesus, I'm not saying you look like her or anything. Just I see the same kind of strength in you she's always had. G&G Components wouldn't exist without her."

"Oh," I said, genuinely touch by the compliment. I was used to hearing good things about how I looked, but Grey's words were foreign and knocked me a little off balance.

"Well, Grey, my dream is to save up enough money to buy a modest vineyard in Italy or maybe California and live out my years making and drinking good wine."

I couldn't believe I'd actually shared that with him. Grace was the only other person who knew my ultimate goal. I smiled as I imagined walking through the rows of vines, feeling the sun that nourished the grapes warming my face.

Grey smiled, taking his first sip of the wine I'd ordered. Someday, I'd be watching people drink wine I'd made.

He swirled the glass of burgundy liquid. "This wine is excellent."

"Wine's been a passion since I was a teenager," I said, joining him in the drinking. "What about you? Did you always dream of selling electronic vehicle components when you were I kid?"

He laughed, flashing those perfect white teeth. Grey was attractive all the time, but he was downright irresistible when he smiled like that.

"Hardly, at around five I was pretty set on being a starfighter," he replied, still smiling.

"As in *The Last Starfighter*?" I asked and he nodded. "I loved that movie when I was little!" I said with a giggle.

I wasn't sure if it was the alcohol, Grey, or that we only had that one night together, but I hadn't ever been so open with a man in my adult life up to that point. Even stranger, I was actually having fun.

"By the time I got to high school, soccer was the dream. Gregory and I were both pretty good, and our parents were really supportive even though they'd always hoped we'd take over the company someday. It's named for us, after all."

"So what happened with soccer, then?" I rested my elbows on the table.

"We both earned athletic scholarships, but by the end of freshman year Gregory decided to quit and focus on school and his soon-to-be wife, Elsa. I stuck with it, and it was looking as though I had a real shot at playing professionally, but I got injured the first game of senior year. Shattered my lower leg and that was it."

There was a hint of sadness in Grey's eyes as he looked down at his hands.

"I'm sorry." I put my hand over his on the table. "I know how tough an injury can be on an athlete. A torn ACL almost lost me my volleyball scholarship, but I got lucky with the timing and made it back a few games into the season my senior year of high school."

"I noticed the scar on your knee." Grey turned his hand to grip mine before he ran his thumb over my knuckles. I shifted in my chair as the effect of his simple touch traveled through my body. I pulled my hand away and picked up my glass. He tilted his head to one side, eyeing me curiously.

"So you finished your business degree and joined the company with Gregory after college?"

"Yeah, I was lucky to have something to fall back on even though it wasn't exactly what I'd wanted at the time. Everything happens for a reason, right?"

"That's what they say," I replied. I'd always been more of the mind that shit just happened.

"I'm happy where I'm at right now," he said, his eyes sparkling as he smiled at me. Jesus. "Being in operations suits me. Traveling to different plants, working overseas, it's been a great experience."

"That's right. How long were you in Japan?"

"Five years in Tokyo."

"Wow, a long time. What was it like living there? Do you speak Japanese?"

"I didn't when I left. I've picked up quite a bit over the years, not that I'm fluent, but I can get by."

"That seems kind of terrifying, living in a place where you don't speak the language."

"So you speak Italian?"

"Um, not really, a little, but I plan to learn." I set my glass down and sat up straighter.

"Even if you don't, I imagine you'll do just fine anywhere you go. Language barrier be damned."

I smiled like a schoolgirl who'd just been praised by her teacher. I needed to cool it with the drinking before I really embarrassed myself.

"So, why did you move to Tokyo for so long? Janet made it seem as though you were wanting to get away from something here." Yep, I definitely need to be cut off after asking such a pointed question and throwing Janet under the bus in one fell swoop.

Grey's jaw flexed. "Someone needed to go and I didn't have anything to keep me here at the time. All the other guys who could have gone had families to worry about. It was easier for me to leave."

He tossed back the last of his vodka and soda just as the waiter dropped off the seafood platter appetizer he'd ordered. It smelled divine.

"I never liked seafood when I was a kid, but my mom forced me to give it a try when we went to Italy and I learned to love it," I blurted after slurping down an oyster. I wasn't sure why I said it.

"Are you close with your mom still?"

I froze. She was definitely not a subject I discussed openly, especially with men.

"Yes, no, um, I mean I was, but not anymore. She died a long time ago."

"I'm so sorry," he said, taking my hand on the table like I'd done earlier.

"It's fine." I pulled away from his grip despite how good it felt to touch him again. "Like I said, it was a long time ago."

Pulling his hand back as well, he seemed to take the hint and changed the subject.

"You've never been married, any kids?" he asked, grinning before he popped a shrimp into his mouth.

I nearly choked on a bite of lobster. "God no, no kids. I have a five-year-old niece I adore but that's it."

"Does that mean you don't want kids?"

"I can't see myself ever getting married, so no. Romantic relationships aren't exactly my thing. I'm not big on disappointment and betrayal."

"Wow, that's a pretty bleak outlook you have there, Ms. Winston."

His use of my father's last name threatened to dampen my appetite.

"Please just call me Claudia from now on."

"All I had to do was kiss you for the privilege," he said with a grin, trying to lighten the mood.

"And you? You mentioned it was easier for you to go to Japan because you don't have any kids. Do you want them?" Why the fuck did I ask him that?

"I think so, but I don't know. I always thought it would have happened by the time I was this old. Now that it hasn't, I wondered if it's just not meant to be."

I nearly cracked up. A busboy approached and cleared the appetizer plates. I smiled at him before turning my attention back to Grey.

"So you're saying you're too old to have kids? How old are you? Thirty?"

"Thirty-three."

"Are you saying I'm old, then? I'm turning thirty-two two weeks from Friday. Perhaps I should start shopping around for nursing homes before it's too late." I bumped his leg with my foot under the table and smiled.

He grabbed it and I squealed before he pulled off my shoe and started massaging. I moaned my approval, wishing he'd move his skilled hands much, much further up my leg.

"Two orders of fillet with peppercorn sauce and roasted asparagus," the waiter said, interrupting our little massage party as he placed the plates on the table. My stomach rumbled at the smell as I pulled my leg back in. "Can I get you anything else?"

"I'm fine," I replied, grabbing my utensils. Having not eaten all day, hunger took precedence over horny and the appetizer had done little to sate me. "This looks amazing."

I couldn't wait. I sliced into the perfectly cooked cut of beef and dipped it in the sauce.

"Oh my God," I said after swallowing the first bite. "This is the best steak I've ever tasted."

"It's very good," Grey agreed, "You have to let me cook for you. I can top this."

"Impossible." I took another bite. So. Fucking. Delicious.

"That sounds like a challenge. Now you'll have to have dinner with me again so I can prove it," he said with a devilish grin. "I make pretty good sushi, too."

The temptation was almost enough to make me consider seeing him again just for the food, but I'd already made up my mind. Somewhere between my sister's driveway and sitting down at the restaurant bar, I decided I just needed one night to get Grey out of my system so I could get my head back in the game.

"If you can cook better than this, you'll have no problem snagging a wife," I said without thinking.

He didn't react, just took another bite of his steak.

I basically inhaled my meal and started eyeing a piece of filet he'd left while he ordered a piece of chocolate cake for us to split.

"Do you want the rest of mine?" he asked with an amused grin.

I smiled sheepishly. "I really do love a good steak."

"I love a girl who eats." He swapped out our plates and watched me polish off his meat. I chuckled to myself, at least I thought.

"What's funny?"

"Nothing, just a dirty thought."

"I've been having those since I saw you get out of that cab this morning."

"Mr. Michaels, that is not appropriate business dinner conversation," I said, biting my lip. The waiter chuckled, setting a piece of gold-flecked chocolate cake between us.

"You started it," he shot back. "Actually, can you just box this up and bring the check?" He passed the plate back to the waiter.

I stuck my lip out. "I was going to eat that."

"You'll still get your chance, but I had something else in mind for my dessert." His voice was husky and full of promise as he signed the check without looking away from me.

My body hummed with anticipation. I wanted Grey like I'd never wanted anything in my life, even if just for the night. The job, the money, none of it mattered, then. It was reckless, and selfish, but I couldn't seem to stop myself even when it occurred to me the home I was about to wreck might just have been my own.

"Jesus, I thought that was you, Grey," a deep voice said from a few feet away as we stood next to our table. "Heard you were back in town."

A tall, sandy-haired man with a neatly trimmed goatee approached. A huge smile spread across Grey's face, making my knees feel weak.

"Hey, Chad!"

It took me a moment to realize the other man was his younger brother as they hugged tight, slapping each other on the back. When Grey pulled back, his smile dropped when he caught sight of the stunning and very leggy blonde who followed behind Chad.

"Hi, Grey, it's so great to see you. It's been far too long," she said softly, moving closer.

She went in for a hug and my blood heated. Grey stopped her by extending his hand for a formal shake. I exhaled my relief while mentally chastising myself for having that obnoxious and unnecessary reaction yet again. Her expression was one of confusion with perhaps a touch of hurt. She looked at me and all the softness and vulnerability in her expression morphed into disdain.

Chad's expression was apologetic as he mouthed "sorry" to his brother before turning to me.

"Who's your friend?" he asked, stepping closer to me, his eyes moving down to my legs, then back up and pausing on my breasts before finally coming to rest on my face.

"Claudia Winston, this is my brother Chad Michaels. Ms. Winston is replacing Janet as Gregory's assistant."

Grey stepped closer to me. I was glad to see he'd gotten past the notion of hiring me as his assistant instead.

"I haven't gotten the job yet." I smiled at Grey, but his expression remained tense. "It's nice to meet you, Mr. Michaels."

I extended my hand but instead of shaking it, Chad Michaels pulled it up to his face and pressed his lips to my knuckles just like Grey did the first time we met.

"Knowing my brother, I'm guessing you're a shoo-in for the gig," Chad said with a smirk.

If Grey and Chad's responses were any indication, I wasn't going to have any trouble catching Gregory Michaels's attention when I finally met him officially.

"We were just leaving," Grey said. His tone bordered on irritation. It seemed the jealous feelings worked both ways, a fact which made my smile a bit brighter.

Chad, who was still gripping my hand, reluctantly let it go and nodded to his brother. It seemed there was a bit of sibling rivalry between them.

"Aren't you going to introduce me?" the blonde said, stepping toward Grey again. He sighed without looking at her.

"Claudia, this is Ashley Slade, an old family friend. Her father is the former CFO of G&G."

"Wow, just an old family friend? I guess that's what five years does," she said. I couldn't quite figure out her tone. It was as if she was mad, hurt, and self-satisfied all at once.

"Yeah, something like that," Grey replied dismissively. "Shall we?" He inclined his head toward the exit.

I nodded and grabbed my purse from the back of my chair.

"It was nice to meet you both," I said to Chad and Ashley as I passed.

"I look forward to seeing you again, around the office," Chad said with a wink.

Ashley responded by glaring daggers at me. I flashed her my sweetest smile.

"We can grab lunch and catch up next week," Chad said to our backs. Grey waved without looking back.

"What was that all about?" I asked when we were out of earshot.

"Just some old family bullshit I don't want to drag back up," he responded, effectively shutting me down. I understood the impulse all too well. Family bullshit was the worst kind. Still, I was curious why he'd gotten so worked up seeing Ashley.

Grey placed his hand on the small of my back, guiding me around the corner to the entrance. His fingers teased the skin exposed by the opening in my dress.

"Shit, it's raining," I said when we reached the door. "My car is parked a block away."

He leaned down and whispered in my ear, "You won't need it tonight. I promise to get you back to it safely, tomorrow."

It was as if the awkward exchange from a few moments ago never happened. Grey was back to his confident, sexy self.

I opened my mouth to protest, there was no way I was staying with him that long, but all rational thought flew out the window when he slid his tongue down my ear and planted soft kisses on my neck. I shivered, squeezing my thighs together as the tension that'd been building all night took on new life. The movement made me acutely aware of the desire pooling between my legs.

I groaned softly when he moved away. I'd never been a fan of PDA. It hadn't really ever been an issue because the only men I saw were married but God help me, with the way he kissed my neck I would have let Grey do whatever he wanted.

A driver appeared in the doorway, umbrella in hand.

"Thank you, Vince," Grey said, his fingertips returning to my back. We walked out and slid into a black town car.

The door hadn't even fully closed and he was climbing over me, or maybe I was pulling him onto me. I couldn't be sure who was doing what. My head banged against the side of the car behind the window. I didn't care. I guess four vodka and sodas and a couple of glasses of superb wine will do that, or maybe it was finally getting to run my tongue over those gorgeous, wine-stained lips.

I grabbed Grey's face and pulled his plump bottom lip between my teeth, biting down just a little before I slid my tongue against his. He tasted like dark, sweet fruit and something else I couldn't quite identify but whatever it was, I wanted more. Grey groaned against my mouth and pushed my legs apart with his knee. My dress rode up over my thighs as he moved his leg forward until my black lace thong was against the denim of his jeans.

I moaned as he moved his leg against me. He slid one shoulder of my dress down, taking the strap of my bra with it.

Rather skillfully, he freed my breast from the formfitting material and pulled my hard nipple between his teeth. I sucked in a breath, bucking against the intense sensation as his tongue worked its magic, and he continued to move his knee against my throbbing pussy.

And then, as quickly and wildly as we'd begun, with me ready to let him fuck me right there in the backseat of the car, Grey released my nipple, moved his leg away and gave me a sweet, gentle peck on the nose as he pulled my dress and bra back up. He flashed a devious, satisfied smile, but his eyes gave away the lust and desire he was feeling. I gaped at him, completely stunned as he moved over and sat back in the seat.

He reached over and brushed his thumb over my bottom lip. "I'm sorry, baby, but there's no way our first time is going to be in the back of a car like a couple of reckless teenagers. I'm going to take my time savoring every bit of you. We'll be at my place in just a few minutes, but we need to make a quick stop first."

Grey opened the divider and instructed the driver to stop at the nearest drugstore. I'd been so wrapped up in him I hadn't noticed or cared whether or not Vince could see us. Modesty wasn't really my thing anyway. When the car came to a stop, Grey gripped the front of his pants and adjusted what looked to be a rather impressive erection before hopping out into the rain. Vince jumped out after him, attempting to get the umbrella open to escort him in, but Grey waved him off and walked in alone.

I adjusted my dress before Vince climbed back in. Checking my phone, I found several messages from Jessica and one from Grace. I didn't bother reading any of them, opting instead to survey my appearance with the camera. My cheeks were flushed and my hair was mussed with several pieces having fallen loose while Grey and I wrestled around. I smiled with my kiss-swollen lips and pulled the pins from my hair, letting it fall in loose golden waves around my shoulders.

Grey slid back in beside me with a plastic bag in hand, sucking in a breath when he saw me.

"You are so fucking sexy." He tossed the bag on the seat before he shifted, groaning as he tried to adjust his erection again. My gaze followed the motion of his hand, and I bit my lip as thoughts of tasting the silky hardness he was wrestling with invaded my mind.

I grabbed the bag, noticing a condom box through the semitransparent material as I pushed it out of the way and slid closer to Grey. It was surprising a man like him didn't walk around prepared. I imagined opportunities for casual sex fell into his lap regularly, a thought which reignited that pesky sinking feeling in the pit of my stomach. Then I wondered if it was just a ploy to gain my trust. It wouldn't be the first time a manwhore tried to pull a fast one on me. Of course, they'd always been marks, so I was the one pulling a fast one. This was unfamiliar territory.

He grinned sheepishly at my eyeing the bag as I slid over to him.

"It's been a long time for me, so I haven't had to worry about keeping these on hand."

I tilted my head, narrowing my eyes slightly as I examined him for any hint of a lie. I saw none.

The sense of relief his confession gave me was disconcerting. I had no business caring who or how often he fucked. Our night together was going to be a onetime thing, and we would go our separate ways as soon as it was over. Grey took my hand, rubbing his thumb lightly over my knuckles as his gaze moved from my eyes to my lips and back to my eyes. I should have pulled away; the action was intimate, too intimate. He touched me as if we were a real couple, not the one-night stand I was determined we were. Instead I pushed forward, pressing my lips against his as he smiled against my mouth. Running my tongue over his lips, I pushed my fingers through his thick hair before he pulled me onto his lap.

As we kissed, a little voice in the back of my mind told me this was dangerous, but I ignored it, convinced I was in control. I told myself again the attraction I felt to Grey was purely chemical; I needed to fuck him once to get him out of my head so I could focus and move on with the job at hand. Between the drinks and the making out and all the emotional shit I had going on in my personal life, I needed release. I needed to be fucked good and hard, so that was exactly what I intended to get.

"We're here," Grey said, breaking our kiss.

I smiled and moved off his lap to fix my clothes as I looked out the window. My heart pounded as the car turned onto the long winding driveway that led to Grey's home. My emotions swirled below the surface as the house came into view. The elegant and inviting property wasn't exactly what I expected for a bachelor. The lawn and landscaping were tasteful and well manicured. The house, while quite large, wasn't flashy or overbearing. It looked like a home.

Holding my hand, Grey helped me out of the car and led me around to a side door, stopping briefly to tell Vince he wouldn't need him again until the morning. I should have stepped in and told the driver to wait because I wouldn't be staying that long.

Instead I remained silent and followed Grey into the house. I would call a cab after I'd gotten what I needed.

"Wow," I said, stepping into the kitchen. It was set up much like I imagined the kitchen of a professional chef would be. Top-of-the-line stainless steel appliances, tons of cabinet and counter space, and a variety of cooking gadgets built in all around. And the smells. I'd stuffed myself at dinner, but the scent of cinnamon and vanilla in the air made my mouth water.

"I told you I like to cook," he said, pulling me along. Good, he wanted to get down to business, which was exactly what I needed.

We entered a large family room and he took me over to the couch. I guess that was better than the bedroom--less personal.

"Give me a minute," he said as I sat.

"Okay, where's the restroom?" I wanted to freshen up after our twenty-minute make out session.

He led me back toward the kitchen, pointing around the corner before he pressed a gentle kiss on my swollen lips and walked away. I watched him stroll back across the room and disappear down a hallway, plastic bag in hand. I slipped into the bathroom and took a moment to survey my appearance in the mirror above the vanity. I was surprised by how I looked. Based on how I was feeling, I expected to be a mess, but I looked as good as I had walking into the restaurant hours before, maybe better with my hair hanging in loose heavy waves. With no need to reapply my makeup, I splashed a little water on my face and ran a hand through my hair.

I slipped out of the bathroom and back to the family room. Grey was nowhere to be seen, so I took the time to explore the room. I stopped to admire an oil painting of a mountain landscape on my way to the fireplace. Landscapes were my favorite. I loved seeing the different perceptions of nature's beauty artists captured. A slight scent of burnt wood tickled my noise, which was surprising considering most people I knew opted for gas. I appreciated the realness of it.

The expansive mantle was lined with photographs that spanned many years. There was one of Grey and his brother when they were boys with a beautiful young woman I assumed was their mother. The twins couldn't have been more than two or three in the shot. Even then Grey had a smile to kill for. His hair was lighter, but the big golden hazel eyes were the same. I moved down the line of photos, which appeared to be arranged chronologically with various shots of Grey and his family. A wedding photo of his parents revealed the source of his good looks. He and Gregory looked a lot like their father, except for the eyes. Those were definitely their mother's. Chad, on the other hand, was like a masculine clone of her, just with lighter hair. There was another wedding photo, one of Elsa and Gregory. I immediately felt a twinge of guilt looking at her smiling face.

What the hell was I doing? I was supposed to be getting her answers about her husband, not fucking his brother for my own selfish reasons. Seeing her was almost enough to make me leave. To run home and confess my mistake to the girls so we could forge a new plan of attack. Almost.

Instead, I lingered as another picture caught my eye. It was of Grey's whole family, except this one included the blonde from the restaurant, Ashley. Grey's arms were draped around her from behind, the two of them looking as happy as any couple I'd ever seen. I had a sudden urge to vomit, followed by a strong urge to break something.

"That was a long time ago."

I jumped at Grey's unexpected presence behind me but didn't turn around.

"How long did you two date?" I asked, my eyes still fixed on his happy expression in the photograph.

"A few years, but I don't want to talk about that right now."

I turned to face him. A mischievous smile lit his handsome face, but there was a touch of sadness in his eyes. I couldn't keep my eyes up for long, considering he'd lost his shirt somewhere in the short time we were apart. All thoughts of leaving evaporated at the sight. He hooked his arm around my waist, pulling me to him. I gasped, but he swallowed the sound, pressing his lips to mine as he pushed me backward. His tongue flicked over mine and then retreated just before he did.

He sat down on the couch, pulling me with him before running his hands down over the bare skin of my knees and then around along my calves. My skin caught fire every place he touched, and I squirmed in anticipation. Kneeling on the floor in front of me, he slipped my shoes off and set them down carefully off to the side. Taking one foot into his strong hands, he rubbed his thumbs up from heel to toe. I groaned at how good his touch felt, unaware of how sore my feet were until then.

"God, that feels good," I whispered, closing my eyes and leaning back against the plush cushions while he continued with his skillful massage. He placed a soft kiss on the inside of each arch and then moved his hands up to my calves.

"You're so tense," he said as he worked his magic on my legs.

"I wonder why." I smirked, lifting my head up to look at him.

My desire flared as bright as ever seeing him down between my legs like that. His eyes were darker than before, clouded with lust as he watched me. I was certain the massage was over, but he kept going, taking his time working out the tension in my legs.

"I want you to fuck me, Grey."

"I know you do." His voice was low and sexy.

My hips rocked back involuntarily at his words. I sat up, reaching for him, trying to coax him up to me, but he resisted. He was so controlled, despite the emotions swirling in his eyes.

"I told you I was going to take my time savoring you, Claudia."

He kissed then licked up the inside of my calf up to my knee and then repeated the action on the other leg. Pushing my dress up to my hips, he spread my legs further apart and pressed his lips lightly against the inside of my thigh before nipping at the sensitive skin with his teeth. I squirmed, pressing my palms down into the couch. My pussy clenched with need. I wanted to grab his head and force his mouth to where it ached, but I resisted.

"I've been thinking about this since you crossed these beautiful legs in front of me in my brother's office. You knew what you were doing to me, didn't you?" He stroked his fingertips just outside the edges of my panties while he looked directly between my legs.

"Yes," I whispered, my voice husky.

"You wanted to tease me, didn't you?"

"Yes, God yes!" I replied as he let his fingers drift just inside the edges of the thin fabric.

"How do you like it, Claudia? Do you like being teased?"

"No, yes, fuck. I don't know, Grey. Please," I blurted out.

He reached under the crumpled material of my dress and gripped the sides of my panties. I raised my hips and he slid them down over my legs and tossed them onto my shoes. Grabbing the backs of my calves, he pulled me closer to the edge of the couch.

"I've been thinking about this pussy all day. I imagine you taste so sweet. Have you ever tasted yourself, Claudia?" He finally rubbed one finger between my swollen lips. "No," I moaned loudly. His touch felt better than I could have hoped.

"Tell me, is it sweet?" he demanded, sitting up and rubbing the same finger over my lips. I opened my mouth and he dipped it inside, letting me taste my own arousal. I closed my lips around his finger, watching him as I moved my tongue around it.

He growled and slowly pulled his finger from my mouth. "Well?"

"Mmm, it's so sweet," I whispered. He groaned and bit his lip as he moved back down.

"I'm not sure I believe you."

I could feel his warm breath against my aching flesh. He inched forward ever so slowly. Finally, when I didn't think I could stand it a moment longer, he ran his tongue over my soft, swollen lips. My loud moan filled the otherwise quiet room.

"God, you're even sweeter than I imagined," Grey said, his voice gravelly.

He spread my pussy with his fingertips, groaning at the sight before he flicked his soft tongue over my clit and sucked it between his lips. I gripped the couch for dear life as he stoked the fire inside me until I was sure I was going to set us both ablaze. He pushed one and then two fingers inside me and I came apart, crying out as my walls pulsed around him.

He crawled up over me, pressing his mouth against mine and parting my lips with his tongue. Tasting myself on his lips, I was immediately turned on again, as if I hadn't just had the most amazing orgasm.

He pulled back and stood up, still wearing his pants.

"I need to be inside you, Claudia," he whispered, watching me as he unbuttoned his pants, which hung low on his trim hips. "Take off your dress."

His body was exquisite, as if he'd been Photoshopped with his perfectly chiseled pecks, well-defined abs, and golden tan skin. My gaze drifted lower to the obvious strain in his jeans and my mouth watered.

I stood and obeyed his command, slipping my dress up over my head and adding it to my pile on the floor. I reached behind my back to unhook my bra and removed the last stitch of clothing I had on.

"Jesus, you are so fucking beautiful," Grey said, running his gaze over my body as he slid the zipper of his pants down.

I watched his hands, biting my lip in anticipation. He hooked his thumbs into the waist of his boxer briefs and slid them off with his pants, his torso blocking my view until he stood back up. I moaned, seeing all of him for the first time. He was fucking perfection, and his cock may have been the most beautiful thing I'd ever seen. I squeezed my thighs together, trying to ease the ache between my legs as we stood there staring at each other. I couldn't take it anymore. Walking forward, I reached for his huge cock but he grabbed my wrist, stopping me just before I could touch him.

I looked up at him, confused. He put his other hand on my shoulder and guided me down to my knees. My mouth watered with his swollen head mere inches away. Licking my lips, I moved forward and then stopped, glancing up at Grey for approval. Jesus, that was a whole new experience. Before then, I was always in control, in and out of bed, but with him, letting him drive was just so fucking hot.

He wrapped his hand around his thick base, pushing his hips forward just enough to brush it over my lips. My tongue shot out instinctually. He moaned as I swirled it around his tip before I sucked it into my mouth.

I can't honestly say I'd ever enjoyed giving head; I was good at it, but it wasn't really my thing until I tried it with Grey. The view of his perfectly sculpted abs, the delicious V cut into the sides of his pelvis like a map to the silky hard cock I was slowly taking further into my mouth. He bit down on his luscious bottom lip. It was the most erotic scene I'd ever laid eyes on. Grey tossed his head back and groaned as my lips moved further down his shaft while I flicked my tongue skillfully over the underside.

"Fuck," Grey moaned as I moved my mouth back and forth over his cock. "Oh fuck, stop!" he said, pulling away. "That felt way too fucking good."

He pulled me up and crushed his lips against mine. He traced my lips with his tongue, first the top and then the bottom, requesting entry. I happily obliged, sliding my tongue against his while his hands stroked my back. He gripped my ass and hoisted me up as I wrapped my legs around his waist.

Still kissing me, Grey carried me across the room. He broke our kiss and started nipping at my neck. I moaned, opening my eyes to see we'd entered a long hallway. The walls were lined with artwork, some famous enough I recognized it, but all coherent thought left me when his fingers slid around my ass and slipped between my wet lips. I gripped his back, steadying myself as he pushed a finger inside me as far as he could, considering the awkward angle.

The next thing I knew, my back hit the downy softness of an overstuffed comforter. Grey crawled over me, placing soft kisses on my belly on his way up. He paused his journey to suck my taut nipple while he massaged my clit until I felt as if I was about to come again. Just as I was about to tumble over that exquisite cliff, he pulled his hand away. I cried out in frustration as he sat up and reached into the night table. My insides tightened as took out and slid a condom over his cock. I was dying to feel every inch of him deep inside me.

Moving back over me, he held himself up on his elbows and stroked the side of my face with his hand. His eyes swam with emotion, but he remained silent. His hardness, trapped between us, pushed insistently up my thigh and over my pubic bone.

Grey lifted slightly, letting the thick weight of him slip down over my swollen lips. I spread my legs, giving him better access as he pressed forward keeping his eyes locked on mine as his tip probed my entrance. I struggled to keep my eyes open as the sensation overtook me and his girth slowly stretched me open. I cried out when he pushed the rest of the way in, the feeling a mix of pain and pleasure. He kissed my lips, my forehead, my eyes, my cheeks, and whispered sweet things in my ears I pretended not to hear. I didn't do mushy sweet sex but God, I loved every second of it with Greyston Michaels.

"Are you okay?" he asked with concern when I winced as he pulled out. The pain was exquisite.

"I'm, aah, amazing. Please don't stop," I begged breathlessly. I felt my orgasm rebuilding, but this one was different. The sensation coaxed from a deeper place as his pelvis rubbed over my clit and his cock hit that special place deep inside.

"I want to see you," he groaned, pulling out and rolling us until he was on his back and I was straddling him.

I started to move slowly at first, letting my body adjust to the change in position before I got into a good rhythm. His cock was easily the largest I'd ever experienced, and it was fucking amazing. He had the power to hurt me, but he seemed to know how to move just right, taking me right up to the edge of pain and eliciting a sort of pleasure I'd never experienced. His hands moved up my body and stroked my belly before finding purchase on my breasts. He massaged them both, rubbing my nipples between his thumbs and forefingers before he sat up and took one diamond-hard peak into his mouth while I continued to ride him.

The experience was like climbing to the top of a rollercoaster, the anticipation, the excitement building with each motion until I could see over the crest right before speeding down, but I didn't come all the way down. He lay back and stroked my clit with one hand as my orgasm peaked, bringing me to another immediately.

"That's it, come for me, baby." He sighed as he lifted his hips.

His body tensed with the approach of his own orgasm. Even as another orgasm overtook me, I couldn't take my eyes off his face. He stared right back; his eyes full of things unsaid, and I wondered if mine were the same. It was like nothing I'd ever felt before and it scared the shit out of me, but I was powerless to stop or escape it. I wanted to be there with him more than I'd ever wanted anything in the world.

He sat up again, rolling me onto my back without breaking our intimate contact. He pulled my legs up over his shoulders, pushing himself even deeper inside me as another orgasm ripped free. He continued to pump into me, his strokes growing harder before he dropped my legs and gave in to his own climax. His cocked pulsed inside me as his weight pressed down on me as he breathed heavily next to my ear. Once the trembling passed, he lifted up, gazing into my eyes. This was typically the point where I started planning my exit, but leaving was the last thing on my mind.

"I could really fall for you, Ms. Winston," he whispered against my lips before kissing them.

A knot of guilt shot into my stomach. I was going to hurt him. His use of that name reminded me of who I was to him, of the lie I was bound to and of all the people I was disappointing by being here.

I stayed silent when he pulled back, giving him a sleepy smile as my only response. I should have told him I needed to leave, but it was the only time I would have with him and I didn't want it to end.

He rolled to the side and pulled me to him so my back was to his front. My body clenched at feeling his lingering erection against my ass and thigh.

"I just want to hold you for a bit. Is that okay?" he said softly as he kissed the sensitive spot behind my ear.

"Sure," was the only response I could manage.

Waking up in the morning, I had that feeling you get when you're waking up from an amazing dream wishing you could somehow go back to sleep and pick up where you left off. Except what I wanted to get back to wasn't a dream.

"Good morning." Grey stepped through the doorway, the dishes clinking on the tray he carried. My stomach growled as the aroma of bacon hit my nose. "I wasn't sure what you liked, so I made a bit of everything." He set the tray down next to me on the bed.

I'm pretty sure my face lit up like a tree on Christmas morning. Several plates were piled with a variety of breakfast meats, eggs, hash browns, pancakes, and pastries, all of which looked divine.

"Oh my God, this is too much." I snatched up a slice of bacon with one hand while holding the satin sheet up over my still naked body. "I usually start the morning with black coffee and toast."

"Sorry, just a sec," he said, standing up. With him still shirtless, I appreciated the view of his muscular back as he strode through the door. A moment later he returned with a silver pot and two cups.

He passed me a cup of the piping hot liquid before pouring his own.

"I've never had breakfast in bed before," I said before taking a careful sip. "Did you cook all of this?"

"Of course, well, except for the pastries. Those are from the store. I'm not much of a baker."

"Still, this is pretty impressive. I can mess up boiling water." I laughed as I grabbed a fork and took a bite of eggs. I'd had a lot of eggs in my life, but those were amazing. He definitely wasn't afraid of seasoning.

"I laid that out for you to wear." He inclined his head toward one of his shirts at the bottom of the bed. "Although I prefer you the way you are." His eyes darkened as they drifted down my body. My own followed to see the sheets were a bit on the sheer side.

Feeling bold, I let the silky material go. It tickled my skin as it slipped back to the bed, leaving me bare for his enjoyment, which was quickly revealed by the growing bulge in his black pajama pants.

"Jesus," he groaned, grabbing the tray and moving it to a table against the wall. He prowled back to me and pulled the cup from my hand to set it on the night table. "You can eat later." He leaned down and captured my mouth, pushing me back against the soft overstuffed pillows. "But I'm going to eat now," he whispered against my collarbone as he sprinkled kisses down my torso until he reached the blonde curls between my legs.

He flicked his tongue over my clit, and I gripped the sheets in both hands as I moaned in pleasure. The man was a fucking genius when it came to giving head. I was starting to think he was good at everything.

He moved his tongue lower, dipping it inside me before moving back up to suck on my clit. My legs trembled at the intense sensation. He pushed one finger inside me and then another and another. I was deliciously sore for our activities the night before. Turning his hand, Grey used his fingertips to stroke upward, hitting my G-spot and making me cry in ecstasy as my orgasm built. I was just about to come when he pulled his fingers out and sat up. I groaned in frustration, which morphed to anticipation when he reached for a condom and slipped it on. He spread my legs wide and slid inside me in one smooth stroke.

"God, your pussy is so fucking tight," he sighed as he pushed into me again. "I could fuck you all day."

I was lost. My fingers dug into his back as he pulled back and plunged back in. I clung to him for dear life as the orgasm radiated out through my body in intense waves. Just as they were starting to subside, he turned me on my side and continued the deliberate strokes of his cock while his hand found my clit and rubbed it in perfectly timed circles.

"Oh my, aah, fuck! That is fucking amazing!" I came hard yet again. I'd definitely found my favorite position of all time as he continue to fuck me and rub my clit bringing me to climax after climax in a way I'd never experienced or dreamed possible. I wasn't sure how long we stayed like that. Time seemed to lose all meaning, and I'd lost count of how many times Grey made me come.

"Fuck, Claudia. That tight little pussy is going to make me come," he groaned and then called out as his cocked pulsed inside me. "You are fucking amazing," he said, collapsing next to me.

I would have laughed if I hadn't been so dazed. All I'd done was lie there while he worked some kind of magical voodoo on my body.

I cuddled into his side and laid my head on his chest, something I couldn't remember ever doing with a man in my entire life, not even back in college. Sex had always been strictly business, even before it was part of my business.

Grey sighed and put his arm around my back, pulling me even closer.

"We should play hooky and spend the day together," he suggested. I sighed. My first thought was how great that sounded. The next was it was impossible. I would already have a ton of questions to field from Grace for not coming home the night before. I couldn't imagine how bad it would be if I didn't show up until late in the day.

"I really can't," I said, genuinely disappointed with my answer. "I have errands I need to take care of this morning, and Janet said to expect a call and possibly a meeting with your brother this afternoon."

"You know, I could still put in a good word for you. It would pretty much guarantee you get the job."

"Please don't do that. Seriously, promise me you won't say anything about last night. I don't need the office gossips telling everyone I fucked my way into a job."

"I'm starting to think you might be ashamed of me," he teased.

I laughed, although I guessed it was true in a way. "Of course it's not that, but I'm a little embarrassed. I don't usually do things like this." Which was true. I hadn't gone to bed with a man who wasn't a mark since college.

"I know your soon-to-be new boss fairly well. He's a progressive thinker. I'm sure he'd just chalk it up to you being a go-getter, really going the extra mile to get the job done."

I pushed his chest playfully. "You're hilarious."

"I won't say anything as long as you don't want me to, Claudia. We can do this by your rules." He nuzzled my neck. "How about dinner here tonight?"

"I can't tonight, I have plans with some friends." A complete lie. "Listen, Grey, if I get the job, we should probably keep our distance for a while, especially around the office."

He pulled back slightly, the corners of his mouth turning down, and he looked away from me.

I was a fucking terrible person. He wanted to keep seeing me and if I was honest, a part of me wanted that, too. Unfortunately, I knew it was impossible. The money was too important. My first responsibility was to Elsa Michaels and even if it wasn't, I couldn't be with Grey. I'd started out with lies, ones he would likely find unforgivable. No matter what came of Elsa's case, there was no getting around the lies I'd already told or the wall I'd built around my heart.

"That's going to be tough but I understand. I hope that just applies to being in the office?" He looked hopeful.

"I think we should play it by ear, especially after last night. The city can feel pretty small sometimes, and I'd prefer not to run into anyone from work like that," I said quietly.

"And romantic relationships aren't exactly your thing," Grey added, quoting our conversation from dinner.

"Something like that." I shrugged.

"I get it, Claudia, more than you know. I've been alone for a long time for a reason. We can keep things casual." He paused. "For now."

An urge to cry overwhelmed me. I sat up and slid to the edge of the bed.

"Nature calls," I said over my shoulder as I grabbed the shirt he'd lain out for me and made my way to the master bathroom on the other side of the room.

I'd thought the guest bathroom was nice. This one was like something from a dream. I ran my fingers over the marbled vanity and awed at the double rainforest shower. This bathroom rivaled a five-star spa.

Looking at myself in the mirror, I could only describe the way I was feeling as shame. I asked myself what I was doing for what felt liked to hundredth time. I'd told myself I just needed to get laid, but it was already so much more than that and I had no clue what I was doing or how to move forward. I slipped into Grey's shirt and inhaled its fresh scent as I worked the buttons. A dress shirt seemed like an odd choice but once I had it on, I had to admit it was sexy.

I splashed some water on my face and smiled at the new toothbrush he'd set out for me. I took my time brushing my teeth and hand combing my hair before finally emerging to find him sitting on the bed with my dress, shoes, and purse neatly arranged on the end.

"I really need to get going soon," I said, hearing the regret in my own voice.

"I probably should, too. I haven't seen my parents yet and my mom has left quite a few messages."

"When was the last time you saw them?"

"About six months ago. My parents came out to visit me in Tokyo every spring. Gregory and Elsa made the trip with them a couple of times."

"What about Chad?"

"Last night was the first time I've seen him since the day I left." He ran his hand through his hair. "It's not as bad as it seems. We talked and video messaged a couple times a month."

"So you're not as close with him as the rest of your family?"

"I guess not. Chad has always kind of done his own thing. He struggled with some shit when he was in college and pulled away from the family for a long time. It was only about a year before I left that he started to get it together and took a job with the company."

I nodded. I wasn't sure why I was so curious about his relationship with Chad. I often went months without seeing my sister. We talked regularly, but Jessica wasn't privy to the more complicated aspects of my life, mainly my business with Homewrecker Incorporated, so it was impossible for us to be as close as I would have liked. She was under the impression I was a private investigator, which was the truth, but it wasn't the whole truth.

I walked over to the bed and grabbed my stuff.

"Thanks for, um, everything, I guess," I said, awkwardly leaning over to give him a quick peck. He grabbed my face before I could get away, turning the quick peck into a long, slow kiss. I didn't fight it, savoring the kiss it instead.

I slipped back into the bathroom and quickly dressed.

"Vince is waiting for you. I'll walk you out," Grey said, grabbing my hand.

We stepped out onto the driveway through the same door we'd come in the night before.

"Last night was amazing," he whispered, pulling me to him as Vince slipped out of the driver's seat to open the door for me. "I think I'm going to miss you."

"Me, too," I said honestly as he leaned in to kiss me. It was sweet, gentle at first, but I pulled him closer, parting his lips with my tongue and pouring all the emotions I would never speak into it. I fought back tears and relished the taste of him, the feel of his full lips before pulling back from what had to be the last kiss we'd ever share.

Chapter 8

"Good morning, John." I waved to the doorman, who'd become something of a friend to the girls and me over the years, as I did my walk of shame across the lobby of my building. As I stepped onto the elevator, my bag vibrated against my thigh.

Grey: I was right. I do miss you.

It hadn't taken him long to make use of the number I'd typed into his phone before I left.

Me: Who is this?? ;P
Grey: Ouch! Forgotten so quickly. I feel cheap...
Me: Hardly, my legs are still wobbly!
Grey: My work here is done...

"The fuck, Claudia? Where the hell have you been?" Grace practically yelled.

I'd been so engrossed with messaging Grey I'd walked into our shared penthouse on autopilot.

"I called you like ten times and sent I don't know how many messages!"

"I'm sorry. My phone died and I left my charger in the office." The lie came easy. "It got late, so I just stayed at Jessica's after dinner."

Grace crossed her arms over her chest. "Bullshit, you were just looking at your phone," she replied, her anger evident. "And Jessica called me after you avoided all of her calls, too."

Fuck.

"This is my burner, Grace. Business only. I was just checking for a message from Janet, she said to expect a call.

"Something else is going on, Claudia. You could have used the phone for one call to me, so I'd know you weren't lying in a gutter somewhere." The anger in her voice turned to concern. "What aren't you telling me?"

My brain went into panic mode. If I told her the truth, she was going to lose her shit and insist I pass the case on to Lydia, pride be damned. I should have been fine with that; it was what needed to happen after last night with Grey.

What happened with Grey? My head was still reeling and despite myself, I smiled when I thought of him. Thinking about him was a foolish indulgence I couldn't afford. I was determined to stay on the case, if only to prove to myself I was still in control. I would have to see him again, but I had to stick to what I'd told him and keep my distance. I prayed he would keep his word. God knows I hadn't exactly been able to resist him when he tried to get close to me. I dreaded the thought of lying to him again, even though it was inevitable. Who I was to him was a lie. There was no getting around it, but it didn't matter. It couldn't matter. He was just a man like all the others despite the way he made me feel. I'd just had a natural response to an attractive, potent male at a time in my life when my biological clock was probably ticking at full steam ahead much to the chagrin of my plans.

Somehow I managed to pretend I actually believed the bullshit going through my head.

"Look, Grace, I'm sorry. I shouldn't have lied about where I was. I just didn't want you to worry." I sighed. "Robert was at my sister's place when I got there, and it didn't go well. I just needed to be alone to clear my head, so I went for a walk around the city and ended up spending a few hours at the Art Institute to calm down. It didn't really work, so I hit up a little dive bar and closed it down with some of the regulars. It was late and I was too drunk to drive and I didn't want to leave my car there, so I slept it off in the backseat."

"Jesus, Claud. Are you okay?" she asked, referring to seeing my father. "And that was fucking stupid sleeping in your car! You should have called me to come get you. I could have picked up Bridget or Lydia on the way to drive your car back."

"Lydia was probably out somewhere drunk herself," I said with a laugh. "I'm fine; everything is fine. Really. It won't happen again." I rubbed my temple, feeling the effects of the drinks from the night before.

"Are you sure, Claudia?" Grace poured me a cup of coffee. "Please talk to me if you feel like you're getting overwhelmed. I meant what I said before; it's not too late if you want off this case."

"I'm good and I promise I'll let you know if that changes."

Another opportunity to bow out no questions asked, yet I let it pass right on by. Again.

Grace walked over and wrapped her arms around me.

"I love you, Claud. I just want to be sure you're okay. So fair warning, I will kick your ass if you ignore my calls like that again."

"Consider me warned," I said with a laugh as I returned the hug.

"You even going to ask how Patty's call with Elsa and her attorney went yesterday?" Grace let me go.

"Shit, sorry, I completely forgot about that. So what did she say?"

"Elsa confirmed there's no way it was the twin in the pictures. He was still in Japan when she got them. She doesn't think he'll be a problem for us now he's back. She's pretty convinced he would be on her side if her husband's lawyers tried to pull a fast one with identifying Gregory on any surveillance. Guess he's had some experience being in her position."

"What kind of experience?" I tried not to sound overly interested, just mildly curious.

"She didn't say, but she wants us to push ahead with the job as discussed. And there's something you're probably not going to like." She looked at me over her coffee cup. Great, now what? "She wants to start surveillance on her husband immediately. I know, I know," Grace continued when I opened my mouth to protest. "She understands the risks, and her bitchy lawyer all but said if we're any good at our jobs we should be able to pull it off discreetly enough to avoid detection by a bunch of amateur paparazzi. Patty already arranged it for him and the twin."

Well, fuck.

"Guess there's no getting around it, then. Client is always right and all that shit," I said sarcastically.

Grace chuckled and took a long sip of coffee.

"Are you feeling up to brunch? The girls are meeting at our spot at eleven."

"Sure, sounds good. Just let me take a quick shower and change first," I said, turning away from her to hide the panic on my face. I hadn't been paying attention when I left Grey's house. Was the tail there already? Could they have seen me leaving? If they did I was royally fucked. Guess I would know soon enough.

With surveillance on Gregory, and Grey by extension, I definitely couldn't see Grey again. Not that I would have anyway.

After a relaxing brunch and a call from Janet to set up a meeting with Gregory at three, I was relieved when our brief call with Patty about the investigators revealed surveillance on Grey hadn't started until after I'd left that morning. Now I found myself back at the scene of the crime, so to speak. If it was possible, I was even more nervous walking through the lobby of G&G than I'd been the first time around.

"Good afternoon, I have a meeting with Mr. Gregory Michaels and Ms. Janet Peterson," I said to the same security guard I'd seen before. He looked as though he could good plow through a brick wall just as easily as I could walk through an open door.

"It's nice to see you again, Ms. Winston." He passed me the tablet to sign in.

I gave him a sweet smile. "It's nice to see you again, too, um, Bruce," I said, glancing at his name tag.

He buzzed me in and I made my way to the elevator.

"Hold the elevator, please!" someone yelled after me. A rather disheveled Bridget rushed in. "Hurry up, close, close!" she blurted, pressing the close door button repeatedly as if she was playing an old arcade game. The doors were all but closed when I caught a glimpse of a tall, very attractive man who had Bridget running scared.

"Who was that?" I raised my eyebrows. "And why on earth would you be running from him?"

"Joshua Slade, the CFO!" she said in a loud whisper as if someone was listening. "Ben sent me up to get his laptop for some work when I got back to the office after lunch yesterday."

"And?"

"And he asked me to go to dinner!" she said as if he'd asked her for a kidney.

I couldn't contain my laughter.

"It's not funny!" she hissed. "Why would he do that? He's so far out of my league and he's a fucking executive. I can barely think around him, let alone form a coherent sentence."

I was surprised to hear her swear. Unlike the rest of us, she tended to use much milder language.

"So what did you say?"

"What could I say? I said, 'um, uh, sure' and then ran off with his laptop." She slumped against the wall of the elevator. "He e-mailed from his phone right after asking me when would be a good time to see him, and I told him I'd let him know. Now how can I get out of it?"

"Why in God's name would you want to? He's hot and you are definitely in the same league. You just need to bring your A game," I said, putting an arm around her shoulders right before the elevator doors opened.

She'd ridden all the way up to my floor. I pressed the button to send her back down.

"I can't believe you didn't mention this at brunch this morning," I whispered as I stepped off the elevator. "We can talk about it tonight. Don't worry. By the time we're done with you, he'll be the one who can't form a coherent thought."

With a wink, I left Bridget looking a bit terrified as the elevator doors closed. I hoped the lucky Mr. Slade managed to find her and get her to commit to a time for their dinner date before she pulled some crazy hack and got herself into the witness protection program. Lord knew Bridget needed a little nudge to put herself out there.

Her dose of early morning drama had actually taken my mind off my own nerves, and I found myself feeling abnormally relaxed as I told the receptionist of my appointment and waited for Janet to come and get me.

"Hi, Janet, it's so good to see you again," I said, extending my hand when she appeared.

"I'm so excited for Gregory to meet you. I think you're just perfect for this job," she said, leading me back toward the offices. I wasn't really sure why she felt so confident about my abilities. I'd barely gotten a word in edgewise during our last meeting, but I'd take whatever help I could get.

Butterflies swarmed in my stomach as memories of my last time in that office surfaced. I wasn't worried about running into Grey this time. He'd texted me after brunch to wish me luck and shared he was going to be out of the office visiting a plant in Elkhart, Indiana for a few days. While I was relieved I wouldn't have to juggle both twins at the same time, a part of me was a little disappointed I wouldn't get to see him. My stomach did an extra flip at the thought of juggling both men. Damn, now that was a nice visual.

"Are you ready?" Janet asked before she picked up the phone to verify Gregory was ready to see me.

"As ready as I'll ever be."

"Mr. Michaels, thank you so much for taking the time." Seeing him again, it was easy for me to tell him from his brother. A wash of something unfamiliar spread over me. Longing, sadness, I wasn't exactly sure, but I didn't like it.

"Of course, Ms. Winston. Please, call me Gregory. It makes things less confusing, especially now my brother is back in town. I've heard only great things from him and Janet about you," he said with a curious smile.

My face suddenly felt hot.

"Janet has such nice things to say about working for you," I said, ignoring his mention of Grey as I tried to hide the tremor in my voice.

Had Grey told him about us despite his promise not to? I couldn't tell, and Gregory moved on from the subject to study the résumé in front of him. I watched him carefully as his eyes passed over the lines of my fabricated work history, nodding here and there along the way.

"Janet, could you get me a cup of coffee, please?" he said through the intercom. "Anything for you, Claudia? Is it all right if I call you Claudia?" He folded his hands on top of the desk.

"Of course it is and no, nothing for me," I replied. "It's refreshing to see such a powerful man so respectful of his subordinates." I tried to sound flirtatious. It came off somewhere closer to awkward. "Like I said before, Janet has said such nice things. It's as if all the employees here are friends." I fidgeted with the pendant on my necklace.

That part of the jobs--the flirtation, the chase--had always come so naturally for me. With Gregory Michaels it was nothing short of forced.

"I'd say we're more like family," he replied casually. "Your résumé is impressive and Janet believes you'll be a great fit here at G&G." He smiled. Even though he and Grey were identical, and he was equally as handsome, his smile didn't have any of the effect on me Grey's did.

"The job is yours if you want it," he said as Janet walked in with his coffee. "Janet, I think we're ready for the offer letter from human resources."

Janet pulled an envelope from behind her back as she set the steaming mug on the desk. She smiled brightly as she set the envelope with my name typed on top in front of me.

"I figured it was best to be prepared." She winked before turning to leave.

"You can take a couple of days to think over the offer if you'd like but as far as I'm concerned, you can start tomorrow." He stood and extended his hand.

"Thank you so much, Gregory," I said, emphasizing his name.

"This might seem like a strange request, but since I hope you'll be joining our little family here, would you consider attending a charity function this Saturday? We bought an entire table and have two seats left open. You could bring a girlfriend along if you like. You would really be doing me a favor. These events can get rather boring, especially when I have to fill a table with my typical business associates. You would bring a little excitement to the group, and you certainly wouldn't want for company."

"Won't Mrs. Michaels be there to keep you occupied?" I leaned forward ever so slightly, putting my acting skills to good use. He'd been sure to specify I should bring a girlfriend, not a date, which was encouraging as far as the job was concerned, but it was still odd for him to make that specification. That's what I was really there for, the job, I reminded myself yet again.

"Unfortunately, Mrs. Michaels will be out of town, so I'll be flying solo for a change."

Guess I was three for three on attracting the Michaels brothers. So much for Gregory Michaels being the exception. He was clearly just as sleazy as every other mark. Not that he would do anything at a function full of acquaintances and business associates, but it would be a good chance to get closer to him. And there was always time after the event.

Gregory's phone chimed.

"I'm sorry to rush you out, but I have an important conference call starting now." He hit the intercom before I'd had a chance to answer about Saturday. "Janet, can you show Claudia out and give her those two extra tickets to the gala on your way? I look forward to seeing you this weekend, Claudia."

It appeared he decided for me.

Gregory picked up the phone, his gaze traveling up my body as I stood. He smiled, looking away as he turned his chair toward the window.

"Chris, how are you?" he said as I stepped out to where Janet was waiting.

"You're going to have so much fun," Janet said, passing me a beautifully decorated envelope. "The gala is one of the hottest tickets in town this weekend." She smiled brightly. "It's a shame Elsa, Mrs. Michaels, can't attend seeing how her foundation puts it on. I guess something came up with one of the schools she's helping to build down in Guatemala. Some sort of hassle about permits, which is just code for a government official looking for a kickback."

At the mention of Elsa, I wondered if Janet knew more about Gregory's indiscretions than she let on. Before I opened the flap and pulled out the tickets, I made a note to ask her out for lunch sometime to see what I could get out of her. Looking down, I gasped when I read the event name and location on the tickets in my hand.

"Oh my God, I can't accept these!" I said, still staring at them. She was right; the World Child Hunger Charity Gala was an A-list event in Chicago. The guest list was a who's who, filled with elite businessmen, congressmen, senators, and celebrities. It wouldn't be a surprise to see the Commander in Chief there, as well. And it was $25,000 a plate. There was no way that event would be boring even if Gregory's table was filled with business associates.

"Claudia, a little tip. When a gift like that falls into your lap, just smile and say thank you. Just think of the networking opportunities. Consider taking the tickets a smart business decision," she said with a wink.

She was absolutely right; it was good business, just not in the way she thought. There would be an obscene amount of wealth in the room, powerful men with mistresses and jilted wives who were potential clients we could pass along to Patty.

"Thank you, Janet. I guess I'm going to need to go shopping before Saturday."

Chapter 9

"I'll only go if you let me drive your car." Bridget folded her arms over her chest.

She was pissed that we persuaded her to leave work early Wednesday and lured her to our penthouse to drag her along on our shopping trip to buy gowns for the gala on Saturday night. Unable to avoid Josh Slade after I'd seen her on the elevator, she agreed to dinner with him, so we were going to get her a makeover and a killer outfit for the occasion.

"Come on, Bridge. You know that car is my baby!" I replied, gripping my heart.

"Yeah, and you know I hate shopping and I don't want to go on this date at all," she responded, her voice melting into a pathetic whine as she finished the sentence. "I don't know how to act around him. He's so good-looking and confident. Why the heck does he want to eat with me? I'll probably spill something on myself or, oh God, on him!" she said, working herself into a panicked frenzy.

"Chill, girl." Grace handed her a glass of wine. "You'll be just fine and if you're not, just shoot me a text and I'll make the infamous bad date bail-out call to give you an excuse to leave."

"Fine, I'll let you drive, but that means only one glass of wine for you," I said, pouring myself a second glass with a smile.

Two glasses later, I slipped in front of Grace into the passenger seat of my RS7.

"Just take it easy," I said as Bridget adjusted the driver's seat.

I had to admit the early birthday present I'd bought the month before looked like a midlife crisis, although I was still way too young for that. At the time, I just needed something new and exciting, so when the sensible sedan I'd been driving for half a decade was paid off, I finally gave in to the constant requests from the dealer I'd bought it from to come check out the newer models. I'd intended to get the new version of my old car, but when I walked into the show room, I fell in love for the first time, and with a redhead, no less.

Seeing Bridget's excitement as she navigated the streets of Chicago was well worth the stress of letting someone else handle what was easily my most prized and most expensive possession. The prior distinction actually belonged to the sterling silver necklace, which had hung around my neck for the last fourteen years. It was an eighteenth birthday gift from my mom. The last of my birthdays she was around to help me celebrate. My heart squeezed tight at the thought of her.

"Is it too late to change my mind?" Bridget whined, putting the car in park in a garage across the street from the exclusive boutique Grace made an appointment at. "That drive was much longer in my head."

"Sorry, Bridge, a deal's a deal." Grace laughed as she slid out of the backseat.

"How fast have you driven this thing anyway?" Bridget closed the door. "I bet my little old car tops out at around eighty."

"Ha, we all know that's by choice. Thanks to Lydia you have more money than any of us did at your age. You just refuse to spend any of it." I took her hand and practically dragged her through the garage to the elevator.

Although I teased her, I admired Bridget's frugal nature and wished mine was better developed. Thanks to my investment in Homewrecker Incorporated and Lydia's talent for day trading, I'd done rather well financially and had quite a lovely nest egg. With a cheaper apartment, a few less pairs of designer shoes and a less sexy car parked downstairs, I probably would have been able to afford my vineyard in Tuscany a lot sooner.

I was reminded of the trip that sparked my dream as we waited for the crosswalk signal to change. The time in Tuscany with my mom had been one of the best of my life. Dad had gone to Italy on business for several weeks, and one day Mom decided she missed him too much. It was completely spontaneous, and while Dad pretended to be furious about Jessica and me missing school, we all knew he was thrilled to have us there. At least that's what we believed at the time.

Several hours and an obscene amount of money later, Grace opened the door to our apartment. True to form, Bridget made a beeline across the open living and dining room space to the glass wall overlooking both the lake and part of the city skyline.

"The only thing I can see from my living room window is my neighbor's blinds," Bridget said wistfully.

"As I said before, your choice, Bridge."

"Not entirely. Neither of you could afford these digs on your own," Bridget replied with a hand on her hip.

"You could always room with Lydia," I suggested, only half serious.

"Yeah right, I can't keep up with her," Bridget responded. She was right. Lydia was a partier and often *entertained* late at night. Living with her would be complicated for Bridget, to say the least.

"Okay, come on, Bridge. Let's see you in your dress again." I clapped my hands like a giddy teenager.

She'd already had her hair and makeup done during our excursion. Both the hairdresser and makeup artist had done exquisite jobs making her look well put together, but in an understated, natural way that was in-line with who she really was.

While Grace helped Bridget shimmy into the emerald green dress, which really set off the color in her eyes, I made my way to the kitchen. With an open bottle of my favorite Cabernet and three glasses, I stopped by my room to grab a pair of heels I'd had in mind when we bought the dress. One glance and I was certain they complimented it as well as I'd imagined.

Returning to Grace's room, I found Bridget already changed. She somehow managed to look absolutely stunning while simultaneously appearing uncomfortable for a beautiful woman wearing a designer dress. So much so I almost regretted roping her into it, but it was for her own good.

She was so lonely; we all knew it. If we didn't give her little pushes now and then, she would likely stay that way forever. It wasn't that I wanted to change her. I loved that girl, and I'd be damned if I let any man near her who wouldn't love her for who she was. That didn't mean we didn't need to bait the hook a little. If there was anything I knew, it was how to get a man's attention. Of course, she'd already managed to capture Mr. Slade all on her own, despite her best attempts to hide her beauty with baggy clothes and messy buns. A little bit of fun with a sexy and successful man like Josh Slade would do wonders for her confidence. Who knew, maybe it would turn into a relationship. Since I'd had zero desire to keep the men I attracted around beyond the scope of my jobs, that wasn't really an area I could help her with. I wondered what Grey was doing for the evening. I hadn't heard from him since he'd sent me the good luck message the day before.

After a heavy-handed pour I handed Bridget a glass, knowing the wine would help her loosen up and adjust to her foreign attire and the idea of going on an actual date more quickly. With the second glass in her hand, Grace herded Bridget into the bathroom to take a look at the full effect for the first time.

"Wow, I look really good." She covered her mouth as if she was embarrassed by paying herself a well-deserved compliment.

"You look amazing, Bridge. Mr. Slade won't know what hit him," I said. Something was familiar about that name, but I couldn't quite place it. The buzzer sounded on our intercom.

"Your car is here," Grace said after answering.

"Just relax and be yourself. He already likes you. Now you just need to figure out if you like him. That's all this is." I helped her slip on a light shrug. "If you decide you don't or you need an out, just text one of us and we'll get you out of there, okay?"

She nodded and reached for the door. "Thanks, for everything," she said softly before taking off on what was probably the scariest adventure she'd had in a long while.

She'd hacked into sophisticated corporate networks, even a few government databases, but that was all done behind the safety and anonymity of a computer screen. If our business taught us anything, men were far more dangerous than computer viruses and firewalls.

"How long do you give it before she calls?" Grace asked as soon as Bridget was gone.

"I don't know. She might make it through the night. You should see this guy; he's pretty hot."

"Aw, our little baby is growin' up." She utilized her Southern accent to the fullest. We both had a good chuckle.

"Maybe we should have had *the talk* with her before she left," I said, turning our chuckling into a full-blown fit of giggles.

"Oh. My. God. I can't. Breathe!" Grace choked out.

My phone vibrated on the counter.

"Shit, it's Patty," I said, trying to stifle my laughter to take the call. "Hey, Patty. What's up?" I asked before putting the phone on speaker.

"I'm sending over a file from the investigator right now," she replied. "Check your e-mail. Mr. Michaels had a very busy day."

I opened the file on my laptop. It contained several pictures, which were taking their time downloading.

"Okay, they're coming through now," I said as Grace huddled in next to me for a better view.

"It's the woman from the other photos," Grace observed.

"Yeah, they met at La Cara for lunch, but it was cut short," Patty said through the speaker. "According to Bobby, she seemed pissed. Tried to touch his arm before he yanked it away. Then she showed him something, and he threw some money down on the table and stormed out. She looked pretty upset. If I had to put money on it, based on the pictures and what Bobby witnessed, I'd say it looked more like a breakup than some paparazzi setup."

"That's great for us," Grace chimed in. "Maybe he was clearing the way before his time with Claudia at the gala Saturday night."

"Here's hoping," I said, trying to sound pleased, although the knot in my stomach told another story. Going into the job, there was a chance Gregory wasn't a cheater, and I wouldn't have to go as far as sleeping with him to get Elsa the answers she needed. If Grace was right, that chance was growing slimmer by the day.

"Yes, I'd say it's excellent for us," Patty added. "If he was already cheating with that woman, Claudia shouldn't have any trouble getting him to do the deed on camera."

If Patty only knew how misplaced her confidence was.

"Where's Gregory now?" I asked.

"Bobby had just followed him to his house when we spoke. He went back to the office after his little date with the mystery woman. But get this, on his way home he stopped at a florist and came out with one hell of a bouquet, presumably for Elsa." Salving his guilt most likely.

"He's covering his tracks," Grace added.

"Looks that way. I'll be in touch if I hear anything more from Bobby. Good luck on your first day at the new job, Claudia."

"Thanks, Patty. We'll talk to you soon."

"I have to admit a part of me was kind of hoping Gregory Michaels would prove us wrong." Grace studied the photos Patty sent more closely. "You can hardly blame him, though. This chick really is something. I'd kill to have the whole "sexy no matter what

I'm doing vibe". Kind of like what you have going on girl." She smacked me on the ass while I poured another glass of wine.

"You're plenty sexy, woman. You certainly don't have any trouble putting asses in the seats, and I'd kill for that whole exotic vibe you've got going on, so quit it with that shit."

"You ever think about what you're going to do when we're done with all this shit? I know you want the whole Tuscany thing, but what about the rest, what about an actual relationship? You've always had a pretty healthy appetite, you know, sexually, but I can't remember you being with a guy who wasn't a job since we started this."

She was right. I hadn't slept with a man who wasn't a mark since college. We'd stayed busy enough with clients that the itch was scratched often enough for me to get by. She and Lydia didn't follow the same line of thinking, but the men Grace saw were few and far between simply because of the nature of our business, and Lydia's never lasted more than a night or two. What we did for a living wasn't exactly something that could be shared with a boyfriend lying in bed at night. Telling a man, "Oh hey, I sleep with other guys for work every once in a while," probably wasn't a good way to move a relationship forward.

"No, I haven't really thought about it, but I'm sure I'll figure something out, for the sex at least. I don't see any need to change the rest."

"After all this time, you still don't want anything more? Don't you worry about being lonely?"

"I've got you and Lydia and Bridget. Who needs a man with all you crazy bitches to keep me company?" I nudged her shoulder. Her expression was a little sad, but the emotion disappeared as quickly as it appeared.

The truth: I wasn't sure about anything anymore. I was trying to be discreet, but I'd looked at my phone about thirty times since Patty called. I still hadn't heard a peep from Grey.

"Hey, I've been meaning to tell you," Grace said, catching me looking yet again. "I got a couple of weird calls today."

"Weird how?"

"The first was on my regular cell--a guy. He just asked if I was Grace Dawson and then hung up as soon as I said yes. The second was on my burner, and whoever it was didn't say anything, just sat there for a second then hung up. Both were blocked."

"That is weird. You should have Bridget look into it and see what she can dig up."

"I'll shoot her a message tomorrow. Maybe she can get to it on her lunch break or something."

"It would probably be a good idea to swap out your burner, too. Lydia could do that for you first thing tomorrow, and then you can just leave the other one with Bridget."

"Can I just say how damn excited I am for this event Saturday?" Grace said, changing the subject.

She tugged on her earlobe, something she always did when she was upset. The calls were bothering her more than she was letting on. It bothered me, too. No one but us girls, Patty, and the people we'd given them to for the Michaels job had the numbers for our burners.

"Yeah, me, too." I tried to match her enthusiasm, but I was more worried than excited.

There was a chance Grey would be there. It would make sense, considering Elsa's foundation was running the event and G&G Components was one of its sponsors.

I could text him and ask if he would be back in town by then, but what if he took the contact as a sign of hope? The last thing I wanted to do was lead him on. Elsa's case was my priority. It had to be. Still, I wasn't entirely confident in my ability to stay away from Greyston Michaels. As much as I hated to admit it, he had an effect on me I seemed to have no control over. I was attempting to hold out hope my one night with him had its intended effect and when I did see him again, the attraction would be less potent--manageable. With another glance at my phone and thoughts of my one night with Grey heavy on my mind, it was hard to imagine anything could make me want him less.

Patty had given Bobby, the investigator, and his partner Jason, who was assigned to follow Grey, all of our numbers to make things easier. She did have other clients and *homewreckers* to juggle after all.

Jason checked in with Grace about an hour after Patty called with nothing of interest as far as the job was concerned to report. Grey was still out of town. Bobby called shortly after.

"I followed my guy and that pretty wife of his to his parents' place. The other brother, the youngest, came by late with a tall blonde," Bobby said through the phone.

"Did you get any pictures?" I asked while Grace gave me a confused look. "The mystery woman is blonde, could be her," I lied. I was confident who it was, but I wanted to be sure. More than that, I wanted to know what the story was between her and Grey.

"Sure, sending them now," he replied.

The photos confirmed my suspicions. It was Ashley Slade. I found myself wondering again if she was dating Chad. I'd assumed they were a couple at the restaurant, but when I saw the picture of her and Grey, I thought they might just be friends. Still, I didn't know Chad or Ashley. Maybe Chad was the kind of guy who would date his brother's ex, and Ashley was the kind of woman who would date her ex's brother. I was in no position to judge.

After discussing the schedule for the next day, I took the opportunity to at least ensure I would be getting a heads-up before the gala.

"Listen, Bobby, can you tell Jason to text me Saturday if his guy starts heading toward the event we're attending?"

"Sure thing," he replied before ending the call.

Grace was still watching me.

"I just want to be prepared for the dynamic of the evening. It might be tricky trying to navigate the two brothers in the same room, trying to tell them apart."

"I doubt they're going to wear matching tuxes, Claud," Grace said. "Although that would be kind of hot." She giggled.

"I can't say I'd mind getting the two of them alone in the same room," I added, which made her giggle even more. The wine had gone to her head. "We should probably call it a night. Tomorrow's a big day. First day at the new job, and it's not looking as if Bridget is going to need us tonight," I said, checking the time.

"You're right. If I drink any more wine, I'm going to regret it tomorrow. Good night." Grace put her glass in the sink and headed around the corner to her room.

It was a bad idea, but I couldn't get Grey off my mind.

Me: Hey, you have plans Saturday?

His response was immediate.

Grey: Hey, nothing I can't get out of for you...

Shit. Now what was I supposed to do. He thought I was asking because I wanted to see him. Maybe I did. It might not be so bad if he was at the gala. What the fuck was I thinking? It would be a disaster if I wanted to actually do my job. I can't imagine Gregory would be interested in me if I spent most of the night dry humping his twin in some dark corner. Either way, I needed to know so I could prepare myself.

Me: I actually have plans. Gregory invited me and my friend to the charity gala.
Grey: I heard you got the job. Congrats!
Me: Thank you! Will you be at the event?
Grey: The whole family will be attending, except Elsa and how could I resist now that I know you're going?

I smiled and then frowned. So I would see him there.

Grey: Don't worry. I'll keep my distance if that's what you still want.
Me: Thank you. I need to get to bed. First day at the new job tomorrow.
Grey: Mmm, now you have me thinking about you in my bed...
Grey: Come over
Me: That's not a good idea

I entertained the idea of going for a solid minute.

Me: It's late & I have to get up early.
Grey: I know, had to try.
Me: Good night
Grey: Good night, beautiful

I wasn't going to need that text from Jason after all. Grey was definitely going to be at the gala. I was so screwed.

Chapter 10

"Okay, Claudia, that's it. Who are you talking to?" Grace eyed me after I checked my phone for the hundredth time since we'd arrived at the nail salon.

"Just Jessica checking in, again," I said, slipping the phone back into my purse.

"How was it yesterday?" she asked with concern.

I imagined she'd been dying to ask how I was feeling because I'd come home from my annual visit to my mom's grave the night before, but she'd resisted the impulse. Bringing up Jessica, who always went with me, opened the door on the subject.

"It was fine. I don't think it will ever be easy, but I think I handle it a little better every year," I said just as the attendant signaled our chairs were ready.

My burner phone buzzed as we sat down for our pedicures, the screen showing it was Janet. "Hey, Janet!" I said, genuinely happy to hear from her.

Much to my surprise, we'd become fast friends. My first two days working at G&G had been uneventful with Gregory in meetings and Grey out of town until Friday night. Most of my time was spent meeting the rest of the office staff, including a couple of angry women Stacy from accounting warned me about. I was grateful when I finally ran into her again, and we promised to make plans for lunch once I was settled in. Beyond that, the only things I accomplished were filling out my new hire paperwork and helping Janet sift through proposals from interior designers bidding to redecorate the executive floor. Apparently, Gregory hired the daughter of one of G&G's largest vendors for the work as a favor, a decision which resulted in a lot of laughs as Janet took me around the office cracking jokes about the young lady's rather unusual taste.

"Hey, Claudia. Gregory wants to send a car to pick you and Ms. Dawson up for the event this evening. Where should I send it?"

"Oh." Covering the mouthpiece of the phone with my hand I turned to Grace. "Gregory wants to send us a car tonight. Janet is asking where to pick us up."

"Send her to *your* apartment," Grace whispered.

She was right. We'd have to get ready at the penthouse and head over to the decoy apartment I hadn't set foot in since signing the month-to-month lease. I gave Janet the address for the building, which luckily wasn't far from our actual building, and told her we would meet the driver downstairs at six.

"Have fun tonight!" Janet said before hanging up.

"Getting ready and getting over there on time is going to be a pain in the ass," I said, rifling through the pile of magazines on the table next to me.

"It's not a big deal. We'll just have to drive over to the other place a bit earlier," Grace replied, leaning her head back and closing her eyes. I wished I was feeling so relaxed.

"It'll have to be a cab. I didn't request a parking space when I leased the other place."

"Fine, we'll take a cab. Crisis averted," she replied with a gasp. Smart-ass.

She was right, but I was so anxious about seeing Grey later that night every little thing was getting to me.

I sat back in the large chair, trying to relax as the technician massaged my calves and feet.

After our mani-pedis we stopped for a light lunch in one of my favorite cafés before we found ourselves seated in yet another salon, this time for hair and makeup. I wore mine partially up with the back hanging down in smooth waves thanks to a set of oversized hot curlers.

Grace opted for a Brazilian blow out and a sleek, flowing style.

"I still haven't heard a peep from Bridget about her date the other night," I said as I held up the small mirror the stylist gave me to inspect the back of my hair before I moved on to the makeup artist's chair. "I saw her for only a second in the office when Janet was giving me a tour Thursday."

"I haven't talked to her either," Grace said, checking her phone. "That means it either went really well..."

"Or so bad she's too embarrassed to tell us," I said, finishing Grace's thought.

"I hope it's the former."

"Maybe we should call her on our way home to get changed," I suggested, feeling guilty for forgetting about what was a pretty big milestone in my friend's life.

"It's probably better if we let her be. She'll talk to us when she's ready," Grace responded. Sometimes Bridget took a little while to open up, even with us.

We walked out of the salon at four thirty, which gave us just over an hour to get home to change and catch a cab over to my fake apartment early enough to avoid having the driver see us go in. My nerves were working overtime. The charity gala was by far the largest and most exclusive event I'd ever attended. To top it off, there was a lot of pressure for things to go well with Gregory Michaels. Now that Patty and Grace were more convinced he'd been screwing around on Elsa, they pushed for me to turn up the heat, so to speak. Getting and keeping his attention while remaining appropriately discreet was going to be tricky in a crowd like that. Especially with Grey around to distract me.

"Grace, can I just say again how absolutely stunning you look?" I said as my best friend stepped out of the town car wearing a long ivory gown with a deep neckline that plunged nearly to her navel, a look I couldn't ever pull off with my large C-cups.

"You're not so bad yourself," she replied as I twirled on the sidewalk in my strapless red dress with a neckline that revealed just the right amount of cleavage. The hem fell just above my knees and it was adorned with intricate silver beading across the waist. The ensemble was completed by a pair of silver strappy heels and a clutch I'd bought for the occasion.

Grace pulled her phone from the purse she was carrying.

"I just got a text from Lydia. She says we look hot in the pictures Bobby just sent her. And Gregory Michaels is already inside." Grace smiled.

I bent down to adjust the strap of my shoe, looking around discreetly.

"Do you see Bobby anywhere?" I asked unable to pin down his location.

"Nope. I suppose that's a pretty good testament to his skills."

It was no surprise; Patty didn't mess around. Her vouching for the investigators meant they knew what they were doing.

"Did Lydia mention if she'd heard from the other investigator, Jason?" I asked, fishing for information about Grey.

"No, the twin must not be here," Grace replied casually. I wished I could be as unaffected as her.

"You ready?"

"Let's do it!" She took my arm and we made our way down the block.

We'd asked the driver to drop us off a little ways down the street from the actual entrance since the line of cars was fairly long and we were trying to draw as little attention to ourselves as possible.

Belston Hall, where the event was taking place, was a breathtaking space with its ultrahigh ceilings, wall-length stained glass windows, and enormous crystal chandeliers. Getting in without being noticed didn't turn out to be much of a challenge because we seemed to have wound up behind a well-known pop singer and her entourage. I presented our tickets in exchange for our table assignment and two glasses of champagne.

"Oh my God, Claudia! Is that...?" Grace whispered just loud enough for me to hear over the harpist and the buzz of conversation filling the room as she inclined her head in the direction of one of her favorite actors. I'd never really understood the appeal. He wasn't unattractive, but he wasn't gorgeous, and he was much shorter in real life than he appeared to be on TV.

"It certainly looks like it, especially with that swarm of women fawning over him," I said as he signed an autograph. "Maybe you can get him to sign your boobs." I nudged her with my elbow.

"You're hilarious," she retorted sarcastically as she took a sip of champagne. "Do you see our table?"

"We're at number twenty-nine. I think that's somewhere toward the center of the room, near the stage." I looked at the order of the tables around us. If I were right, we'd have some of the best seats in the house. According to my program, the singer we'd followed in was performing later in the evening.

"Claudia, I'm so pleased you could make it." Gregory took my hand and kissed my knuckles as we turned toward him.

"You must be Ms. Dawson," he said, repeating the gesture with Grace. Her face flushed, her eyes as wide as saucers as she took him in. He definitely looked good in the tailored black tuxedo. Somehow Grace kept it together and flashed him one of her bright smiles.

"Mr. Michaels, it's such a pleasure. Thank you so much for the invitation. This event is breathtaking, and I can't believe some of the people here," she said, her eyes drifting back toward that actor.

"Please, call me Gregory." Gregory leaned in closer to follow her line of sight. "Are you a fan?"

Grace nodded, looking a little unsure.

"I'll introduce you," he said.

Grace gasped. "You know him?"

"As I'm sure you know, my wife's foundation puts this event together and G&G has been one of the sponsors for years. He's a big supporter. I wouldn't say we're friends, but he's an acquaintance."

I liked he wasn't pretentious about the connection like so many men tended to be when trying to show off.

"Let's wait until the crowd dies down some. Can I escort you to our table?" Gregory stepped between us and offered us each one of his arms.

I took it, trying not to be obvious as I scanned the room for Grey. I was surprised he wasn't with Gregory to greet us. My stomach sank as I wondered if he might not come at all. I should have been wishing for precisely that, but I never seemed to do what I should when it came to Greyston Michaels.

The first hour of the evening flew by in a whirlwind with Gregory introducing us to our table mates, even though we had yet to make it to the table, which consisted mainly of his business associates and executives from G&G. Amongst them was the rather handsome Mr. Slade, who'd taken Bridget out on her first real date a few nights before. Our last stop was to finally see the only man Grace had eyes for since we'd walked in. She even got her autograph, although just on the back of a program, much to my chagrin.

When we finally arrived at the table, one chair remained empty, painfully obvious to me, at least. No one else seemed to notice or care.

Attempting to convince myself Grey's absence was a good thing, I mentioned I was a little light-headed as I sat, hoping Gregory would sit and talk with me at the table.

"I'll send over a waiter with a tray of hors d'oeuvres. You probably need to eat something with all that champagne," he replied with a smile before leaving us.

We watched Gregory carefully as he spoke easily to a variety of people throughout the event, from businessmen to celebrities to politicians. Nothing seemed to throw him off his game, until she walked in.

"Isn't that her?" Grace said in a loud whisper, pointing toward the entrance as I popped a stuffed mushroom in my mouth.

"Yes, it's her." I watched the voluptuous blonde we had yet to identify head straight toward Gregory. Noticing her approach, he excused himself from the group he was with to meet her. The easy melody of a waltz filled the room and a few couples whirled around the dance floor on the side of the stage next to our table.

"He's definitely not happy to see her," I whispered to Grace after Gregory gripped the woman's arm rather roughly and escorted her through the door to a side hallway. It seemed risky for him to behave like that at an event where he was one of the most sought after guests in the crowd, but Grace and I seemed to be the only ones paying attention to him at the moment.

"I'm going to use the restroom and see if I can hear anything," Grace said. The hallway Gregory had chosen, presumably for a little privacy happened to be where the bathrooms were located so it provided the perfect excuse to eavesdrop. I decided to follow her lead and headed that direction just as she ducked through the door. If I'd timed it right, I could pick up listening where she left off without being obvious.

Weaving my way through the tables, my gaze landed on Chad as he descended the stairway at the entrance. It seemed he preferred to be fashionably late. It was nearly ten when he arrived at the restaurant the first time we met, and Bobby mentioned him showing up late for dinner at his parents' house. He must have spotted me because he headed in my direction. A warm smile covered his face as he approached. I didn't know if I should stop to greet him or keep moving. The choice was made for me. I squealed when a muscular arm snaked around my waist.

"Hello, beautiful," Grey said against my ear as he pulled me toward the growing group of dancers on the floor. I dragged my heels as I looked around, wondering if anyone else was watching us, mainly Gregory.

"I was starting to think you weren't coming." I sounded far happier to see him than I intended. It didn't matter. Even if my tone hadn't, the flush of my skin betrayed my true feelings. My heart pounded so loudly I was sure the whole room could hear it over the final bars of the waltz.

I really needed to get it together. How could he affect me so much in a matter of seconds?

"I got tied up, but I couldn't stay away knowing you were going to be here."

"I'm here with my friend, Grace. She's in the restroom. I was just on my way to join her," I said, fighting my instinct to get closer to him.

"I've missed you," he whispered, leaning in closer.

"I need to find my friend. She's probably looking for me by now." I scanned the room for Grace. It was just for show. I could have looked right at her and I wouldn't have seen her. All I could see was Grey.

"Dance with me first. I haven't been able to stop thinking about the way your body feels against me," he said, pulling me around to face him.

Warmth spread low in my body as I looked up into those gorgeous eyes. A slow smile spread across his face, and I made the mistake of looking at those lips.

"Grey, we agreed to be discreet at work." I attempted to put some space between us.

My resolve waned as he pulled me closer and moved us to the rhythm of the foxtrot the band started playing.

"Lots of people are dancing, no one is going to think anything of us sharing one dance, Claudia." He smiled down at me.

"One dance." I placed one hand in his and the other on his shoulder. His smile turned triumphant. Despite myself, I laughed.

I caught sight of Chad watching us with a knowing smirk. His eyes moved to my right and my gaze followed. Gregory was walking toward us, looking rather ruffled. Grey didn't seem to notice his brother's approach until Gregory was right next to us.

He whispered in Grey's ear, but I couldn't quite make out the words. Grey's gaze shifted toward the exit. His expression was impassive, but his body tensed slightly. There was a hint of panic in his eyes. I turned to see the source of his anxiety. There was Ashley, looking absolutely stunning and staring directly at Grey from across the room.

"You'll have to excuse me and my brother, Claudia. There are some people I need to introduce him to," Greg said with an unconvincing smile. He was tense, even more so than Grey, a far cry from the poised man I'd spent the bulk of the evening with.

"I'll see you later," Grey said hopefully as his brother practically dragged him away. Gregory stopped briefly to say something to Chad who turned and walked toward Ashley, cutting off her pursuit of Grey.

"That shit was awkward," Grace said, returning to the table where I'd been waiting.

I looked up from my phone. Lydia texted to let us know Grey was on his way to the event. It was a little late for the warning.

"Did you hear anything?"

"Not really. They got quiet when I came through the door. I know Gregory saw me, but he acted as if he didn't even know me. He was definitely upset about whatever they were talking about. I did hear him call her Kristen right before the bathroom door shut. I tried to listen from inside, but I couldn't hear anything. They were gone when I came back out."

"He came back in, but I've haven't seen her again," I said, attempting to be casual as I looked around. I hadn't seen Grey since Gregory carted him off. "I wish we could follow her. We need to know who she is and what's up with her and Gregory."

"Already got it covered." Grace smiled proudly. "I sent Bobby and Jason a message when I was in the bathroom. They're calling in another colleague to keep an eye on her."

"I don't know what I'd do without you."

"Excuse me, ladies, I'm sorry to bother you, but I was wondering if this beautiful young woman wouldn't mind making an old man's night by dancing with me." A rather attractive older gentleman with kind eyes held out his hand to Grace.

"Of course I wouldn't mind. It would be my pleasure." Grace stood to take his hand as he grinned at her.

As if my body somehow felt his presence, I turned to see Grey coming back into the room. He was looking all around the room, at the tables, and then he said something to an older couple who'd walked in before him. The three of them made their way across the room, having to stop several times as other attendees roped them into conversation. Finally, they met up with Gregory near the bar. I averted my eyes when Gregory pointed my way and all of their eyes landed square on me. It was like being on stage under a spotlight. I looked away, pretending I hadn't seen them.

A waiter stopped by to clear some glasses and dishes from the table. I cursed under my breath at the emptiness of all the seats around me. Everyone else was dancing, getting drinks, or mingling with other guests.

"Mom, Dad, this is Ms. Claudia Winston." Gregory said as they approached. "She's taking over as my new assistant when Janet retires." He turned to his parents. "Claudia, this is my father, Carter, and my mother, Bethany. Of course you already know Grey."

"It's nice to meet you." Carter raised my hand to his lips, apparently a signature move he'd passed down to his sons.

"A pleasure," I replied as butterflies fluttered around my stomach so hard I was sure there were actual creatures trying to escape my body. I resisted the urge to look at him, but I could feel Grey's gaze boring into me as his brother introduced me to their parents.

"Claudia, so great to meet you. I apologize in advance, but I'm a hugger." Bethany Michaels pulled me into her arms. I chanced a glance at Grey who was smiling wide as he watched me with his mother. I, on the other hand, was completely freaking out. At least internally.

"Janet has been singing your praises," Bethany said, finally pulling away. I wasn't much of a hugger, but she was certainly good at it. In just a few seconds she'd made me feel as if I'd known her forever. For a brief moment, it reminded me of hugging my mother. I swallowed hard against the knot forming in my throat.

"I'd love it if you came by for dinner sometime so we can get to know you better," Bethany continued glancing toward her sons. I took a calming breath, pushing back my sad thoughts as I wondered if Grey mentioned me to his mother.

"That's an excellent idea," Carter added. "Janet has always been like family to us, no reason you shouldn't be as well."

"I'd love to."

"And who's this gorgeous creature?" Bethany looked behind me at Grace returning from her dance.

Grace beamed at the compliment.

"This is my friend, Grace Dawson. I dragged her along as my plus-one tonight."

True to form, Bethany pulled her into a hug and Grace looked at me, eyes wide with surprise. I raised my hand to my mouth to stifle a laugh.

"It's so nice to meet you, Grace. I'm Bethany Michaels and this is my husband Carter. I believe you already know my boys." She gestured toward Gregory and Grey. With tuxedos of opposite color schemes, Gregory's being black and Grey's white, it was easy to tell them apart, not that I needed the help. I would know Grey anywhere.

"I've had the pleasure of meeting Gregory," she said, looking at Grey who stepped forward, extending his hand.

"Greyston Michaels, but my friends call me Grey," he said as she took his hand. His eyes cut to me. "Any friend of Claudia's is a friend of mine."

"It's nice to meet you, Grey." Grace flashed him one of her signature smiles before glancing at me curiously.

"What do you say, Mom? You want to go show them how it's done?" Grey said after releasing Grace's hand.

Bethany chuckled and took his arm.

"I'd never miss a chance to dance with one of my boys." She brushed some stray hairs back from his forehead. Grey was easily a foot taller than her and she had to reach up on her tiptoes. I couldn't help smiling at the adoration in his eyes as he looked down at her.

"How about it, Ms. Dawson? Since my wife seems to have left me for a younger man, would you do me the honor?"

I'm pretty sure Grace blushed, although with her rich skin tone it was hard to tell. I couldn't blame her; Carter Michaels was basically an older version of his very hot sons. I shivered, thinking of what Grey would look like at that age.

"Looks as though you're stuck with me then, Claudia." Gregory offered his arm.

I took it as Grace smiled back at me. From where she stood, it couldn't have worked out better. I was supposed to be there for Gregory, but I found myself wishing for a different partner as he led me around the dance floor. I stole a glance at Grey. He stared back at me, and I recognized the look in his eyes. They reflected exactly what I was feeling, and it scared the shit out of me. So much so I felt a newfound determination to put an end to whatever was going on between us. Everyone was counting on me--Elsa, my friends, even myself. I couldn't let some ridiculous and completely out of character infatuation ruin everything. I was so close I could practically taste the first glass of the wine I was going to make.

With new resolve I turned my attention to the reason I was there. My mark.

"You're an excellent dancer, Gregory."

"Thank you. Elsa insisted we take ballroom dance lessons before we were married, and we liked it so much we continued for a few years after until Dad retired. It's hard to find the time with the business expanding the way it is."

"Well, the lessons have certainly paid off." I inched closer. "I've been wanting to take dance classes again. I trained some when I was younger, but I got into volleyball, and because I was good enough to actually hope for a scholarship, it became the priority."

"How did that work out?" He seemed genuinely interested and impressed.

"I got a full ride to the University of Illinois and played all four years while I earned my business degree," I replied, holding my head high.

"That's very impressive," he said. "I'm worried with your education, you might not find working as my assistant quite challenging enough, but I want you to know it's something Janet and I discussed when we reviewed your résumé and there are certainly opportunities for you to move up at G&G if that's what you want."

Thank God Bridget used real facts of my education when she compiled my new identity.

"I appreciate that, Gregory, but I imagine with everything you do, being your assistant will be plenty challenging."

He nodded as the song ended and we all walked back to the table. I tried not to be disheartened by his lack of response to my attempts at flirting. That event was the last place where he would take such a risk, but it was strange he'd been so enthusiastic introducing me to his parents.

"Ladies, if you'll excuse us, I need to borrow my sons for a few minutes," Carter said after each of the men held out our chairs. I avoided looking at Grey where he stood behind his mother as I picked up a fresh glass of champagne.

"Well, I'm not one to sit back in the shadows while the boys have all the fun," Bethany said as the men walked away. "I say we find some more drinks and mingle. You girls stick with me. I'll show you how to have a good time at one of these swanky events."

I liked Grey's mother almost instantly. We spent the next hour or so getting into all sorts of mischief with her, including placing a ridiculously large bid on a silent auction item I'd had my eye on from when we'd first arrived. It was an eight-person wine tasting tour in Napa Valley, and although it was a serious long shot for me to win with the amount of wealth floating around that room, I decided to give it a try.

"Having fun?" Grey slipped up behind me while I was waiting for his mother to finish writing her bid on a local artist's original oil painting of the Chicago skyline.

"A blast," I replied, leaning back into him without thinking.

I realized my mistake almost immediately. It was all he champagne and the atmosphere. People were dancing, chatting, and donating insane amounts of money. If I wasn't already drunk on champagne, I would have been drunk on the air in that room. The classical band had packed up for the pop singer's performance, which ended fifteen minutes earlier. One of the city's top DJs had taken over and the crowd thinned out as some of the older guests started calling it a night while many of the younger crowd were just getting revved up for the evening. Grace was among the latter out on the dance floor getting down to a mix of the latest chart toppers with a decent crowd of admirers trying to move in on her. I recognized one of them as a Cubs player. I caught a glimpse of Gregory heading our way and moved away from Grey. Gregory looked our way and smiled as he went by. Shit. The evening had been fun, but not nearly as productive as I would have hoped where he was concerned. I'd hoped for some hint of him wanting to get together after the event.

"What was that all about?" Grey sounded a bit irritated.

"What was what about?" I asked, feigning ignorance.

"You stay away from me whenever my brother is around."

"I'm just trying to be professional. He's my boss," I replied, turning toward him. There was a storm brewing behind his eyes. I hated I could read him so well, feel his moods as soon as they shifted.

"Bullshit. When you first met me and you thought I was him, you didn't seem to care a whole lot about being professional around him or that he's married. Very happily, I might add. Then you don't want anyone at work to know about us. Are you worried how it will look to everyone or just him? Do you have a thing for unavailable men? Because I can assure you, sweetheart, my brother is too unavailable, even for a hot little number like you."

I spun around to face him.

"Who the fuck do you think you are?" I spat.

"I'm the guy who's stupid enough to be falling"--he stopped and ran his hand over his face in frustration--"*to be interested* in a woman who is doing everything in her power to push him away."

His breath smelled of whiskey and his eyes were glazed. Was he about to say falling in love? My heart surged at his near confession. I should have walked away, the small piece of rationality still functioning in my equally alcohol addled mind told me as much, but I ignored it. I'd gotten in over my head with Grey, but I could still get it under control.

"You sound ridiculous. You don't know me, and I wouldn't put so much stock in your brother's character." I turned away from him.

"What the fuck is that supposed to mean? What do you know about my brother or his character?"

"Nothing, I just know men. You're all the same."

"Wow, some old boyfriend really did a number on you, huh?"

"Not even close."

"Then what is your deal? This..." He stepped in front of me and gestured between us. "I've never felt anything like it and I know you feel it, but you insist on fighting it. So, please, if it's not that you have some weird thing for my brother or married guys in general, what the hell is it?"

"My deal is I don't do relationships. I like my life the way it is and I don't need a boyfriend or any of the shit that goes along with one. We fucked once--"

"Twice." His eyes blazed as he stepped closer to me.

"Whatever, twice. It was fun but that was all it was, okay?"

I saw my words cutting him, but I just couldn't stop myself. He'd struck a nerve. I was drunk, and he was screwing everything up for me. I needed to end it, rip off the bandage and be done with it once and for all. The thought sent my heart crashing into my stomach, but I gathered every ounce of willpower I had in me to ignore the sensation. It was for the best, even if it was what I wanted; there could never be anything between Grey and me. We started on a lie--a pile of lies--and that was nothing we could build anything real on.

"Hi, Grey, can I talk you for a minute?" Ashley tapped Grey on the shoulder. Neither of us noticed her approach. I had an uncontrollable urge to punch her in the face for touching him.

He looked at me, his eyes full of hurt and defeat and sighed.

"I do know you, Claudia."

"Apparently not. You two should talk. I need to find my friend." I looked past him, pretending to search for Grace. His eyes stayed focused on me, but I kept looking past him.

"Fine. Ashley, why don't we go somewhere more private." He shook his head at me as he took her arm.

It was as if he kicked me in the gut, but it was what I wanted. Right? I drowned in regret as she smirked at me. Staring at their backs as they moved through the crowd, I wanted to run after him and tell him everything I'd said was a lie, but I just stood there. I told myself it was for the best even though tears stung my eyes.

"Hey, Claud. I need to talk to you," Grace said in my ear, putting an end to my foolish notion of going after Grey.

He snatched a glass of champagne off a passing waitress's tray. She stopped, staring at him wide-eyed while he gulped it down and took another before he and Ashley disappeared from view.

"I think Gregory's about to leave, and Bobby just texted that he needs to talk to us."

"Can we just sit here for a moment?" Grace said to the driver when we got into the car.

"Of course, miss. I'm at your disposal for the night."

The night definitely didn't go as planned, but Grace didn't seem to notice. She'd been too busy having the time of her life.

She closed the privacy partition.

"Driver, we're going to be making two stops on the way back," I said in a voice slightly louder than normal. He didn't respond or turn back, assuring us he couldn't hear us talking, so Grace dialed Bobby's number and placed the phone on speaker.

"Hey, Bobby, what's up?" Grace said curiously.

"Just wanted to fill you in on the mystery woman. She left right after you messaged me, but she just sat outside in a car and then got out a couple of times and paced around texting on her phone before she got a call. She got back in the car for another ten minutes or so, kind of like she was waiting for someone, before she finally left. Our associate made it here in time to follow her, but I haven't heard anything yet about where she ended up. Do you want him to stay on her for the night?"

"Yes, please stay with her. We need to figure out who she is," I replied.

"Okay, we'll take care of it," he said before hanging up.

"I'm going to head back in and see if I can get some more time with Gregory before he leaves." I checked my appearance in my compact mirror. Grey was busy with the pair of legs named Ashley. There was no reason I shouldn't take the opportunity to finally do my job.

"Okay, I'll send the car back here for you after I get dropped off," Grace replied as I opened the door.

"Sounds good. Don't expect me home tonight, I'm guessing I'll be using the other apartment."

"Shit, well good luck, then."

"Since when have I ever needed luck with men?" I gave her a wink before closing the door.

Chapter 11

"Jesus, Claudia," Lydia said when I stumbled into the office. "You look like shit."

"Has anyone made coffee?" I asked without addressing her statement.

It was bad enough we were working on a Sunday. I knew I looked like shit. I'm definitely a woman who can hold her liquor, but when I went back into the gala to find Grey and Ashley gone and Gregory engrossed in a conversation with a couple of local politicians, I started pounding the champagne.

I did finally get to talk to Gregory again when he and Chad carried me out to the car and sent my drunken ass on my way. God, I hoped I didn't say anything stupid, but I couldn't be sure because the details were fuzzy. After the driver helped me upstairs, I passed out on the couch still in my dress and shoes. Waking up at four in the morning to vomit while visions of what Grey was likely doing with Ashley flashed in my mind certainly didn't help with my hangover.

"Here you go." Bridget walked into the conference room with a piping hot cup of coffee for me. God, I loved her.

"The investigator followed the woman from the pictures back to an apartment building," she said as I sat down and took a healthy sip of the sweet, sweet caffeinated nectar.

"She stayed there all night. There were a few people in and out, but no one he recognized. There's a doorman so he couldn't get inside discreetly. I ran the plates on her car," Bridget continued. "It's a rental under the Clarion Corporation. I haven't found much on the company yet, it appears to be a shell owned by several other corporations, which are owned by even more corporations, so it'll take a bit more digging to find out who's really behind it all. I did find an apartment leased by the same company in the building, so it's safe to assume that one's hers. I still haven't been able to dig up a last name, but I'm working on it."

"Is there anything on Gregory's calendar with her name on it?" I asked.

"No, I checked this morning when Grace told me her first name. The lunch he had with her was just blocked out as busy, no location or other attendees designated," Bridget said. "I did find something else, though. I ran a program to cycle through some of the old G&G security footage going back six months using facial recognition and got a hit for her about eight weeks ago. She signed in and got off on the executive floor. I'm trying to dig up the security logs for that day to get a full name."

"Bridget, you could rule the world if you put your mind to it," Grace said, walking through the door. I'd wondered where she was. I'd expected to at least have a message from her asking how things went after she left the gala, but I hadn't heard a peep. Based on her appearance, she's almost as hungover as me. I guessed there was a story behind that because I knew she didn't have enough to drink at the event to be in such a state.

"It was actually pretty simple. All I had to do was tap into the..."

I zoned out when Bridget started rambling about a bunch of technical jargon.

My mind wandered to Grey. I wondered how he was feeling since he'd definitely had his fair share of alcohol. Then I remembered Ashley and hoped he felt even worse than I did.

"So, are you going to tell us how your date went?" Grace asked Bridget, her voice gravelly, pulling me from my thoughts. I'd completely forgotten about her dinner with the handsome Mr. Slade.

"Wait a fucking minute!" Lydia turned in her chair to stare Bridget down. "You had a date and no one told me?"

"It wasn't that big a deal," Bridget replied. The color rushing to her face told a different tale.

"Did you finally do the deed?" Lydia waggled her eyebrows. Grace pinned Lydia with a hard stare, warning her to stop teasing Bridget.

"No! We just had dinner and hung out for a little while before his car took me home. It was--nice." Bridget's voice trailed off as if she was lost in the memory. She sounded happy.

I'd been a shitty friend, yet again. A date was a big deal for her, and I was so preoccupied with my own bullshit I'd forgotten she even had one.

"Fine, keep your fucking secrets, Bridget." Lydia pouted. "So are you two at least going to fill me in about the gala since you left me sitting at home, bored and alone, on a Saturday night?"

Luckily, Grace was more than willing to fill her in with all the details of the night, hangover be damned, which included my losing the only item I'd bid on. I was surprised to hear she'd given a guy her number and made a note to ask her about it later when I was in a better mood. I wondered if he had something to do with her mysterious hangover.

"Girl, I don't know how they expect us to concentrate with all these gorgeous men running around here," Paul, the interior designer Janet and I settled on, said as I set down three cups of coffee for him and his assistants. He was the perfect stereotype of what most people would imagine when thinking of a male interior designer with his skinny jeans and brightly colored shirt, which was more like a blouse. His dark brown hair was cut short, except for the long wisp of white-blonde bangs hanging to one side of his forehead.

"You don't have to tell me." I laughed, playing along. "I started last week and I'm still drooling all over myself half of the day."

"Here, honey"--he tossed me a monogrammed handkerchief--"for the drool. I've got two."

Closing the door behind me, I covered my nose with the gift to lessen the effect of the paint fumes as thick plastic covering the floor crinkled under my feet. Janet wanted to get the redecorating done well before her departure so after settling on a firm, she insisted they begin over the weekend painting the offices on the west end of the floor.

I stepped through a makeshift door at the end of the hallway made from the same plastic that was on the floor and turned to make my way back to Janet's office.

The morning flew by as she filled me in on the intricacies of working for Gregory Michaels. He liked to give everything a personal touch, so a good chunk of my time was spent learning the names of G&G's top vendors and dealers.

"Is it okay if I step out to grab some lunch?" I asked as Janet flipped through some swatches Paul asked her opinion on.

"Of course. Can you drop these off to Paul on your way and tell him to go with this one?" She handed me the stack.

"Sure, do you want me to bring you back something to eat?"

"No thanks, I pack my lunch most days," she replied with a smile.

"Okay, I won't be long," I said before heading back to the office where Paul was working.

"Hey, Paul," I poked my head in the door. "Janet wants to go with this one." I handed him the swatch. "I'm running out for lunch. Can I pick something up for you guys?"

"Thanks, hon, but we brought food. Need to keep working," he said as he adjusted a clock he was mounting on the wall. "Don't you go and get yourself kidnapped by one of those sexy boys on your way out." He winked. "Or do and just be sure to call me with all the details!"

I laughed and closed the door. He wasn't wrong about the level of hotness in the building. The three Michaels men would have been enough to keep all the women and *Paul* talking but in my days working there, I'd seen a few others who'd have no problem turning heads in their own right.

I was standing waiting for the elevator.

"Claudia, wait."

A shiver skated over my body at the sound of his voice. I sighed with relief or was it resignation? I didn't know, but I resisted turning around.

"Can we talk? Maybe have lunch?" Grey asked, sounding defeated. "I need to apologize for my behavior at the gala."

"I'd rather not." I was such a liar but it sounded convincing.

"Please, I want to apologize."

"You just did. Apology accepted," I said, crossing my arms over my chest.

"Okay, but I still want to talk to you. To explain." He placed his hand on my shoulder and my resolve melted away.

"Fine."

The chime of the elevator sounded and we stepped on.

Grey stayed behind me close--so close I could feel the warmth of his body through the knit blazer and sheer blouse I wore. My stupid body responded to his nearness as it always did: my skin flushed, my panties dampened, my breath quickened, and my heart pounded. So much for getting him out of my system.

I was grateful he didn't touch me. I would have lost myself in his touch, and I couldn't afford to let that happen again. I had to stay strong, in control and remember why I was really there, whom my loyalties were to.

We remained silent until arriving at the restaurant.

"Two for Michaels," Grey said to the hostess.

He shrugged and flashed me a half smile when I looked at him. He'd known I would agree to lunch. Cocky bastard. I couldn't help but smile back at him, seeing the glimmer of hope in his eyes. Not to mention those delicious lips of his but again, I needed to stay focused. Damn it.

Once we were seated and our drink orders were taken, I finally broke the silence.

"We need to make this a quick lunch. I told Janet I wouldn't be long," I said, pretending to be worried. Janet wouldn't care if I was late, especially if I told her Grey took me to lunch. In reality, I didn't trust myself to be alone with him for too long.

"This won't take long," he responded. The waitress dropped off our drinks and took our lunch orders.

I sipped my water and looked around at everyone in the restaurant, except Grey. I could sense his gaze on me, but he remained silent until the waitress returned.

"Can I get you anything else?" The petite brunette batted her eyelashes at Grey, clearly very interested in what he needed.

"No, I'm fine," he said.

I finally looked at him. He raised his eyebrows in question.

"Oh no I'm fine, too," I said, turning to the waitress who smiled at me curiously. I imagined she was wondering what the hell my problem was.

I was happy to realize her interest in Grey wasn't bothering me. I chalked it up to getting a better handle on my attraction for him after having the weekend to stew over it. It had nothing to do with the fact he didn't even look at her.

I inhaled deeply, the scent of pepperoni and cheese filling my nostrils. I was absolutely famished. I hadn't eaten breakfast and my appetite over the weekend had been spotty at best. I'd decided on an Italian grinder, so I could eat it on the go if I needed to make a quick escape.

"I'm sorry for ambushing you the other night and for the way I acted after." He looked at me sincerely. God his eyes were entrancing. "The things I said to you, about my brother, I had no right. I don't know what I was thinking but you have to understand, I've never felt like this about anyone before. Not even about the woman I almost married."

"What happened? Why did you just *almost* get married?" I asked, leaning in.

"She didn't show up to the wedding," he whispered, his gaze moving down to my hand and the silver necklace I was twirling.

"It was Ashley, wasn't it?" I asked gently.

He nodded in affirmation. "I wondered after I saw that picture of you together. Why do you keep it?"

"I guess I didn't have a chance to get rid of it. I left right after everything happened."

"She's the reason you went to Japan?"

"Yes, the joint venture had been in the works for months before and there were a few potential candidates to go and oversee the project, but I needed to get away. I was on a flight a week later, and I hadn't been back until the day we met."

"Why did she change her mind?"

"I suppose it was an extreme case of cold feet. Looking back, there were signs. She didn't feel as if I was ambitious enough. When my father named Gregory as CEO of G&G, we got into a huge fight. She wanted me to challenge the decision, but I'd never wanted the job in the first place. Like I told you, the family business was never my dream. I joined out of necessity and I'm glad I did, but I was never suited for Gregory's role. I need more freedom than that."

"Can I ask you one more thing about her?" He nodded. "Is she dating Chad now?"

"No, he wouldn't do that. I think I mentioned our families are close when we saw her at dinner?" He looked to me for affirmation.

I nodded.

"Well, in addition to being G&G's former CFO, Ashley's father is my dad's best friend and her brother, Josh, is our current CFO. My family isn't the type who would write her off because my relationship with her didn't work out. That's another reason I left. To make it easier on everyone. Let the wounds heal."

That was why Joshua Slade sounded so familiar to me. He was Ashley's fucking brother. My positive feelings about him chasing after Bridget dissipated entirely. His sister was obviously a complete bitch. She had to be to leave Grey standing at the altar, so the odds were good he was a complete asshole.

Grey stopped to push around the pasta on his plate, but he didn't actually eat. I was tempted to ask him what they talked about after the gala. I was more tempted to ask if they did anything more than talk right before I lost my appetite.

"We all grew up together and my parents always loved her like a daughter. I think they were just as hurt as I was that day. My mom never thought we were right for each other. I think she was almost relieved when Ashley didn't show up."

"Was there someone else?" I asked.

"Are you asking if she ever cheated on me or if I cheated on her?" he asked, pinning me with his intense gaze. "So we're clear, I would never do anything like that. Ashley was unfaithful, one time I know of, a few weeks before the wedding. She confessed right away, swearing it was the biggest mistake of her life. She said she was just scared about getting married, and I was foolish enough to forgive her and try to work through it. I think subconsciously she was trying to end things without really having to end them."

"What about the guy? Did you know him?"

I didn't know why I kept pushing on what was obviously a painful subject. There was no way in hell I would share all of my bullshit so openly. I admired him for it and for some reason, I wanted to know all of it.

"I don't know who she cheated with--I never wanted to know. I never told any of my family about it, although Elsa had her suspicions and asked me flat out. She never liked Ashley. She thought she had a thing for Gregory when we were teenagers, but my brother only ever had eyes for Elsa after she transferred into our school in the eighth grade."

"Jesus," I said, sitting back in shock.

It was an odd reaction for me. I knew men were cheaters by nature, although I doubted Gregory's propensity for it more each day. Granted, I had yet to bring my A game where he was concerned, but he hadn't given me any real signs of interest.

I also knew women could be just as disloyal as men. Still, it was hard to believe a woman would cheat on a man like Grey. I reached for his hand across the table and then stopped myself, realizing I would be sending the wrong message. Again.

He noticed my hand but didn't say anything.

"What about you? Is that why you're so antirelationship? Did someone cheat on you?"

I laughed. "No, I've never given anyone the chance." I took a bite of my sandwich.

Hearing him talk about Ashley, I wasn't worried about her anymore. Why was I worried about her in the first place? Grey wasn't my boyfriend, and I'd told him there was no chance with me. What did I expect him to do?

"So something when you were younger--your family?"

My heart started to pound and the food in my mouth was impossible to swallow. I took a big gulp of water to wash it down and waved for our waitress. "Can I get a box and the check, please?"

"Claudia, I'm sorry. I didn't mean to pry." Grey leaned forward with a desperate look in his eyes.

"It's fine. I just need to get back to work." I pulled out my credit card.

"Let me buy you lunch, please?"

I nodded as a swirl of strange emotions ran through me. Part of me wanted to open up and tell him the things I never talked about, not even with my closest friends or my sister. The prospect terrified me, and it was an incredibly foolish notion. A few weeks from now the job would be over and depending on its outcome, Grey could end up hating me. There was no getting around it. For the tiniest fraction of a second, I thought of confessing everything and asking him for things he wouldn't want to give while making promises I knew I couldn't keep. I had to get away from him.

"I'm sorry, Grey. I just--I need to go," I blurted as I stood and grabbed my purse.

Fuck the stupid sandwich. I wasn't hungry anymore anyway, and I couldn't stand there another minute.

"Wait, Claudia, at least let me give you a ride back." He stood, his posture full of the intent to chase me down the moment I fled.

"Grey, please, I just want to be alone for a few minutes. I'll grab a cab. Stay and enjoy your lunch."

I needed to put some distance between us as fast as possible. With the things I was thinking, I couldn't trust myself to be alone with him.

He must have seen how much I meant what I was saying because, despite the tension in his body saying it was the last thing he wanted to do, he sat back down and let me walk out.

After my near meltdown at lunch with Grey, I was desperate to get the answers Elsa needed and move on with my life as quickly as possible. The rest of the day working with Janet dragged along, and I didn't see Gregory once the entire day.

Back at Homewrecker Incorporated, things didn't look much better. None of the surveillance turned up anything we could use to figure out what, if anything, was really going on with Gregory. Bridget was still working to find out Mystery Kristen's, as she liked to call her, last name and whom she was working for. I was embarrassed to report I hadn't made one iota of progress with Gregory on my end.

Other than the mystery woman and Elsa's photos, nothing pointed toward Gregory currently cheating or that he was looking to start, but we didn't have a definitive explanation for any of it to verify he wasn't cheating either.

"Any of you want to go grab a drink or something?" I asked as we were packing up for the night. It was nearly seven and I didn't want to go home just yet.

"Sorry, I have a date tonight," Lydia said, which was no surprise. When she wasn't on a job, she stayed plenty busy with a slew of casual sexual partners around Chicago.

I looked to Bridget and Grace.

"I've been fighting a killer headache for most of the day. I just want to lie down and call it a night," Bridget replied without really looking at me. Something was up with her, but I didn't push. I had more than my fair share of secrets.

That left Grace, who smiled sheepishly.

"Sorry, Claud, I can't go out for a drink, but I'll have a glass of wine with you at home before my date."

Now that was news. Grace hadn't had a date, *an actual date*, with a man who wasn't a mark in at least a year.

"Holy shit! Who do you have a date with?" It was official. I was turning into the worst friend ever. Two of my friends had major things going on in their personal lives, and I'd been too wrapped up in my own shit to take any real interest.

"Just a guy I met at the gala. He called earlier today and asked me to dinner," she said, her expression happier and lighter than I'd seen in a long time.

I should have known. I had a sneaking suspicion it wasn't the first time she was seeing him since the gala. Grace wasn't like me. Despite everything she saw with our work, she still believed in love. For the first time, well, ever, I found myself wondering if she might be right to still have that hope. What the fuck was happening to me?

"I suppose it will be a celebratory glass of wine, then," I said, trying to shake off the nagging and unfamiliar feelings plaguing my thoughts.

As promised, Grace and I toasted with a nice glass of a Chardonnay we'd discovered on a tasting in New York. She practically floated around the apartment in all her excitement and anticipation as we sipped wine. It was infectious; at least it would have been if I were in better spirits.

Once she left for the evening, I headed to the other apartment where I'd decided to stay most nights until we finished Elsa's case. Inside the sparsely decorated space, I was left alone with my thoughts. I started on my third glass of wine as I racked my brain for a way to move things along with Elsa's case.

I started paging through the file on Gregory I'd grabbed before I left the penthouse, looking at the logs Bridget put together from the daily video feeds from G&G. I examined the few photos our surveillance came up with on him and double-checked the printed calendar we'd pulled from the network.

It wasn't long before my search shifted, and I was looking for Grey's name in the video logs, studying pictures of him. There was one of him and me at our lunch earlier, which I'd explained away easily as a business lunch he'd asked for to discuss a gift for his brother--my boss. I was surprised by how at ease and pulled together I looked, knowing I was on the verge of falling apart when the photo was taken.

I jumped when there was a knock at the door.

Since I'd already slipped into my pajamas, I grabbed a robe from the bag I'd packed and threw it on over the somewhat sheer nightgown.

The only people who knew this address were the girls, Janet, and Gregory's driver. I knew none of the girls would be stopping by unannounced, and I couldn't imagine any reason Janet would. That only left one possibility. My heart sank as I approached the door. It was going to be Gregory. That's what I wanted. That was the whole point, wasn't it? Still, if Gregory were standing on the other side of that door, I knew I'd do my job and it wouldn't just be Elsa's heart that was broken by the end of the night.

"I'm sorry to sneak up on you like this," Grey said through the door as I peered through the peephole. I felt a brief wash of relief. "I just want to talk for a minute, please."

I seriously contemplated climbing down the fire escape before I accepted the fact I needed to face him.

"How did you get my address?" I asked and slowly opened the door.

Grey's eyes went down to my body, and I thanked God for the robe, although it was a bit on the sexy side, just not nearly as bad as the nightie it covered. I needed to make this conversation quick and concise without losing my head and doing something stupid again. I told myself that while my eyes practically devoured Grey's appearance as he leaned against the jamb of my door. He was in a pair of faded jeans with a gray Cubs T-shirt tucked in sloppily. It was the most casual I'd ever seen him. Well, next to being naked. Apparently he was sexy in anything.

"I might have bribed my brother's driver for the info." He flashed me a crooked, but unsure grin. "I was discreet. He won't say anything."

"And how exactly did you figure out which apartment was mine?" I stepped back to let him in so I could close the door. I didn't move from the foyer, hoping the conversation would be short and not give him any ideas about getting comfortable staying.

"Charmed the doorman"--that damn grin of his turned confident and sexy--"and gave him five hundred dollars."

I turned away from him to hide my smile and walked to the kitchen. I pulled a bottle of water from the fridge and offered it to him before grabbing a second for myself.

When I faced him again, I saw the wheels turning in his head. He ran his hand through his thick hair and his smile slipped.

He looked fucking adorable trying to figure everything out. I put my bottle of water on the table next to me. I considered opening the door and telling him to leave, instead I did something incredibly stupid.

"Look, can we just--"

I gripped the front of his shirt and pulled him down to meet my lips as I stood on my toes. The bottle of water he'd been holding bounced on the floor and his arms snaked around my waist before he pulled me closer. I moaned as his tongue slipped between my lips and my arms drifted up and around his neck. I didn't know what I was doing, but I just needed to kiss him that moment. I was so weak around him, which I loved and hated at the same time. I wanted to ease the confusion and frustration he was feeling and maybe ease the same emotions in myself. Being close to him seemed to be the only way to do that. I broke the kiss and laid my head against his chest. Hearing his heart beating as he held me, I felt the urge to cry. I didn't want to break his heart, but I knew if I let things continue with him the way they were, that was exactly what would happen.

"Listen, Grey," I said, finally pulling away but keeping my arms around his neck. "I can't deny I'm attracted to you, but this is something I just can't do any more, even if I wanted to. I just can't."

I pulled my arms down and took a step back.

"I meant it when I said I don't want to do this because of work," I said, which was true, just not the work he thought. "But you were right before, when you said something must have happened with my family. I'm just not capable of being in a relationship. I warned you this would happen--that you would regret me. It's just how it is. As much as I might want you, it just can't happen."

"You're wrong. Even if I never see you again, I wouldn't regret you." He took my hand. The simple touch sent a shiver across my skin. "What happened with your family?"

"It's not something I talk about," I said, pulling my hand away. "But I need you to respect what I'm telling you and stop trying to make this thing happen."

"Then why did you just kiss me?" That was a good question.

"Consider it a good-bye kiss, Grey."

He narrowed his eyes at me. "Bullshit, Claudia," he said, moving closer. "I get you have some shit to work through, but I'm sick of you pushing me away when it's clear you feel more for me than you're willing to admit, and I refuse to let this be the end for us."

I shook my head, opening my mouth to persuade him it had to be, but he didn't give me a chance to say anything.

"Don't say anything yet. I'm going to ask you one question but before you answer, understand I won't allow you to push me out of your life completely. Do you understand?"

I shook my head.

"If you aren't comfortable being in a relationship, what would you be comfortable with?"

What the hell did he mean? What else was there? The only people in my life were my sister and my friends. Shit. I looked at him. Could I be friends with a man? With Grey? I guessed there was one way to find out, and it seemed to be my only way forward at the time.

"What if we tried being friends?" I bit my lip.

He watched me for a moment. "With benefits?" He grinned.

"Don't be a smart-ass." I put my hands on my hips.

"Okay, friends. For now." Grey extended his hand for me to shake. I took it and he pulled me into his arms, hugging me tight. "Hey, friends hug, but I promise I won't push you for more."

I sighed, letting him hold me as my suggestion sunk in.

Friends. I'd never had a male friend. It was an intriguing idea. No, it was a fucking terrible idea, but as much as I'd tried to convince myself I needed to, I wasn't ready to say good-bye to Grey, and appeared he wasn't going to let me anyway.

Chapter 12

"Kristen Page." Bridget slapped down a small manila folder on the table triumphantly. She'd called a lunch meeting back at Homewrecker Incorporated to reveal her latest discovery. "And, after sifting through mountains of corporate charters and bullshit, I found the company she works for. Arrow Components."

"What's Arrow Components?" I yawned.

I'd barely slept after Grey left my apartment the night before.

"Only G&G Components' biggest competitor," Bridget responded.

"So what does this mean? Is she some kind of corporate spy who started sleeping with him to get intel?" Grace asked, playing with her hair as she paced the floor.

"I don't think he was ever screwing her," I replied. "I haven't had as much time with him as I would have liked and though I hate to say this, he just doesn't give me that vibe I usually get with marks. Maybe the pictures were some kind of blackmail to get information?"

"Maybe, but you remember the Zimmerman case? We were convinced he wasn't a cheater until we finally figured out he was fucking the first PI his wife hired and she was helping him cover his tracks. Why wouldn't Gregory have told Elsa about the photos if it was just blackmail and he didn't screw Kristen? If he's faithful, nothing we do should change that. So until you know something for sure, I think we need to keep pursuing all the angles. Are you good with that?" Grace looked to me.

"Of course, why wouldn't I be?" I asked defensively.

"I don't know, Claud. You've just seemed off your game lately. Forget I said anything," she continued. "I'll talk to Patty so she can fill Elsa in. You go back to the office, keep working with Janet and let Gregory get comfortable with you being around. See if he slips or reveals something we can use."

She gave me a reassuring smile.

"You've got this, Claudia." Lydia looked up from her tablet.

"I know. I've looked through Gregory's schedule for the next few weeks, and I've found some times when I think I can get to him outside of the office. He's pretty booked up. There's a convention in Kentucky he's leaving for this Friday, and another in Dallas late next week, but there are some evening business dinners planned after he gets back from Dallas. I could easily be dining in the same restaurant and bump into him after he's had a good meal and a few drinks to loosen him up. Not to mention Janet wants me to start doing more on my own with Gregory. That will give me plenty of excuses to see him and work on getting closer."

"If he's gettable, you'll get him." Grace nudged my shoulder. "No man can resist your charms. Hell, I don't know how

I keep my hands off you." She winked and stood. "I have to get going, have a lunch date to get to."

"The mystery man from the gala?" I raised my eyebrows. She just smiled. "Did you even make it home last night?" I asked, pushing her arm.

"I went home. I won't say what time, but I did go home," she replied with a laugh.

"You're going to have to give me the details tonight." I smacked her ass.

She just shook her head and walked out, although it was more like floated out. That must have been one hell of a date.

"Guess we should head back to the office." I turned to Bridget. "We can share a cab."

"Or you could let me drive your car?" she said, a question in her tone.

"No way. Once was enough," I replied, laughing.

"Um, Claudia, there's something I need to ask you about." She twisted her hands in her lap. "Last night Jason called me because Grace was on her date and I guess your phone was off or something."

Fuck, fuck, fuck! The tail on Grey; I'd completely forgotten about it.

"He said he followed Greyston Michaels to an apartment building and he went up and stayed for about twenty minutes. It was your building--your *other* building."

"Bridge, it's not what you think," I replied, trying to figure out what the hell to say.

"I don't know what to think about it," she said quietly.

"I met him the first day at G&G and he has a little crush on me, but I made it clear I wasn't interested and I needed to keep things professional. He didn't get the message the first time around and just showed up last night. He bribed the doorman to get up without being announced. I let him in for just a few minutes and made sure he understood he had no chance with me."

"Is that really what you want?" Bridget asked. I must have looked confused; in truth, I was confused by her question. "I mean, do you--you know, like him?"

"It wouldn't matter if I did, Bridget. We've got a job to do, which potentially includes me fucking his identical twin brother and capturing it on tape. Not exactly the stuff romances are built on."

"Oh," she said, "I just thought maybe, um, I don't know. Maybe you'd changed your mind about that stuff or something. I've kind of always wished you would so you could be happy."

"I don't need a man to make me happy. I've got you guys." I smiled. "I will tell you something strange, though. He asked me, since we couldn't be together like that, if we could be friends."

"What did you say?"

"That's the strange part. I said yes."

"But won't that end when the job is over?"

"Of course it will, but he was pretty clear he wouldn't accept anything less, and it would make my job a lot harder if he was actively pursuing me every chance he got, especially around the office where his brother might see. At least this way, I have a little control over the whole thing and can keep him at a comfortable distance."

What I didn't share was how much I actually liked talking to him and how I wasn't sure I could let go of him just yet. Being just friends, it would hurt less when things ended, as they inevitably would.

"So what now?" Bridget asked.

I wasn't sure if she meant for Grey and me or about work.

"Well, I hate to ask you this, but can you keep this just between us for the time being? I don't want to freak the others out. Grace is already worried about me and I've got it under control."

I sounded convincing, even to myself. I could do my job and be friends with Grey in the meantime. If Gregory was innocent, there was even a chance I could do it without hurting him any more than I already had. With the bonus we'd get from Elsa when the job was over, I'd be a lot closer to affording my vineyard, and if I could talk Grace into selling the penthouse, I'd definitely have enough. I could get out of the game, say good-bye to Grey, and move on without him ever having to know the truth.

"I won't say anything, I promise. You can always talk to me if you need to, about this, or whatever," Bridget replied, touching my arm. That girl was one in a million.

"Ditto, Bridget. I haven't asked you about Josh because I know you're a private person, but I'm here if you ever need to talk. Now I guess we should get out of here and get back to our fake jobs," I said, smiling down at her.

"Speak for yourself. I'm actually working really hard!" she said. "Ben has been running me around like crazy setting up their new inventory system. Which reminds me, he's probably going to want me to travel to some of the plants over the next few weeks. I could probably stall for a while. It's not as if I'm going to be staying on there after you're done with the case."

"No, don't stall. I think Lydia's got a handle on the camera feeds, and I have access to most of Gregory's files now."

I didn't want to bring it up just yet, but with Grace's new man in the picture and me thinking of starting the search for a vineyard, Bridget might want to consider extending her employment at G&G just in case.

As promised, Grey stopped pushing me for anything other than friendship, and he was playing it pretty cool in that regard, as well. He'd stopped to talk to me in the office only once since showing up at my apartment. Janet had stepped out for a doctor's appointment on Wednesday afternoon and Gregory was meeting with a vendor across town, so I'd popped in to talk to Paul for a few minutes before lunch. He was busy hanging an interesting tapestry on the wall, but stopped to fill me in on a little office gossip he'd picked up from the receptionist. Nothing on Gregory, unfortunately.

"Ms. Winston, can I get your help on something for my brother's schedule." Grey poked his head in the door of the office the designers were working in.

Paul mouthed, "Oh my God!" to me before I followed Grey out.

"Way to keep it discreet," I said out of earshot as we walked down the hall.

"What? I really want to talk about my brother's schedule," he deadpanned.

"Oh, sorry. I, um, I--"

He cracked up laughing.

"You asshole!" I said teasingly, although my face was hot with embarrassment for being so presumptuous.

"Sorry, I couldn't resist. I just wanted to grab you for a second to see how you're doing, you know, since we're friends. I haven't talked to you in person in a couple of days," he said, giving me a genuine, warm smile. "I noticed you seem to be making a lot of friends around here. You and that little redhead from IT seem pretty chummy." There was a question in his tone.

"Bridget actually helped me get the job. We've been friends for a couple of years. She's a great kid," I said, meaning it wholeheartedly.

"Kid, huh? You're barely older than her and you're calling her a kid." He laughed as we entered his office.

"There's enough of an age gap I can get away with it. I'm turning thirty-two next week."

"I think I remember you mentioning something about a birthday coming up." He pulled a bag from behind his desk. My heart thudded. For a moment I thought he'd gone and bought me something, but seeing the restaurant name on the bag, I realized the appetizing smell I'd noticed when we first walked in was coming from it. "I know you want to keep things professional, aka, are ashamed of being seen out with me in public." The corner of his mouth lifted. "So I figured we could eat in every once in a while as a friendly compromise."

"I think I can live with that," I said, peeking into the bag. "I love Italian food."

"I know," he replied with a proud smile. Of course he knew. I'd mentioned going to Tuscany and even shared that I hoped to live there someday.

"So can I ask you something?" I said as he pulled out a loaf of Italian bread wrapped in paper and set it on the table in the sitting area of his office. "Joshua Slade, is he a good guy?"

Grey looked at me quizzically.

"Yeah, Josh is great. I've known him since we were kids. Why do you ask?" He looked more than a little worried, maybe even jealous.

"My friend Bridget mentioned they'd gone out once, and I was just wondering. I can't have my friend dating a complete douche bag on my watch, and I just thought given who he's related to--"

"You mean Ashley. Trust me, he's nothing like his sister. He's one of the nicest guys I know, maybe a bit on the nerdy side, but your friend would be lucky to have him."

Nerdy was definitely good for Bridget, and I was relieved to hear Grey speak so highly of him. Although other than the brief discussion we'd had about her date back in the office, Bridget remained silent on the subject. For all I knew, it'd just been that one date but as curious as I was, I didn't want to press her about it.

Now Grace was another subject. She'd seen her mystery man three times in under a week and couldn't stop talking about it. Well, the dates at least. She didn't really offer much about the man himself. I was happy for her, if not a little jealous. Her situation was considerably simpler than mine, especially if this job was indeed our last as Homewrecker Incorporated. I knew Grace was as ready to retire as I was, but we hadn't discussed it. I didn't see the point until I was more certain. With a connection like Elsa Michaels to help her and the money she'd get selling the penthouse, she'd be well on her way to starting the charity she'd talked about since college, and she'd be free to be pursue whatever kind of relationship she wanted. Of course there would be some concern the details of our former business could come out later but before Elsa's case, we'd taken steps to protect our anonymity, so it was up to Grace if she wanted to share that information with her significant other.

"I'm glad to hear it." I sat down on the couch in front of the place setting Grey made for me. He pulled over a chair from in front of his desk. He sat in it and pulled the lever, a whoosh of air following as he dropped down to the chair's lowest setting. I couldn't help but smile at him. It was so easy being around him, so natural, even though I was constantly reminding myself to keep my thoughts focused on friendship and not how sexy he looked when he smiled.

"So what's the deal with your necklace?" He pointed toward it with his fork before he took a bite of salad. "You always wear it."

My hand shot to it instinctually. I was surprised he'd noticed but he was right, I never took it off.

"It was a gift from my mother. The last one she gave me," I replied, letting my fingers slide over the delicate detail of the rectangular filigree locket. It looked like a typical pendant at first glance, but it slid apart to reveal three pieces, each with a tiny photograph tucked carefully inside. The front photograph, which faced toward my heart, was a picture of my mom on the day I was born. The next, which faced toward her, was of me, and the third was of Jessica, both taken while we were in Tuscany. When I was younger, I would open it often and stare at my mom's picture but in recent years, I'd allowed myself to open it only once a year on my birthday. It was an early birthday gift. When Mom gave it to me a few days before my birthday. She said it was because she wanted me to have it with me--to keep her in my thoughts while I was away at college.

"I'm sorry, I know you don't like to talk about your family."

"It's okay." I slid the panels of the locket between my fingers to open it. "This is a picture of her."

I turned the pendant around so he could see it but because of how small it was, or maybe just because he wanted to, he came and sat next to me on the seat to get a closer look. He took the pendant from me and studied my mom's picture before looking into my eyes.

"You look like her," he whispered so close his breath teased the skin of my face.

I wanted to kiss him so badly I could hardly stop myself, but I had to. I had to steer clear of the attraction I felt for him, so I thought of the one thing that could pull me from any other feeling.

"She committed suicide," I whispered so low it was barely audible. "Fourteen years ago," I continued. My voice sounded a bit stronger despite the tear that slid down my cheek. It'd been a long time ago but for some reason, I hadn't really been able to move on. I still felt the pain of her loss. Probably because I lost my father, and any chance I ever had of trusting a man, that day as well. Until Grey.

Grey didn't say anything; there was nothing to say. Instead, he pulled me into his arms and I buried my face against his chest and sobbed.

On my way to pick up food on Friday for my third consecutive lunch with Grey, I thought about how strange it felt opening up to someone, about how something awful changes the dynamic of a relationship. Everything was just easier with him.

While the attraction between us simmered below the surface, waiting for a chance to ignite the flame once again, we both managed to stick to our agreement and remained strictly friends. He quickly became a very important part of my day, so much so I was sometimes able to forget it would have to end soon.

Whenever I did let myself consider the impending end of our friendship, my chest tightened and my eyes stung, only a tiny preview of the pain I was going to feel when it actually happened. Somehow I ignored it all and decided to enjoy the time I did have with him. It wouldn't be long before Gregory would be spending a lot more time in the office, and with me.

He was leaving in the afternoon for the convention in Kentucky he and Gregory were attending over the weekend, so I'd volunteered to pick up lunch for the second day in a row.

"Have a nice day," the girl who'd put together my order said as I passed her the signed credit card slip and picked up my bag of food.

I was excited to get back and share a sampling of some of the best sushi in Chicago with Grey, knowing it was going to be three days until I saw him again.

"Cynthia? Fancy meeting you here," a voice I'd hoped to never hear again said from beside me, far too close for comfort. "Surprised to see me?"

"Wow, Eric. What are you doing here, in Chicago?" I asked, trying to hide the fear that was prickling all over my skin. Not only was I running into a former mark at home, but it had to be Eric Bennett, the only one whom I'd ever actually been afraid of.

"I could ask you the same thing. One day we're having a good time and I tell you I'm falling for you, and the next you're gone, your phone is disconnected and I never hear from you again. I checked at your job, and they said you'd quit, didn't even leave a forwarding address for your last check."

I smiled, looking around casually for a way to escape--a cop nearby I could grab. But what could I say? Eric hadn't actually done anything to me, and they couldn't exactly arrest him because he gave me the creeps.

"I'm really sorry, Eric. I meant to call you, but things just got really crazy for me after the last time I saw you. I came back here for a family emergency, and I dropped my phone rushing through the airport. It got crushed under some big guy's shoe and I lost all my contacts. I ended up just taking on an extra line my sister already had on her plan instead of forking over the money for a new phone."

"Things got really crazy for me, too, Cynthia. I'm getting divorced--thought you might be interested to know that little tidbit--but I'm actually here to check out possible locations for a new hotel." His tone was calm, but there was something brewing behind his eyes I couldn't quite read.

"Wow, that's crazy. Are you okay?" I tried to sound concerned and surprised.

"I'm great. Why don't you give me your number and we can get together later, talk about everything in a more *private setting*?" he said, moving closer to me.

I pulled the bag of takeout in front of me to hold it with both hands as if it was getting too heavy for just one.

"Actually, why don't you give me yours? I left my phone back at my sister's place when I ran out to pick up lunch for us, and I don't have the number memorized yet. How long are you in town? I can give you a call tomorrow or maybe this weekend."

"Or I could just follow you to your sister's and then you can give me your number, too, and I'll know where to find you."

The hairs on the back of my neck stood on end.

"That's not a good idea; things are a mess there. Her husband had an accident and just came home from the hospital today." I prayed he would drop it.

"Fine." He pulled a pen and business card from his inside breast pocket and wrote his cell number on the back.

He stepped forward and slipped the card into the pocket of the fitted trousers I was wearing as he stared down into my eyes. His gaze then shifted to my lips. I smiled up at him, trying to muster every ounce of skill I had to maintain the act of a woman who was actually attracted to him while in reality his nearness made me want to vomit.

"I'm in town until Monday. Don't wait too long to call." He ran his fingertips down the side of my cheek.

"I won't. I'll be here helping my sister with the kids and taking care of the house for the next couple of weeks. Then I'm heading home to Kansas to visit some other family, but I'll be back in L.A. by the end of the month. I have a couple of auditions lined up." I backed away; thankful I still remembered the backstory I'd fed him. "I really need to go. My sister will start to worry, especially since she can't call to check on me."

Eric gave a single nod and stared at me until I turned and walked through the door. I could still feel his eyes on me as I walked down the sidewalk out of view from inside the restaurant. I'd walked from G&G, but I couldn't risk Eric following me, so I hurried around the block and hopped into a cab.

"Can you just drive around for a little while and then I'll give you the address?" I said to the driver.

He drove around downtown and along Lakeshore for about fifteen minutes while I watched the cars behind me, looking for Eric or any sign of someone following me. Finally, when I was confident we hadn't been followed, I directed the driver to G&G, gave him a big tip, and hustled into the building. When I was inside, I stood by the mirrored glass, watching again just to be sure

I didn't have a tail before I ducked into the lobby restroom and dialed Grace on my cell.

My hand trembled as I raised the phone to my ear. Grace picked up on the third ring and she giggled before she said hello.

"Grace, holy fucking shit! He's here, in Chicago! He just tracked me down in a restaurant and told me he's getting divorced, and I'm fucking freaking out. How the fuck did this happen?" My voice shook.

She said something to someone. Her voice was muffled so I couldn't hear what exactly, but I heard the low tones of a man's voice respond.

"Okay, Claud, slow down. What the hell are you talking about? Who's in Chicago?"

"Eric Bennett!" I whispered loudly.

"Holy shit!" Grace responded. "Did he tell you why he's here?"

"He said he's in town scoping out a location for a new hotel, but he wants to see me and, Grace, something was off, more than before."

"Maybe it's time you tell me what really happened in L.A."

Fuck. I'd just wanted to forget him and everything that happened between us. Now he was here in my hometown and there was no escaping the past.

"Yeah, okay. We'll talk tonight when I get home."

As soon as I ended the call, my phone vibrated in my hand.

Grey: Hey, what's taking so long? I'm starving here!
Me: In the lobby, be right up

I sat the bag of food and my purse on the counter. I needed to get myself together before I saw Grey, or he would know something was up. That was the last thing I needed.

Grace wrapped her arms around me as soon as I stepped through the door.

"Jesus, Claud, are you all right?" She held on to my shoulders and looked into my face.

"I'm fine. Seeing Eric like that, here at home, just scared the shit out of me. What if I'd been with someone when he called me Cynthia--like Gregory," I said. *Or worse, Grey,* I thought.

"Just be happy you weren't."

She stepped away and passed me a glass of wine she had in her hand. I dropped my bags and followed her to the couch to sit.

"He said he's only here until Monday but if his company is building in Chicago, he'd be around for months."

"We'll cross that bridge when we get to it. Bridget can keep an eye on his company's website and their public filings so we'll know if and when the time comes," she said, taking a drink.

I stuck my nose in my glass of Cabernet, inhaling the deep scents of earth and chocolate before taking a long sip, preparing myself for what was next.

"Actually, I think I need something a bit stronger for this." I headed to the kitchen.

I returned with a bottle of bourbon in one hand and two glasses with ice in the other and sat back down next to Grace. She took one of the glasses before I opened the bottle and covered her ice with the dark amber liquid. I filled and emptied my own glass once before I started talking again.

"I assume Patty told you about the stuff on the tape: the ropes, the handcuffs, the floggers, all the kinky shit he was into," I said while Grace watched me with rapt attention.

"Yes, she told me."

"For the record, none of that is really my thing, but I did whatever it took to get the job done. Anyway, does she also mention how the tape cuts off at the end while I'm still tied up?"

She nodded.

"It wasn't a glitch, I deleted the rest."

Grace's eyes were filled with concern as she shifted in her seat on the couch, but she stayed silent.

"After the parts Patty saw, he got really angry for absolutely no reason. He said I'd displeased him, so I needed to be punished. I played along at first, but then he put a ball gag in my mouth and I couldn't use my safe word and then he flogged me again--a lot harder. So hard that he drew blood. I tried to scream at first, but that only seemed to encourage him so I stayed silent while he kept going."

"Oh God," Grace said through the hand covering her mouth.

My eyes stung, but I refused to waste any tears on that piece of shit so I swallowed hard and continued.

"Then, just like that, he stopped, turned off the light, and walked out. He left me in there, alone in the dark, for what felt like hours. My arms were numb by the time he finally came back and untied me. When I was free he acted as if nothing happened, and I played along because I was terrified of what else he might do. Then he asked me if I wanted a drink, gave me my stuff, said he had an amazing time before he kissed me, and walked me to the door."

I poured myself another glass of bourbon.

"He called me several times the next day and left crazy messages about how he was falling in love with me, how he wanted to leave Alaina for me. I had to turn the phone off; it was insane. I even left the apartment and stayed in a hotel that night before I flew back here. I was certain he was going to show up looking for me."

"My God, Claudia. I had no idea. No wonder you were so scared today. Where did you run into him?"

"It was at that little sushi place I told you I liked--about five blocks from G&G. I was careful when I left. I took a cab and drove around for a while before I went back to the office. I'm sure no one followed me. Guess I won't be eating sushi for a while," I joked, trying to lighten the mood for my own sake.

"I know this isn't what you want to hear, but maybe you need to take a long weekend. I could call Janet for you on Monday, tell her you have the flu. Gregory is out of town until Tuesday anyway."

She couldn't have been more wrong. It was exactly what I wanted to hear. Grey was going to be out of town, too, so I had zero desire to go to G&G, or anywhere else for that matter, until I knew Eric Bennett was gone.

"I'm good with that."

"Oh, well, great then. I'm going to have Bridget do some digging and see if Eric was telling the truth about leaving Monday."

"Jesus, I don't want her hacking an airline just because I got a little freaked out. It was just the worst coincidence in the history of coincidences," I said, although part of me didn't care if she had to hack a NASA satellite to figure out what Eric was up to.

"We'll try it the old-fashioned way first, give his administrative assistant a call and see if we can get her to divulge anything about his schedule."

"Good thinking, you're so smart," I said in an overly sweet, slightly sarcastic tone, although I meant every word.

"What do you say we veg out on the couch with some popcorn, some more alcohol, and a Ryan Gosling movie?"

"I'm not hating that idea," I said, jumping up. "But I get to pick the movie!"

I ran and grabbed the remote as she chased after me.

"I'm not going to sit and pass you tissues while you sob your way through that super sad one. I don't care how epic you think the love story is."

"You're such a bitch." She poked my side.

"I know, how about *Crazy, Stupid, Love*? It's funny and there's plenty of romance like you love."

"I can live with that." She stood and went to start the popcorn while I turned on the television.

Chapter 13

"Bridget checked with Eric Bennett's assistant this morning and she confirmed he was due back in the office tomorrow morning, so it should be safe for you to head back to G&G first thing," Grace poked her head into my room. "And, I know you said you didn't want her hacking any airlines, but she confirmed he was booked on the red-eye tonight."

A weekend of hanging at home ordering great takeout, drinking some delicious wine, and watching all of our favorite movies was just what I needed.

"What did Bridget say when she called his office?" I asked out of pure curiosity.

"That she was calling from Mr. Bennett's doctor's office to confirm an appointment." Grace started to laugh. "She even rescheduled the appointment for later this week!"

"That cheeky little minx," I replied in my best British accent, courtesy of our British movie marathon on Saturday, which included *Bridget Jones's Diary*, *Love Actually*, *Pride & Prejudice*, and *Sense and Sensibility*. Clearly, Grace picked the movies that day, although I actually didn't mind all of the romance for a change.

"So I think we need to talk through your game plan for the day and a half you do have this week before Gregory leaves again for Dallas. Unfortunately, Bridget hasn't been able to find anything about what Kristen Page and Arrow Components are up to yet, and the investigators haven't had anything of interest to report from Kentucky. Gregory has spent the whole weekend meeting with vendors and dealers or hanging out with his brother," she said, pacing the floor by my bed. "Not to mention Elsa's attorney wants to meet later this week. Patty said she's really concerned about what Arrow Components and Kristen Page might be up to, so much so Patty had to talk her off the ledge. She was ready to call the whole thing off and tell Gregory about all of it--the pictures, hiring us, you."

"Shit." I rubbed my fingertips over my necklace. If Elsa told Gregory about me, Grey would find out, too.

"Patty persuaded her not to do anything rash, reminded her what was on the line for her foundation if she made the wrong call. She agreed to see what the investigators can dig up and to give you more time to test Gregory. Even if it turns out all of this has something to do with the business, Elsa's always going to wonder if it was more than business with Kristen. Why else would he keep it from her?"

I didn't want to think about Grey learning the truth about who I was, nor did I want to think about the fact I had less than two days to see him that week, which might turn out to be my last week on the job. I wouldn't see him more than the private lunches we had in his office but because he was gone with his brother, he'd been texting less and less and I'd actually started to miss him. Definitely a first for me.

"I'm open to any ideas you have," I said, walking past Grace to the bathroom. I grabbed my toothbrush and toothpaste and turned on the water. "There's not a lot I can do, I can't exactly ask him if he's interested in a roll in the hay or if he's being blackmailed by a competitor. Not to mention, he's more dedicated to work than any mark I've ever worked. It doesn't seem as though he's been doing anything outside of the office except going home to Elsa."

"I've considered that, so I say you make a pass at him the next time you're alone in the office. Nothing too forward, but make sure he gets the hint and see what he says," she said as I brushed my teeth.

I shook my head and went to spit.

"The worst thing he can do is fire you, which means we'd lose the bonus since we wouldn't be able to close the case."

She thought I was shaking my head because I was worried about the money and truthfully, part of me was but mostly, I wanted to stop trying to lure Gregory into cheating, and not just because I was worried about hurting Grey. Gregory wasn't really like any of the marks I'd worked before. I actually liked him and not just because of his brother. He was a good boss--kind, considerate and fair even with those who didn't seem to deserve it.

"I don't think he'll go for it, Grace. He just doesn't strike me as a cheater."

"Shit, who the hell are you, and what have you done with my cynical, "love doesn't exist" chanting best friend?" she asked.

I threw a washcloth at her. "Shut up. I'm still here, but you know I can read people pretty well--men in particular. He's not giving off the traditional vibe I get. Besides, have you considered if Elsa is the one who calls it off, we'll still get paid the bonus?"

"I wouldn't admit this to Patty, but this case is about more than the money for me. You know what Elsa could mean for me, for the foundation I want to run, but it's not just that. I admire and respect her, and I don't want to see her running back to her husband still wondering or, worse, find out later he's not the man she thinks he is and end up losing everything she's worked so hard to build. Besides, I have two words for you: Wesley Zimmerman."

She was right to bring that case up again. We'd almost given up on the Zimmerman case. He had me all but convinced until I got ahold of his phone and Bridget worked her magic to retrieve his deleted messages.

"You're right. We can't be sure of anything yet and there's too much at stake."

Of course I knew closing the Michaels job meant for Grace and the things she wanted to do for her brother and other families like hers. I'd been selfish in dragging my feet with Gregory because as much as I hated to admit it, the reason had nothing to do with the case and everything to do with getting more time to live in my doomed fantasy friendship with Grey. It was ridiculous and it needed to stop. Grace was right. Elsa had questions about a man she'd known and loved for her entire adult life. Who was I to decide her fate based on a brief acquaintance with that man, which was tainted by my feelings for his brother?

"Okay, Grace. You're right, just because Gregory seems like a nice guy right now doesn't mean anything. If he's a cheater, all we need to do is present him with the right temptation," I said, feeling determined to do just that. It was time to stop fucking around, use all the weapons in my arsenal to turn Gregory's head, and get him to show me he was just like all of the other marks I'd worked in the past.

With renewed resolve, I strode into G&G on Tuesday morning in a red skirt suit I knew looked hot but was still professional. The two buttons I left undone on the jacket and the lacy somewhat sheer black camisole I wore underneath made it less so, but I was on a mission so I was pulling out all the stops. My hair was up in a loose twist with a few tendrils hanging down to frame my face, and I'd opted to leave out my contacts and wear my glasses instead. The overall look was very naughty librarian, but it worked.

If I wasn't certain about my wardrobe choices before I walked into the building, the fact the lobby security guard, Bruce, elbowed his coworker when he saw me and could barely talk by the time I made it to his post gave me the extra boost of confidence I was going to need.

"Holy cow," Bridget whispered, catching up to me as I arrived at the elevators. "Guess the long weekend did you some good. You look fantastic!"

"Where'd you come from?" I smiled down at her. "I didn't see you on my way in."

"I was in the bathroom." She twisted a chunk of her long red hair around her finger. "I always get a little nervous when I come here."

"You look really nice too, Bridget. Are you wearing new perfume?"

She nodded.

"Is it for anyone in particular?" I asked, trying to be nonchalant.

"I don't know. I just like the way it smells, no real reason," she replied, but the look in her eye and the little smile on her face said there was a very specific reason for the change and his name was Josh.

"Well, I like it."

The doors opened.

"Hey, you want to grab lunch tomorrow?" I asked when she stepped out.

"Sure, that sounds good. You already have plans today?"

"Yeah, I have a meeting with Gregory. I'll text you tomorrow if I don't see you," I said as the doors closed.

Between my meeting with Gregory and my lunch with Bridget, I'd be able to avoid Grey until he left Thursday morning for the convention in Dallas.

"Hi, Anna." I waved to the receptionist as I walked by, pulling my phone out of my bag.

Me: Can't do lunch today, have a meeting

I figured it would be easier to tell him via text so I wouldn't have to worry about him stopping by to ask me.

Grey: That sucks. Tomorrow?
Me: Sorry, Bridget already asked

I worried he would press me to cancel it.

Me: Seems she really needs to talk
Grey: Guess we can catch up Monday then

I was a little surprised he was so understanding, although I shouldn't have been. He'd been true to his word about being just friends and acted accordingly. I felt a little sad I hadn't seen him in so long. I missed him, but I needed to keep my distance and get back on track. The job wasn't about me, which I had to keep reminding myself of every time I was tempted to get out of my meeting with Gregory. The morning flew by, probably because I was so nervous about what I had to do.

Janet decided to take a rare lunch out of the office to give me a chance to work with Gregory on my own since she announced her last day, which was six weeks away. I felt guilty, knowing her time training me was in vain and she'd be left scrambling to find a replacement.

I pushed those thoughts aside as I approached Gregory's office. We were supposed to be going over his tentative schedule for the rest of the month and some information he'd asked Janet and I to compile for a presentation he was giving at the upcoming convention. I could hear him talking on the phone so I knocked lightly.

"Come on in."

He was still on the phone when I stepped through the door. He looked up at me, his expression a little surprised, and then he smiled and continued talking.

"That sounds good, Chris. I'll have Nick get back to you later today," he said before hanging up the phone.

"Wow, Claudia, you look great. Are the glasses new?" He stood and walked around the desk to greet me as I set my notebook and tablet down on his desk.

I extended my hand, but he pulled me into a quick hug. That was new and definitely a good sign. Maybe Grace was right about it being like the Zimmerman case. While he made his way back around the desk, I took a seat and discreetly popped open another button on my jacket, letting it hang open to reveal the maximum amount of cleavage I could show without making me look like a total hooker.

"No, I just ran out of contacts," I lied as I pulled up the PowerPoint presentation on my tablet.

"This looks really great," Gregory said when I laid it in front of him.

"So you're good with the font and the color scheme?" I asked. "It's really easy to change if you prefer something else. Here, let me show you." I walked around to stand next to him. Instead of crouching down, I bent over at the waist so he'd be sure to get the maximum effect if he turned to look at me while I demonstrated the software. I was pretty sure he knew how to use the program just fine on his own, but he indulged me.

"I actually think I prefer this one," Gregory said after he'd toggled through a couple different themes.

"I think you're right." I leaned even closer to him. My left breast was touching his shoulder, but he didn't seem to notice. "That looks much better; you have a great eye." I pretended to admire the change without moving away. I wondered if I would need to get on his lap to get his attention.

"Ahem."

I jumped at the sudden sound from the doorway. Grey leaned against the jamb, glaring directly at me. I tried to control my features as a twinge of guilt tightened my stomach. I took a small step away from Gregory.

Grey strode into the room calmly and smiled at his brother. "Sorry to interrupt your *meeting*," he said to Gregory.

My heart was in my throat and the blood rushed so hard behind my ears, I could barely make out what they were talking about. Something about their trip to Dallas and a call that afternoon. They must have finished because Grey started walking out, and my heart slowed just a little.

"Ms. Winston," Grey said, looking back with a smirk, "Janet sent over a list of potential assistants for me, I'd like your opinion on a couple I like. Stop by my office when you're finished here," he demanded before finally walking out. He didn't bother to wait for a response or close the door. I wondered if it was to be rude on purpose or he thought I needed the lack of privacy to control myself with his brother.

"I wonder what's gotten under his skin." Gregory said rhetorically after his brother left. "Well, with that change, I'm happy with everything, Claudia. I really appreciate all of your work, and it seems as though Janet is finally getting excited about retirement now she's not worried about who's going to take care of me." He chuckled as he passed the tablet over, looking at me for the first time since I'd stood beside him. His gaze remained focused on my face.

"Thank you, Gregory. It's been a pleasure working here so far," I said, finally stepping back around the desk.

"Can you send Janet in to see me when she gets back from lunch?" He smiled before he studied some paperwork on his desk, effectively dismissing me. I felt sick when I walked out. I couldn't talk to Grey yet, not until I got ahold of myself because I was pretty sure he didn't actually want to talk about assistant candidates. I ducked into the bathroom and hid in a stall for God knows how long before I felt calm enough to face him.

"You wanted some help deciding on a candidate?" I tried to keep my voice from shaking as I stepped into Grey's office. I was usually so happy in that space, but in that moment I was nothing short of terrified. I knew what was coming. Grey was looking out the window.

"Not really," he said, swiveling around in the chair. His eyes were dark. He stood and stalked toward me where I stood just inside the door, not stopping until there were just a few inches between us. He didn't touch me or grab me like I'd expected. Instead, he reached behind me and pushed the door closed. Grey didn't move back for several seconds. He just kept staring down into my eyes as though he was daring me to look away and trying to see into my soul at the same time.

My fear turned into anger. Who did he think he was? He didn't own me and he certainly wasn't going to control me. I don't get intimidated.

Still holding his gaze, I finally spoke. "Did you summon me here to have a staring contest then?" I said, challenging him. That probably wasn't a wise move.

"No, I think you know I want to ask what the fuck you were trying to do with my brother." His breath was even, no expression graced his face.

"We were going over his presentation for Dallas." I lifted my chin.

"Bullshit. What is it, some kind of fetish?" His voice grew louder. "You were practically sitting on his lap!"

"You're delusional," I replied, feigning conviction when all I felt was guilt.

"Am I?" He looked down. "Funny, two more buttons were undone when you were leaning in Gregory's face." He hooked his index finger in the front of my jacket and pulled it out. Despite myself, I shivered when his finger brushed the top of my cleavage and my panties dampened. "What? You didn't want them on display for me? And you never answered my other question. Do you have some kind of fetish for married men? It certainly seems that way?"

It was a reasonable question under the circumstances; my response was less so. Before I knew what was happening, I smacked the side of his face. He didn't even look surprised--in fact, he smiled.

"So that it, then? Catching a single guy must be too fucking easy for a woman like you. You must need the challenge of destroying a family to get off."

His words stung, a feeling I clearly wanted to share. I swung my hand at his face a second time, but he caught my wrist before I could make contact and crashed his mouth down over mine.

His tongued pushed between my lips, not waiting for an invitation. He released my wrist and gripped my hips, digging his fingers into my flesh. My body relaxed against him and I moaned into his mouth. It must have been the response he was waiting for because as soon as I gave in he let go and stormed out of this office, leaving me there horny and confused.

Chapter 14

I stumbled through the rest of the day. As much as I wanted to pack up and go home, I couldn't. Janet wouldn't mind, but I couldn't face Grace yet, so I headed to my other apartment to hide out for the night. She would want to talk about what happened with Gregory, which was a big fat nothing. Whether he just wasn't attracted to me, or there was something else going on, Gregory clearly wasn't taking any bait I was casting.

To head off Grace's inevitable inquiry, I shot her a quick message.

Me: It was a no go with Gregory today. Meeting got canceled
Me: Going to try and reschedule.
Grace: Bad luck, where are you?
Me: Other apartment.
Grace: You okay?
Me: Absolutely :) Who knows, maybe he'll show up here ;)

Grace: Fingers crossed!

I didn't see or hear from Grey that night or the next two days. I wasn't even sure if he'd come into the office on Wednesday. I considered texting him to apologize or try to explain, but what could I say? Nothing I could tell him would make any sense. Besides, I didn't want to lie to him again. Silence was the best alternative.

It was no surprise the surveillance reports revealed nothing of interest once again. We hadn't gotten anything new since finding out Kristen worked for Arrow Components.

"With Gregory gone, we can slip a bug into his office. No one would bat an eye at me stopping to see you while you're working in there now," Bridget suggested on Friday when we were out for our third lunch that week. "We can swing by Homewrecker Incorporated and pick up the equipment on our way back to G&G."

"That's a great idea," I said as I pushed bits of salad around on my plate. It couldn't hurt to listen in on all the calls Gregory made from his office.

"What's wrong, not hungry?" Bridget asked, her brow furrowed.

"Not really, guess the stress of the job is getting to me. I've never had to work so hard for it before. I'm just ready for it to be over."

"I know," Bridget said, her expression soft. She was the only one who knew about the added frustration that was Greyston Michaels.

After lunch and short taxi ride, I walked into my office at Homewrecker Incorporated while Bridget gathered the equipment she needed.

I stopped cold when I saw the box on my desk. I'd completely forgotten it was my birthday. I had a pretty good idea who it was from since I got one every year. I was just about to toss it in the trash, like always, when there was a knock at my door.

"Hi, Claudia. I swung by your other place on my way in to pick up your mail. Happy birthday, by the way," Lydia said with a smile as she handed me the two packages wrapped in identical paper. One was small and rectangular; the other was much larger and flat.

I looked at the other box on my desk and sighed, picking up the card next to it.

Opening it, I scanned it quickly. Despite my intention to just read who the sender was, I made the mistake of reading "My dearest Claudia" in handwriting I hadn't seen in over fifteen years. I closed the card as tears stung my eyes and tossed it into the trash can beside my desk.

"Here, you can have whatever this is. Just wait until I'm gone to open it. I don't want to know what it is, and you have to promise not to mention it again." I handed the box from my desk to Lydia.

"Shit, really?" Lydia said and then nodded and walked out when she saw my expression.

With the annual gift from my father out of the way, I was curious who'd sent the other gifts. The girls usually went in on something together, but they would wait until we were all together to give it to me, and Grace was nowhere to be found.

I peeled the second envelope open and pulled out the card.

Happy birthday, Claudia.
I'm sorry.

Grey

He shouldn't have been the one apologizing. I'd slapped him for asking what were fair questions under the circumstances, after all.

Pulling the paper off the small box, my breath quickened when I recognized the signature robin's egg blue box. I flipped open the lid and gasped at the exquisite diamond and ruby tennis bracelet inside. It must have cost a small fortune and I absolutely loved it, but there was no way I could accept it. I considered calling him to tell him as much but thought better of it. I couldn't talk to him yet.

Instead I carefully pulled the wrapping of the other gift.

"Oh my God," I said into the silence of my office as I stared down at the mountain landscape painting I'd admired in passing at Grey's house. I didn't even realize he'd seen me looking at it.

For someone who didn't really cry, I seemed to be coming close a lot lately.

Me: Thank you for the gifts. They're beautiful
Grey: Happy birthday
Me: But I can't accept them
Grey: What about the apology?

I accepted it, but I really didn't understand why he offered it. I didn't understand why he wanted anything to do with me.

Me: That I accept

I knew if I didn't accept his apology, he would just keep trying whether I deserved it or not.

Grey: Now it's your turn
Me: I'm sorry for slapping you

He deserved that much at least, but the friends thing wasn't really working anymore.

Me: Let's just forget the other day and move forward professionally
Grey: So not even friends now?

Was that what I was saying? The thought made me feel sick, but either way it would all be over soon.

Me: Maybe that's for the best
Grey: Mom wants you to come to dinner Sunday

Shit. I'd agreed to dinner with the family at the gala.

Me: I don't think that's a good idea
Grey: If you're turning down an invitation from Bethany Michaels, you'll have to tell her yourself

How did it all get so complicated? Oh yeah, because I was a selfish idiot.

Me: Fine. What time?
Grey: 5
Grey: I'll send my car for you at 4:30

I was probably going to regret this.

Me: Okay. I'll be in front of my building at 4:30

I usually waited until right before bed, but I needed to see my mother's face at little early that birthday. I sat in my chair and slid the panels of the locket open.

"I love you, Mom," I whispered as I stared at the tiny photo.

❖

My phone buzzed again. I picked it up thinking it was Grey texting again, but it continued to vibrate in my hand with Jessica's name flashing on the screen.

"Hey, Jessica," I said attempting to sound cheerful.

"Auntie Claudia!" Izzy yelled, followed by an adorable performance of Happy Birthday.

"That was great, Izzy. Thank you so much!"

"Okay, bye. I love you, here's Mommy," she said, followed by some muffled rustling.

"Happy birthday," Jessica said finally.

"Thanks, Jess."

"How are you doing?"

"Good, I was just about to head home," I said honestly. I was starting to feel better.

"Izzy has been begging to come see you. Maybe we could stop by Sunday so she can give you your gift. She made it and she's extremely proud."

I smiled, thinking about my niece. My last visit was so brief I barely got to see her.

"I have to be somewhere Sunday evening, but it would be fine if you came early."

"Great, we should be there around nine," Jessica said.

"So, how have you been?" I asked. We'd talked for a while after our trip to the cemetery, mostly reminiscing about Mom and all of our antics from when we were little. It'd become something of a tradition over the years. We just talked about the happy times, careful to avoid the heavy shit.

"I've been okay," she replied. I could tell there was more she wanted to say.

"Just okay? Is something else going on?" I asked with concern.

"Yes. I know it's your birthday, and it's the worst time to ask you this, but can you please call Dad? He's sick."

I didn't say anything for what seemed like forever. Nor did she.

"There are things he needs to say to you, things you need to know about him, about Mom."

A tear slipped down my cheek. "Jessica, I...I just can't talk to him. I know you don't understand. You may think I'm unreasonable, but I just can't. Whatever I need to know, you can tell me."

"Claudia, they aren't my secrets to tell. Just think about talking to him before it's too late."

"Fine, I'll think about it but don't hold your breath," I said, surprising myself.

"I guess that's a start. Thanks, Claudia. I love you."

"I love you, too."

Grace walked in just as I slipped the phone into my bag and stood to head out for the night. "Hey, I thought you were hanging with your new friend all day today." I said, waggling my eyebrows at her.

"Come on, you know I can't let your birthday go by without taking you out for a celebratory drink!" She hooked her arm in mine. "So let's go upstairs and get changed. Bridget and Lydia are meeting us there."

Grace suggested we keep it low-key because we were just having drinks and dinner at one of our favorite pubs, which was pretty casual. Neither of us were up for a late night of the club scene or the inevitable hangover that would follow.

I'd slipped into a printed sundress with a little black shrug just in case it got cool in the evening. Grace chose a cute romper with a light jacket.

We were able to hail a cab right as we stepped out of the building. It was a nice evening, and still pretty early, so we probably could have walked to the restaurant, but we'd both opted for heels, which weren't exactly conducive to a long early evening stroll on the city sidewalks. Although with the pungent smell in the cab, I might have been willing to deal with sore feet instead.

"No way, my treat." Grace slapped my hand when I opened my wallet to pay the driver. "It's your birthday."

She didn't have to tell me twice. I escaped out into the fresh air and waited for Grace to join me.

"The place seems pretty dead for Friday night," I said as we approached the door.

"Good." She held the first door open for me. "It will make for a nice quiet night."

I pushed through the second door and approached the hostess stand.

"Just two of you?" the young, chubby cheeked girl asked, flashing an excited smile. Someone clearly loved their job.

"No, we're meeting some friends. They should be here already," Grace said from behind me.

"Oh, yep, they're already seated," she said cheerfully, leading us around the corner to the main dining area. I looked back at the stand as we walked away, noticing she didn't grabbed menus or place settings for us.

"Surprise!"

My hand shot to my heart as the whole room yelled in unison.

"You bitch," I said sarcastically to Grace as she pulled me into a hug.

"I know, I know, but I couldn't resist," she said in my ear.

"What'd you do? Have them close the place down just for us?" I said, moving back.

She just shrugged one shoulder nonchalantly as if it was no big deal.

Before I could chastise her for spending that kind of money, Lydia and Bridget pulled me into a tight hug.

"Happy fucking birthday!" Lydia said, clearly having gotten her party started a little early. She tilted her head to the side, eyes wide in a "look over there" expression.

When I did, an unexpected swarm of butterflies appeared in my stomach. Grey beamed at me from across the room where he was standing with Joshua Slade. My stomach, butterflies and all, dropped to the floor. Why the hell was he there? My eyes darted around the room in search of Bridget, or a place to hide. I caught sight of her coming out of the bathroom. She must have seen the panic on my face.

"It's okay," she mouthed, looking toward Grey before giving me a thumbs-up, which was a bit corny, but reassuring. I let out a breath. She must have let Joshua bring Grey along.

With the panic gone, I looked back to Grey. His eyebrows were tight as he watched me. Though his presence made me a bit nervous, I grinned at him so hard I must have looked like a complete idiot but God, however fucked up it was, I'd missed him. I wanted to go over and throw my arms around him and feel his around me. Luckily, another pair of masculine arms pulled me out of the trance that was Grey.

"Happy birthday, Claudia," John, the doorman from our building, gave me a warm hug. I chanced a glance at Grey when John released me. His jaw was tight as he glared at John. John's wife, who I'd met at the building Christmas party, wrapped her arms around John's waist from behind and the tension in Grey's face disappeared. I gave him a quick smile and then turned back to Grace.

"I can't believe you did all this," I said, waving my hands around at all the decorations.

"John and Gina did most of the work," Grace replied, smiling at the couple.

"Thank you both." I gave Gina a quick hug.

"You're welcome, Claudia. It was our pleasure," Gina said.

"Auntie Claudia!" Izzy yelled, running through the small crowd. I scooped her up into my arms and squeezed her tight.

"I'm so glad you're here, pumpkin." I kissed her cheek. "Hi Jess, hi Shawn, I'm so glad you're here." I fought hard not to look at Grey. The last thing I needed was for him to talk to Jessica.

My sister watched me nervously. I put Izzy down and pulled my sister into a hug. "I suppose you asked to come over Sunday to throw me off the scent of this little party?"

"Grace made me," she replied as I went on to hug Shawn.

I wondered if Grace really thought the party through, and if Bridget consulted her about our surprise guests, considering we were working a job at home. My sister and Shawn didn't know what kind of work we really did and I wanted to keep it that way.

"Happy birthday, Claudia. This is really great," he said, looking around the restaurant.

"Yeah, my friends are the best."

"We can't stay very long, need to get this one home to bed at a decent time," Jessica said, hoisting Izzy up on her hip.

"But I'm not tired!" Izzy humphed, her little eyebrows pinching together.

"I know you're not, but you will be pretty soon. We can stay and have fun for a bit as long as you're good." Jessica put her back down. I was glad to hear they weren't staying long. Izzy shot off between Lydia and Grace who were standing nearby.

Jessica and Shawn followed. They'd never been the kind of parents who let Izzy run around unsupervised, no matter how many other adults were around. Considering it looked as if it was an open bar across from the main dining area, leaving early was a wise choice.

"I can't believe the sexy twin is here!" Lydia whispered loudly in my ear as she sidled up next to me.

"Jesus, Lydia!" I hissed. "You mind keeping it down; my family's here."

The DJ started playing songs from the eighties. I knew that was all Grace. She loved that decade. "Sorry, I'm just wondering how he ended up here? Who invited him?"

"I'm guessing it was Joshua over there next to him," I said, keeping my eyes on Grey.

He laughed at something Joshua said, but his eyes drifted back to mine for a moment. He was doing a pretty good job of not staring. I, on the other hand, needed to work on that or someone was going to notice.

"Then who invited him? He's pretty fucking hot, too?" Lydia continued, clearly on the prowl.

"That would be Bridget." I looked away from Grey long enough to spot her again. It wasn't hard; I just followed the line of Joshua's gaze.

"Shit, is every guy who works at that place hot? Did she invite more?" Lydia asked, scanning the room.

"I doubt it. He's the guy she went on a date with, or I guess maybe the guy she's dating now by the looks of it."

"Holy fuck! That's the guy? Way to go, Bridge." Lydia tossed back the rest of whatever drink she had in her hand. "At least the other one is single."

I loved Lydia, I really did, but as I watched her adjust her shirt to show more cleavage, I wanted to punch her in the throat.

Of course, I would need to find a more diplomatic way to keep her from pouncing on Grey.

"Slow down there, killer. We're still on a job," I said, stepping in front of her to stop her from eye-fucking Grey.

Lydia stuck out her lip. "Fine, guess I'll have to find some company for the night elsewhere." She headed to the bar.

When Bridget finally went over to talk to Joshua, I smiled at Grey and motioned toward the bar with my eyes. We arrived at the same time.

"Vodka and soda," I said, smiling brightly.

Grey chuckled beside me. "I'll have the same." He set his empty glass on the bar. "Happy birthday, Claudia. This is quite the party."

"It is, although they don't seem to have been very selective about the guest list," I said, nudging his arm.

"Ouch." He grabbed at his heart. "Old age is making you bitter."

Touché.

"You're such a smart-ass." I picked up my drink and took a healthy sip. "Seriously though, how did you end up here?"

I had a pretty good guess, but I was curious why Joshua would have brought him along to crash a party for someone he'd never even met. I'd seen him in passing around the office, but somehow we'd never been formally introduced.

"Your little redheaded friend invited Joshua, and I happened to be sitting next to him in the most boring convention imaginable when he got the e-mail. I told him I couldn't stand another minute of that shit and if he let me tag along, we could use the company jet to fly back. That was enough to persuade him since he's pretty shy around new people and wanted someone he knew with him, and the fact Bridget said it was okay after he insisted on asking her first," he said, laughing. "I think he's got it pretty bad for her."

"Why wouldn't he? Bridget is great." I said proudly.

"I'm sure she is if she'd earned the right of friendship with you," he said with a smirk.

"Stop making fun of me; it's my birthday."

"Did you like your gifts?" he asked quietly.

"Yes, I love them but if I'd known you were coming, I would have brought them to give back. It's too much."

"Please keep them, just a friendly token and an apology, nothing more."

"If you give gifts like that to all your friends, you must be pretty popular."

The vodka was clearly starting to kick in.

Grey leaned on the bar with is elbow. "You're more special than my average friend," he said, giving me a sexy half smile. His eyes were dark, lids hanging low as his gaze drifted to my mouth.

I bit my lip.

"God, don't do that."

"Do what?" I asked with a shrug.

"Bite your lip like that. It makes me want to do it, too."

The lightning of desire spread through my veins. God, I wanted to kiss him, bite him, lick him. I needed a fucking intervention. I was relapsing and Grey was my drug of choice.

"Hey, Claudia," Bridget said, walking up with Joshua in tow. "I don't think you've met Josh yet."

I was grateful for the reprieve before I lost my head and did something stupid again. I needed to slow down on the alcohol and drink some water.

"Happy birthday, Claudia." Joshua offered me a bottle of wine with a card attached. "I didn't want to show up empty-handed, and Bridget said you really like wine."

Seeing him up close and hearing him talk, I had to adjust my initial impression of him. He was more adorable than hot; there was an inherent sweetness about him I'd missed before. I could definitely see how well his temperament suited my fiery-haired friend.

"Thank you, Josh, that's so considerate. It's so nice to finally meet you. I can't believe it didn't happen sooner with me being on the same floor at work. Guess this guy and his brother must keep you locked away doing all the real work and making them look good."

Even in the dim lighting of the pub, I could see a hint of color rise in his cheeks. Definitely adorable.

Someone must have asked the DJ to crank things up because the music suddenly got louder. I recognized the beat. Grace was out on the dance floor holding a microphone while the "Cha-Cha Slide," one of our favorite songs from college, blasted through the speakers.

"Claudia, happy birthday, girl! It wouldn't be a party if we didn't dance to this at least once, so get your sexy ass out here!"

I glanced at Grey, who smiled wide, waiting to see what I would do. Bridget was already shaking her head in refusal as if she'd read my mind, but I ignored her and grabbed her hand to drag her with me through the tables and join Grace. Grace and Lydia were already lined up and doing the steps, which Grace and I forced the two younger girls to learn, by the time we weaved our way through.

We fell into line when they did the first half-turn in the dance and followed along to the commands in the song. Pretty much the whole room watched us. I laughed when we finished "cha-chaing real smooth" and turned to see Grey and Jessica with Izzy in her arms joining in. The area set up for dancing was fairly small, so the other guests probably couldn't fit without running into some of the tables, although I could tell Shawn was seriously considering squeezing his way in anyway.

The song ended and another favorite came on. Izzy ran around the edge of the dance floor and I bent down to greet her.

"Mommy says we have to go," she said with her bottom lip sticking out.

"I know, pumpkin. It's getting late. I'm so happy you came, and if you're really good for your mom and dad, I'll come pick you up in a couple of weeks and take you to the beach and movie I promised last time. Would you like that?"

She nodded her head enthusiastically. I followed her off the floor to say good-bye to Jessica and Shawn.

"Who's the guy?" Jessica asked. Since she knew everyone there other than Grey and Joshua, I was pretty sure whom she was talking about.

"Just a guy Bridget is dating and his friend," I responded casually.

"Yeah, okay," she replied with a knowing smile.

I ignored whatever implication she tried to make and gave her and Shawn a quick hug before rejoining everyone on the dance floor. Grey slipped away back to Joshua who stayed close to the bar. It wasn't long before Bridget followed suit.

We were in the middle of grooving to "We are Family" when Grace grabbed my arm.

"Oh my God! He came!" she yelled in my ear.

I followed her gaze to the door where a man, who I assumed was the mystery man from the gala, was smiling in her direction. She then turned her back to him and kept dancing, giving me a wink as she did. I raised my eyebrows.

"Can't seem too eager," she said, leaning in close.

Good, I was glad she was playing it cool and not rushing things. It'd been a long, long time since she'd had more than a casual date, but the looming prospect of retirement clearly had her hoping for something more serious.

I gave her the international sign for drink. She shook her head, so I walked to the bar alone while she continued dancing with Lydia and Gina who were still going strong.

"I think we're going to head out," Bridget said when I got close. "I have to get up early tomorrow."

I smiled at her, waiting for her to elaborate, but it seemed that was all I was going to get.

"This was a great party; thanks for letting us crash." Joshua shook my hand.

I could feel Grey's eyes on me, much like they'd been the whole night, but he'd managed to be fairly discreet so no one other than my sister seemed to have picked up on anything.

"It was nice to see you again, Claudia," Grey said, briefly touching my forearm. Because he'd come as Joshua's guest, courtesy of Bridget, it was only good manners he left with them. I didn't really want him to go, but I knew it was for the best. I'd paced myself pretty well with the drinking, but I wasn't foolish enough to think I was only vulnerable to Grey's charms under the influence.

"Nice to see you, too," I said and then bit my lip for good measure. He shook his head and smirked.

"Don't forget dinner on Sunday," he said quietly over his shoulder as he walked by.

"Looking forward to it."

The plan for pacing my alcohol consumption flew out the window around eleven after Lydia ordered a third round of shots for those of us who'd stayed at the party. I vaguely remembered John taking his shirt off and dancing on the bar after doing a body shot off Gina. I managed to lose one of the designer heels I'd taken off by the dance floor at some point. Grace and her new man disappeared sometime between me going to the bar and when Grey left. She didn't bother with so much as an introduction or a good-bye, which seemed more than a little weird. She'd been spending a lot of time with this guy and I had yet to meet him. I began to wonder if she was hiding something.

I'd been lucky to make it to my room in the first place, so I had no clue if she was home when I stumbled through the door with a little help from John and Gina, who probably weren't much better off than I was. I really hoped he wasn't on duty the next day.

It was nearly noon on Saturday when I finally crawled out of the bed in desperate need of some aspirin and a cup of coffee. The bottle of aspirin and a bottle of water sat by the coffee maker on top of a note and an envelope

Sorry for bailing last night. I hope the gift makes up for it, it's from all of us, and don't worry, I didn't win it. I'm hanging out at the pier with Jared today. Take some aspirin, drink the whole

bottle of water, skip the coffee, and go back to bed until you feel better.

Love, Grace

Inside the envelope were four tickets for a Napa Valley wine tasting, the exact thing I'd bid on and lost in the silent auction at the gala. It made sense she'd specified she hadn't won it because I would have been pissed if she'd paid more than what I bid on it, which was a lot.

It more than made up for her skipping out on the party. Of course, I'd had so much to drink I probably wouldn't have noticed if everyone had left me there dancing by myself anyway. A sad fact I was paying for dearly. I was grateful I didn't have any plans or commitments for the day, which allowed me to follow Grace's instructions and go back to bed.

Chapter 15

After sleeping away most of Saturday recovering from my party, I felt pretty great getting up Sunday morning. So much so I threw on my running shoes, compression pants and a jacket and headed up to North Avenue Beach for an early morning run. It was just a little after five, so the place was all but deserted.

On the trail, my thoughts turned to Grey. Everything was so confusing. I had no idea how to proceed with him. A part of me wished we could move on as friends after the job was over, possibly more, but there were too many lies. Too much baggage stacked up between us, and I wasn't even sure if I was capable of giving him what he and, if I was being truly honest with myself, I wanted.

I was coming around the curve of the peninsula on my way back to the mainland when I caught sight of a man running my way.

I stopped cold, my chest heaving as I tried to catch my breath.

"What, what are you doing here?" I said, looking up at Grey in his blue pullover hoodie as I pulled the earbuds from my ears.

He laughed, gesturing toward his clothes as if to say, "Isn't it obvious?"

"I came out for a run to clear my head. I used to run this trail all the time before I left for Japan, seemed like it was time to get back in the habit," he replied, stepping closer.

I don't know if it was the endorphins from my run, all of the pent up emotions I'd been battling with since the first time I laid eyes on Grey, or just the joy I felt seeing him so unexpectedly but for whatever reason and, despite my better judgment, I threw my arms around his neck, pushing up on my toes as I crushed my mouth to his.

He tensed for a moment before his arms slid around my back and he pulled me closer, his tongue dancing in perfect unison with mine.

The pound of another runner's shoes against the pavement pulled us from the moment.

"Come on." I grabbed Grey's hand and tugged him in the direction of the parking lot.

We cut across the sand, something I normally wouldn't do, especially since I'd driven there in my baby, but I couldn't bring myself to care about a little sand in my car with visions of all the things I was considering doing to Grey flashing in my head.

"Wow, nice car," he said when the lights flashed as we approached.

I opened the back door and practically pushed him back on the leather seat. He slid over to the other side, pulling me with him as I reached back and closed the door. The space was more than a bit cramped and I was sweaty from my run, but I didn't care. Grey didn't seem to mind at all either.

I straddled him and I unzipped my jacket before fumbling to get free of the sleeves while Grey struggled with his hoodie. I laughed and he grabbed my face, pulling me down to his mouth while my arms were still trapped behind me in my jacket. It was early and my car was parked alone on the far side of the parking lot, so there was no one walking by to see what we were doing, not that I would have cared if they did.

"I guess I didn't really think this through." I laughed against his lips.

I lifted up as much as I could in the cramped space, finally getting my arms free. Grey wadded up his hoodie and tucked it under his head against the seat.

"I could stay crammed in here all day if it means being with you." His eyes swam with emotion. He searched my expression, a hint of concern in his gaze. He was right to worry. With that brief moment to think, everything else barreled back into my thoughts.

"I'm sorry, Grey. I don't know what's wrong with me." I backed up against the door, pulling my jacket up over my chest as I struggled to get control of the emotions flooding my mind.

"Talk to me," he said, sitting up on his elbows as he watched me intently.

"I'm not sure I can do this. I need some space, some time to think and clear my head."

Grey sighed, pulling his leg from under me to sit up all the way. "This feels way too familiar, Claudia." He slipped his arms back into his hoodie before he looked at me again. "I agreed to be friends, said I wouldn't push for more, but you keep sending me mixed signals. Is this a game to you?" He placed his hand on his forehead while his elbow rested on top on the seat back. "Because it's starting to feel as though you're just playing with me."

"No, Grey, it's not that." I inched closer and put my hand on his knee. "This is all new to me. I know I'm fucked up and this isn't fair to you, but I--" I turned away from him and put both hands on top of my head. "Ugh! I just don't know what to do. I don't know what I want!"

"Well, I do. I want you; I think I've made that abundantly clear. And I think you do know what you want, you're just scared to admit it to me, maybe even to yourself."

I stared at the red stitching on the back of the seat in front of me, not wanting him to see the tears welling in my eyes.

"I'm not sure if you've noticed, but I'm not going anywhere. Well, I'm going to leave now and go for a run, or maybe grab a cold shower..."

I chanced a glance at him and saw a smirk turning up one side of his mouth.

"What I mean is I'm not going to let you push me away." He reached over and stroked his thumb over my cheek. "Someday you're going to figure out this is real, that you can trust me. I'm willing to wait for you to get there."

I nodded, unable to speak over the knot in my throat.

He leaned over and kissed my cheek before he opened the door. "You're still coming to dinner tonight, right?"

I nodded again.

"Good, I'll see you then." He stepped out of the car and closed the door behind him.

I stayed there, watching as Grey jogged back toward the running trail, wondering what in God's name was happening to me before I finally zipped up my jacket and drove home.

The car Grey promised arrived promptly at four thirty, though I'd wondered if he would show up himself instead. When we'd made the plans he was going to be flying home the same afternoon, but he'd come back early for my birthday. I supposed he was giving me the space I'd insisted I needed.

I'd decided on a gray pencil skirt and black ruffly blouse for the occasion. I left my hair down and finished the look off with a pair of cherry-red heels and the tennis bracelet Grey gave me.

He would appreciate the gesture, although I had no idea what message I was trying to send. My head was telling me to stop, to finish the job, and leave before I made things any worse. My heart was telling me something else.

After riding for about thirty minutes, we turned off the road and drove up a long, winding driveway through some trees to what could only be described as a mansion. The landscaping was exquisite with a fountain showcased in the center of the round driveway of the courtyard.

We came to a stop where Grey was waiting dressed in a pair of khakis and a polo, leaving me feeling a tad bit overdressed.

"Your parents' house is amazing," I said, taking Grey's offered hand as I slid from the car. "I hope I'm not overdressed."

"You look beautiful." He did a double take of my wrist when I threaded my arm around his elbow. "I'm glad you decided to keep it."

"I liked it too much to return it," I said, running the fingers of my other hand over the stones in the bracelet he'd given me.

"Claudia, it's so nice to see you again!" Bethany Michaels pulled me into a hug as soon as we entered the dining room.

"Thank you so much for inviting me, Bethany. Your home is breathtaking," I said, looking around the tastefully decorated space.

In a whirl, I was practically passed around the room from one Michaels family member to another, starting with his father Carter and then his younger brother Chad.

"It's good to see you again, Claudia." Chad took my hand, but a glance at Grey made him drop it without a Michaels signature kiss to the back of a lady's hand.

It'd been a really long time since I'd been part of a family dinner. The last was probably for Jessica's birthday a few years before.

I could feel Grey's eyes on me as Gregory approached, his hand on the small of Elsa's back as they walked toward us.

"Claudia, this is my wife, Elsa," Gregory said with nothing short of pride and love in his tone and his eyes.

Elsa didn't skip a beat.

"It's lovely to meet you, Claudia. I've heard such wonderful things," she said with a genuine smile.

"Likewise." I shook her hand. I couldn't detect any hint of confusion in her eyes, if anything she seemed amused by my presence. I wondered if she knew Bethany had invited me.

"Grey, why don't you give our guest a tour of the house," Bethany suggested. "We still have some time before dinner will be served."

"Shall we?" Grey offered his arm. I took it, glancing at Elsa who was smiling at me with a knowing expression. I had no fucking clue what was happening.

"You look gorgeous," Grey said, stopping before we walked out of one of the five guest bedrooms in the home.

"You mentioned that already," I replied, nudging him.

He flashed me a big smile. God he was sexy, especially when he smiled. He ran his thumb over the tennis bracelet adorning my wrist. "I love seeing this on you," he whispered, stepping closer.

I'd had all day to think, and I still wasn't much clearer on what I was doing.

Fuck it.

Those were the words running through my head when I gripped the back of his head and pressed my lips to his. He smiled against my mouth, and I seized the opportunity to trace the inner seam of his lips with my tongue before I pulled back.

"What are you doing to me?" he whispered against the side of my face. He gripped my waist with ardent possession.

"I could ask you the same question." I slid my hands over the front of his shirt.

He pushed his fingertips through my hair and captured my mouth again with his delicious lips. I moaned and he snaked his arm around me, pulling me closer as his tongue swirled around mine.

"We should get back before someone comes looking for us," he said, pulling back with a smile, his eyes dark with unquenched desire.

The walk back into the dining room felt a bit like a walk of shame when all heads turned our way. I was certain everyone knew something happened between Grey and me. If they did, no one said a word. I'd seriously gone off the deep end. It was as though no matter what was at stake, no matter the consequences, I couldn't control myself when it came to Grey. From the first time we met, it was as if we'd gotten trapped in each other's orbit with no prayer of escape. No matter how I tried to push him away, he couldn't stay away for long.

Since the dawn of mankind, humans had been fighting against the forces of nature but one way or another, nature always won. Perhaps it was time I accepted that. Even though the thought scared me, I found myself smiling.

Everyone was already seated at the table, conversing and laughing when we took our seats. I chanced a glance at Elsa. She was talking to Gregory but watched me with a curious expression. The kitchen doors swung open as three workers carried in family-style bowls and platters of salads and appetizers. The aromas filling the spacious room were positively heavenly, so much so my appetite flared despite my anxiety.

I was just about to take a bite of a strawberry salad when the doorbell chimed. A few moments later Ashley Slade appeared in the doorway.

"Sorry I'm late," she said, surveying the room. Her gaze stopped on Grey and her eyes glinted, like a predator first sighting their next meal. Her expression changed significantly when she saw me sitting next to him.

"Ashley dear." Bethany got up and walked over to her. "I thought you couldn't make it to dinner this week."

She looked at Grey and then me apologetically. Why would she feel the need to apologize to me?

"My plans fell through and I was in the neighborhood, so I thought I'd stop by."

I could feel the tension rolling off Grey as Ashley stared at him.

"Hi, everyone," she said to the room. "Hi, Grey."

I don't know what came over me, but I grabbed Grey's hand under the table and leaned closer to him. Gregory noticed and nudged Elsa. Grey relaxed and looked at me, smiling that easygoing, sexy smile of his.

Ashley's expression fell to disgust before she stormed over to the table to take an empty seat by Chad, which thankfully was on the opposite end of the table.

Grey held my hand off and on for most of the meal, only letting go when both hands were necessary for eating. Sometimes he stroked my thigh. Sometimes I stroked his. We couldn't seem to stop touching each other. I'd flipped a switch I wasn't sure I could un-flip, and I wasn't sure if I wanted to.

Despite Ashley's hostile presence, the evening was pretty great. The food was delicious, and Grey's family was beyond welcoming.

Grey excused himself to use the restroom just before dessert was served. Ashley stood, presumably to follow, but Elsa intervened, asking her something about a class she was taking.

Bethany came over to me right after Grey disappeared down the hall.

Leaning down next to me, she said quietly, "It's been a long time since I've seen him this happy."

I didn't know how to respond, so I just smiled. She squeezed my shoulder before walking back to her seat. She sat down and whispered something to Carter who glanced at me and winked.

"I missed you," Grey whispered next to my ear before he took his seat.

"You were gone two minutes," I replied with a grin.

"So, I still missed you," he said, touching my knee.

Ashley seemed to have had enough at that point and dropped her napkin on the dessert she hadn't touched.

"I'm actually not feeling well. I think I'm going to head home," she said, looking around. Her gaze landed on Grey, who didn't even acknowledge her.

"I hope you feel better," Bethany said, standing again. "Let me walk you out."

Bethany returned a moment later and smiled at me again.

I devoured my slice of chocolate mousse pie and may have had a second piece, before I squeezed Grey's hand and leaned over to him.

"I should get going."

"Come home with me?" he whispered.

"I shouldn't. I just need a little more time to figure all this out." I stood to leave before he could protest.

"Thank you for inviting me to dinner. I had a lovely time and the food was excellent, but I need to get home."

All of the men stood. I looked up at Grey, he was about to speak, but Gregory beat him to it.

"Let me walk you out." He came around to escort me to the car. To say I was surprised was an understatement. Elsa, whom I'd found impossible to read all night, gave me a little wave and a smile. I looked to Grey as I took Gregory's arm. Instead of the irritation I expected, his expression was calm, pleased even.

"I wanted to thank you, Claudia, for what you did for Grey," Gregory said as we stepped outside. "The whole situation with Ashley, it's hard on him, hard on all of us because of our family connections. I think it's why he stayed away so long. She really hurt him and it took a long time all of us to forgive her, but we did because that's what we do. She has always been like family, and we don't turn our backs on each other in this family."

Unconditional love, it was a novel concept for me.

"There's no need to thank me."

"He really likes you. I could see that the first time we met," he said with a smile.

Not knowing what else to say I smiled back.

"I think Ashley wants him back. My mother certainly thinks she does, but none of us want to see that happen, not even Ashley's parents."

My confusion tugged at the corners of my mouth. They didn't know about Ashley's affair so why didn't they want her with Grey.

"We all love her, but Ashley is a complicated woman. She's selfish and impulsive. Even before she left my brother, there were problems we could all see, but he wouldn't listen to reason. I think someone new might be just what he needs to keep history from repeating itself," he said, smiling down at me as he helped me into the car. "Have a good night."

"You, too, thank you, Gregory."

He closed the door and I sunk back against the seat.

I hadn't liked Ashley from the first moment we met, before I knew who she was to Grey, but hearing Gregory suggest I'm what he needs made me realize I'd been exactly what they all thought she was and more. I was selfish, impulsive, untrustworthy, and more convinced than ever Gregory was innocent. If they ever found out the truth, they would all hate me. Elsa was family. They could forgive her for her part in my deception, and who would blame her anyway after those pictures she received? But me, I wasn't family. I was there for money; there would be no forgiveness for me.

"How'd it go tonight?" Grace asked before I'd even closed the front door. I'd just stopped to pick up some clothes before I headed to the other apartment. Grace was going to be having company, and I wanted to stay out of her way.

"It was really nice," I replied honestly as she followed me back to my room.

"How did Elsa seem?"

"She seemed, happy," I said, thinking back to her demeanor during dinner.

Grace frowned.

"You should have seen them together. You know me; I wouldn't exaggerate. Gregory adores her. I think he might actually be the exception to the rule."

"Well, shit. Are you sure they didn't brainwash you at this dinner?"

"Ha, no, but I'm certain we need to focus our energy on the business angle of this case, find an explanation for those pictures and why Gregory hasn't told Elsa about any of it."

"It's your call. If you can't turn his head, then I can't imagine anyone ever will." She smiled.

"Speaking of turning heads, you look nice," I said. "When's Jared coming over for *dinner*?" I waggled my eyebrows as I stuffed a few things into my bag.

"He had to work late, but he should be here soon."

"What did you say he does for a living?" I asked, although I knew she hadn't mentioned it before.

"Oh, um, he works security. That's what he was doing at the gala when I met him."

Something was definitely up, but I was exhausted and decided to let it go. "I'll get out of your hair, then." I walked back toward the kitchen. A loose floorboard I'd been meaning to get fixed for months squeaked under my feet as I passed by.

"Are you sure you don't want to wait and at least say hi?" She picked up the corkscrew and a bottle of wine.

"Maybe next time; I'm so tired. I've been up since a little before five. Have fun."

Standing in the elevator, I was relieved I wouldn't have to talk any more about my night or the job or anything. I could just sink into a nice hot bath, drink a glass of wine, or maybe the whole bottle, and go to bed. I needed a good night's sleep and hoped maybe things would suddenly be clear in the morning.

Twenty minutes later, I was in my other apartment and slipping down into the tub until the water covered everything but my head. I reached a soapy arm out to grab my glass of Cabernet as the sultry sounds of my favorite old Fiona Apple album filled the air. It'd been the soundtrack to my teenage years and seemed appropriate because I hadn't been so confused and unsure of myself since I was that age.

Thinking I'd heard something, I turned down the music with the remote. I'd been soaking for so long my fingers were soft and pruney, so I decided to get out and head to bed. Just as I'd slipped on my robe, I heard a faint knocking sound. The hairs on my arms stood as a variety of scary scenarios involving poltergeists and killer dolls briefly flashed through my mind. I tended to be a little jumpy when I was alone at night. Laughing at myself, I tied the waist of my robe and tiptoed down the hallway to investigate the noise. As I got closer to the kitchen I heard a light knock on the door. I moved closer and peered through the peephole.

"You don't have to let me in, but I couldn't stop thinking about you," Grey's deep voice said through the door.

I smiled, realizing I'd been hoping he would come over since the moment I'd walked out of his parents' house. I wasn't entirely sure I deserved him, but I wanted to find out if someday I could. I looked down at the water that dripped down my legs and puddled by my feet. What was there to fight anymore? The job had changed. I could honestly say I believed Gregory was faithful to Elsa, and between Bridget, Lydia and the investigators Patty hired, it wouldn't be long before we knew exactly what was going on with Kristen Page. I'd have to find a way to explain everything to Grey eventually. I still had no idea what I would say or how he would react, but I was slowly finding my way and I felt a kind of hope for the future I'd never imagined.

Opening the door, I didn't say a word before I backed up a little and tugged the belt of my robe. The tie came undone easily and the satiny fabric parted a few inches in the front. Grey hissed and stepped toward me before crashing his lips down on mine. I pushed my hands into his thick hair as he backed me into the room and kicked the door closed behind him. I tugged at his shirt, pulling the bottom free from his khakis as we kissed wildly. He followed my lead, breaking our kiss for just long enough to pull it over his head and toss it somewhere while I moved to the buckle of his belt.

I pulled him down the hallway as I slipped the belt free and let it fall to the hardwood floor. He pulled my robe off my shoulders and let it drift to the ground. Goose bumps covered my bare skin. Backing away from him while he kicked off his shoes and pants, I sat on the bed, legs spread wide. I traced my hands slowly from my knees and up my inner thighs while he stood in the doorway, his large cock hung heavy to one side. I moaned as I let my fingers drift ever so lightly over my swollen clit and then down between my wet soft folds.

Keeping my eyes on Grey, I put my fingers in my mouth slowly and sucked off the moisture. He growled low in his throat but remained where he was, watching me with eyes darkened by desire. I moved my hand back down between my legs, circling my clit slowly.

"Stroke your cock," I commanded in a breathy voice.

His eyes grew heavy with lust as he did what I'd asked. I moaned seeing him grip the thickness in his strong hand. He moved his hand slowly over the silky hard skin with his gaze pinned on my hand and its motions.

I stopped touching myself and slid back on the bed as I crooked my finger at him, calling him to me. He didn't need to be asked twice. My body tingled with anticipation as he stalked toward me before crawling onto the bed and over my body. He grabbed my hands and pinned my wrists on the pillow above my head.

"You like to tease me, Claudia," he groaned against my ear and then dipped his tongue inside and up the outer rim. "Do you want me to tease you?"

"No, Grey, I want you to fuck me."

"I'm not going to fuck you," he replied, moving to look into my eyes.

I squinted at him, confused and on fire with the need to feel him inside me. I squirmed beneath him, my body trying to persuade his to give me what I wanted despite what he said.

"I'm going to make love to you, Claudia," he whispered and gently kissed my lips.

Those were words I'd never heard, and I didn't know what to do with them. I honestly didn't know what to do with Grey or any of the feelings he incited in me. I felt the sting of tears in my eyes and panicked, trying to turn away from him before he could see.

He released my wrists and turned my face toward him. "Don't do that. Don't hide from me, Claudia. I want all of you-- your joy, your ecstasy, your sadness, your anger, your fear." He pressed his lips to mine and whispered, "Your love."

I couldn't speak; I was too overwhelmed. Instead I lifted up and pressed my lips to his, trying to pour all the words I couldn't say, the words I was too afraid to say, into that one simple action.

Grey stroked my face as he lay on top of me, returning the kiss.

"I need to feel you--" I finally whispered when the urge to cry passed "--inside me."

He nudged my legs further apart and gently rubbed my clit with his fingertips for several seconds before sitting up to scoot off the bed. He grabbed a condom from the pocket of his pants, then climbed back onto the bed and slipped it on.

He covered my body with his, his erection pressing against my sensitive flesh. I reached between us, guiding his width to where I needed it. He pushed inside me slowly, achingly so, staring into my eyes the whole time.

I held his gaze, getting lost in the emotions I saw reflecting back at me. I liked the way I looked in his eyes. He made me want more, made me want to be more, to be better, for him and the possibilities I saw in the way he saw me. I held on to that, gripping it and him tight as we moved together, both coming apart slowly but completely in each other's arms.

Chapter 16

Waking up in Grey's arms, I didn't panic or feel the need to rush him out.

Something changed and I knew what I had to do.

"Where are you going?" Grey pulled me back against him as I tried to slither out of bed unnoticed.

"Sorry I woke you. I just need to make a phone call. Are you hungry?"

His hand slid over my belly and landed between my legs.

"For this," he murmured against the side of my neck before he feathered the sensitive skin with kisses up to my ear.

I squirmed against him and his growing erection pressed against my ass. Any other phone call could have waited, but the one I was about to make needed to happen before I did anything else. And before I had a chance to lose my nerve or change my mind.

"Hold that thought. I'll be quick, I promise," I said finally, wiggling free.

He groaned in disappointment as I ducked into the bathroom and slipped into another robe.

I didn't have Elsa's number in my phone, but it was in the file I'd brought from my office at Homewrecker Incorporated. I tiptoed down the hallway, picking up Grey's shirt and my other robe along the way.

I grabbed the file from my messenger bag and my phone from the table and carefully opened the front door. I pulled it closed gently behind me so Grey wouldn't hear I'd left the apartment. I opened Elsa's file and dialed her number. My mouth was dry, my palms sweaty. I hadn't really thought through what I was going to say. I seriously considered hanging up, but she picked up on the first ring, surprising considering how early it was.

"Hello?" she answered, sounding half asleep. Shit, I didn't think. She was probably in bed lying next to her husband. My options for talking were suddenly very limited.

"Elsa, it's Claudia. I'm so sorry to call you so early and out of the blue like this," I blurted.

"Hi, no, it's okay. I was expecting to hear from you," she replied, her tone unreadable. Shit, what did that mean?

"I don't really want to do this over the phone, could you meet me later to talk?"

"Yes, of course. How about we have lunch? We could meet somewhere close to the office around noon. There's a little French bistro just around the corner."

"I know the place. I'll see you at noon. Thank you, Elsa." I hung up the phone. I took a deep breath, which felt like the first I'd taken in weeks, before I slipped back into the apartment and put her file back in my bag.

"Everything okay?" Grey asked, scaring the shit out of me when I walked past the kitchen. "Sorry," he said, seeing me jump. "Just thought I would make us some coffee while I waited."

"Yeah, sorry, everything's great. Just had to take care of something."

He seemed satisfied with my response.

"I just realized I never asked how you take your coffee. I gave it to you black the last time." He looked a little upset by the revelation.

"That's how I like it," I said with a smile. "How about you?"

He carried a mug over to me where I was leaning against the island. He moved around behind me and kissed the side of my neck as he set it on the countertop in front of me and took a seat.

"Same," he whispered, his warm breath tickling my ear. "How long have you lived here, the furniture's a little...sparse?"

I moved in closer so I was standing between his legs as I sipped my coffee.

"I just moved in about a month ago. I was living with my friend Grace before that, but it was time for me to have my own space."

My insides twisted at the lie, but I needed to talk to Elsa and my partners before I could tell him the truth. I fought the panic brewing inside me as I considered how he might respond.

"Listen, I'm sorry to do this, but I have to work today. I assume you do too." I hoped he got the hint even though I really didn't want to let him out of my sight.

"I think you should take the day off and spend it in bed with me. I am technically your boss." He flashed a cocky grin.

"As my boss, do you really want me to be the kind of employee who blows off work to stay in bed with my boyfriend?" That just slipped out. My stomach flipped.

His grinned broadened into a megawatt smile. "Yes, that's exactly the kind of employee I want you to be." He rubbed the tip of his nose over mine.

I poked my index finger into the front of his chest. "You're awful." I laughed. "But really, I have a lot to do today. I promise I'll make it up to you later," I said, waggling my eyebrows.

"Fine, I'll get out of your hair as soon as I finish this coffee, but I'm going to hold you to that promise."

"What's the big emergency? Why are we meeting so early?"

Lydia groaned, flopping into the chair next to Bridget. I looked around the room at all my partners--my friends--who were regarding me with curiosity and maybe a touch of annoyance for getting them out of bed so early.

"I'm not sure where to start." I stood and paced in front of the table.

Confusion was the general expression of the room with the exception of Bridget, who was looking down at the table, smiling.

"After this we need to call Patty. Then I'm meeting with Elsa Michaels for lunch, and I'm going to tell them everything I'm about to tell you."

"Claudia, what the hell are you talking about? " Grace leaned forward.

"I should start from the beginning. The first day, when I went to meet with Gregory's assistant, Janet, I saw Gregory staring at me down in front of the building. I don't know how to describe it, but I've never felt chemistry like that before. I panicked. I wasn't ready to meet him like that. I felt too out of control, so I hid in the bathroom until the coast was clear. When I finally went upstairs to meet Janet, he showed up and the pull I felt toward him was even stronger once I met him up close."

Grace and Bridget exchanged a look before I sat down and continued.

"He didn't try to hide his attraction to me when he took me into his office and once the door was closed, I did what I do best. I flirted, I seduced, but he gave as good as he got. I can't stress enough how it was unlike anything I've ever felt before."

I stood and started pacing again.

"Then Gregory Michaels walked in."

I was facing away from the group. When I turned around, Grace was trying to hide her smile behind her hand. I furrowed my eyebrows, wondering what the hell she thought was funny.

"The man I was with, the one I felt things I'd never imagined with wasn't Gregory Michaels; it was his twin, Grey. By the time I realized the truth, I'd already agreed to go to dinner with the wrong man."

All of them looked around at each other but said nothing, so I went on detailing my secret relationship with Grey--the time at his house, dinner with his parents, the night before, all of it.

Finally, when I'd spilled it all, Grace spoke. "So, let me get this straight. You're going to call Patty and tell her you're meeting with Elsa Michaels to officially breech our contract and forego the bonus for a man you've known a few weeks?"

It sounded pathetic when said altogether like that, but it was exactly what I intended to do. I nodded and shrugged. What else could I say?

"You know what this means?" Grace continued, looking around at the other girls.

"Claudia Mason is fucking in love!" Lydia answered, crude as ever, earning a round of laughter from the room.

Shit. I didn't actually say the L word, did I? Did I even think it? But what else could it be? I was willing to blow up my entire life just for a chance with a man who might not want me back in the end. If that wasn't love, I wasn't sure what was.

Grace got up and rushed over to throw her arms around me.

"So, you're not mad?" I asked, not sure how to respond. I kept waiting for one of them to get pissed, like they were all entitled to be. "You were all, *we* were all counting on that money."

"Girl, I would gladly *pay* money to see you happy for a change." Grace nudged my arm. "We've made more in the last few years than I'd ever expected. I know my foundation is going to happen. What's a few more years compared to my best friend's happiness?

"I never imagined having as much money as I do now," Bridget said quietly. "And I've never had any big plans. I just love working with all of you."

"Yeah, I'm with them. It's just money. Don't get me wrong, it would have been nice but like Grace said, it's nothing compared to you being happy for a change."

"Again with that! What do you mean for a change?" I asked, trying to sound offended, but as I scanned back over my life for the past fifteen years, I couldn't point to a time when I could honestly say I was content. I'd tried to act as though I was, put on a brave face, so to speak. Clearly my efforts weren't as successful as I thought.

"Look, you're strong, you work really hard not to let your feelings show, but whether you realized it or not, we could see you wanted more."

"Even I could fucking see it, and you know I'm not big on all that touchy-feely shit," Lydia added.

"This isn't quite as much of a surprise as you think." Grace glanced sideways at Bridget, who immediately turned red. I pinned her with a hard stare, but I couldn't be mad at her for sharing what she knew about me and Grey with the other girls. We were partners, and it was wrong of me to ask that of her.

"I'm sorry for putting you in that position, Bridget." I put my hand on her shoulder. "I shouldn't have asked you to lie for me, especially not to family."

"Do you know what you're going to say to Elsa?" Grace asked.

"Well, considering she was at dinner last night, she's probably got a pretty good handle on the situation. I'm just going to be honest about what I've done, my feelings for Grey, and my perception of her husband. I know he's not a cheater. Seriously, you should see the way he looks at her, especially when she's not looking. He adores her and not to overstate my charms, but I think I could have stood completely naked in front of him without getting more than an offer of his jacket to cover myself."

"I've seen the look you're talking about," Bridget added. "Grey looks at you that way."

My heart fluttered in my chest at the mention of his name. Did he really look at me that way? Would he still when he knew the truth?

"I feel so guilty about all of the lies I've told him, and I'm terrified of what he will think of me when I tell him the truth. What if it changes things for him? What if he can't love me when he knows?" I said, confessing the fear I realized had been dancing in the back of my mind since the day Grey and I first met.

"If he really loves you, nothing you share with him about your past will change that. What matters now is the future. At least that's what Jared said when I told him," Grace confessed, biting her lip as she looked at all of us.

"Jesus, Grace! Why didn't you say anything before?" I said, pushing her leg.

"It's a long story and I'll fill you in later. Right now, we need to talk to Patty and then you need to meet Elsa and go get your man!"

The call with Patty wasn't as bad as I anticipated. She'd almost seemed amused when Grace started the call by blurting out I was in love with my mark's twin. According to her and Grace, we weren't necessarily in breach of contract with Elsa because I assured them I was confident in my assessment of Gregory. I just had to persuade her to give us little more time to dig into Kristen Page.

"I'm so glad you called, Claudia," Elsa said, standing to hug me. I returned it easily.

I took my seat across from her at the table out on the patio of the quaint little bistro.

"I took the liberty of ordering drinks for both of us," she said as the waitress set down two glasses of white wine.

"Thank you." I picked up my glass. "I'm not sure where to start," I said with a sense of déjà vu.

I took a long sip of wine, a very nice Pinot.

"Actually, I want to ask you something before you say anything else," Elsa said, stopping me. "Do you love him?"

I nearly spit out my wine.

"Grey, are you in love with him?" she asked again.

I probably looked as if I was having a seizure with the way my eyes fluttered from the surprise of her question. I'd assumed she expected there was some sort of relationship between Grey and me, but for her to jump to that conclusion after only seeing us together once... I was shocked to say the least.

I took a breath, gathering myself before I responded. "Yes."

It was as simple as that in the end. No dressing it up with excuses or explanations. That one answer was at the heart of it all. I loved Greyston Michaels.

She regarded me closely and then smiled wide.

"Thank God!" she said, taking a drink. And I'd thought I was shocked by her question. Her reaction was even more surprising and doubly perplexing.

"So, you're not mad?" I asked as the noise of the city moved around us as if my entire world wasn't shifting on its axis.

"Not at all," she continued. "I'm not sure if you're aware, but Grey and I have always been rather close. Gregory and I were best friends, and Grey had always been his best friend before me, so our connection was a natural result. I've known him as long as I've known Gregory, and he leaned on me when Ashley broke his heart all those years ago. He didn't want to tell his family about all of the messy details because of her connection to them. Grey's good like that."

God, even after everything Ashley had done to him, he tried to protect her.

"After dinner last night he pulled me aside, and let's just say he's fallen for you--hard. I encouraged him to go after you."

"Why? Why would you do that?"

"Because for a long time I worried, we all worried, what happened with Ashley was it for Grey. In five years away, he hadn't so much as had dinner with someone romantically. He'd thrown himself into the work, which had never really been his style. Don't get me wrong. He's a hard and very capable worker, but family always comes first for him. Ashley hated that about him. Despite coming from a wonderful, loving family, she's most concerned with status and power, so she pushed Grey toward things he didn't want. I think when we all got over the initial shock of what Ashley did, we were relieved she'd left Grey. I'd always worried they weren't right for each other, and then you came along and I was certain they weren't."

"But I was supposed to be working for you, not falling in love with your brother-in-law," I said, feeling guilty.

"You may not realize it but in following your heart, you showed me mine again." She smiled as she looked down at her ring.

"Last night wasn't the first time a man mentioned you to me. Gregory told me about you the very first day you showed up in the office. All he could talk about was the way his brother was looking at you. That's why he asked you to the gala. We usually have to drag Grey to the event, but he changed his tune when he found out you were going," she said, laughing.

I nodded along, clinging to her every word as I finished my glass of wine.

"The day before your partner met with my attorney, Gregory came home so excited for his brother and so happy to see me after my time away in Guatemala. We spent the evening watching one of our favorite movies as we snuggled on the couch and then when he was away at conventions, he would call me and we'd stay up talking all hours of the night like we hadn't done since we were teenagers. I almost asked him about the photos a million different times, but I couldn't find the nerve. Then Patty told me about Arrow Components and I knew there was an explanation, but Patty persuaded me to hold off."

Elsa put her hand over mine. "I saw the way Grey looked at you last night and how a simple touch from you pulled him out of Ashley's dark cloud in a heartbeat. When I turned to my Gregory, he had that same look in his eye. All I could see in them was love, the same love that had been there since we were teenagers. It might have changed, grown deeper over time, but it hadn't faded. I don't know why I let someone else persuade me it had or why I let someone else turn me away from my heart."

"You asked him about the photos, then?"

"Yes," she said, smiling. "The woman, Kristen Page, showed up one day pretending to be seeking a job with the company. Her résumé was impressive, so he met with her to discuss potential opportunities. He quickly realized she had an ulterior motive after human resources did a background check. He confronted her at their next meeting, which she'd requested be in her hotel restaurant, and she admitted to working for Arrow Components. She claimed she was only sent there to feel him out about a potential acquisition. She even had an offer and letter of intent prepared. He turned her down flat."

"So then she sent the photos to you?"

"No. Right after he left the meeting, Gregory received an anonymous e-mail with the photos arranged under a tabloid headline accompanied by a threat to release the photos if he didn't reconsider the offer."

"But why didn't he just tell you what happened?" I asked, trying to understand.

"A second e-mail followed with two more potential headlines. One about my family, more specifically about my father leaving for another woman, and the other about my inability to give Gregory a child, which it asserted was due to an abortion I'd allegedly had in college."

"Oh my God," I whispered, covering my mouth.

"There was a copy of some paperwork that documented my visit to a women's clinic which performed abortions, but I was actually there for a blood test to confirm my pregnancy. I miscarried a few days later."

"I'm so sorry, Elsa."

"They threatened to release all three of the stories if Gregory didn't comply. As you can imagine, the scandal would have a huge impact on the foundation given the beliefs of some of its largest donors."

I nodded.

So all of it was a ploy to force Gregory into selling the company. As strange as it was, I was grateful for their attempts. If it wasn't for them sending those photos to Elsa, I probably would have never met Grey.

"What I saw as Gregory becoming distant was him trying to protect me. He's been stalling Kristen and Arrow Components for the last few weeks while a team of investigators worked to dig up anything he could use to back them down, and they are finally making some headway." She leaned back in her chair, looking relieved.

"I'm embarrassed I ever doubted him but even worse, I let something Ashley told me years ago affect me and make me doubt my husband and one of my best friends."

"What do you mean?"

"After Grey left for Japan, Ashley came to the house, crying her eyes out. We'd known each other a long time, although we'd never been very close. She broke down, telling me leaving Grey was the hardest thing she'd ever done but he'd given her no choice. She claimed he was the one who cheated on her and that was why she didn't shown up at the church."

As if I didn't already have enough reason to dislike Ashley.

"Grey was gone and the relationship was over, so I kept that information to myself, just like I'd done when Grey told me she was the one who cheated. When these pictures showed up, I wondered if she was telling the truth and it was really Grey who was the cheater. If he could do it and then lie to me so convincingly, it wasn't a stretch to believe Gregory could as well."

Doubt was a tricky, nasty bitch.

"Elsa, what about the rest? About hiring us? Did you tell Gregory about that as well?" I held my breath, waiting for her response. If Gregory knew, he would likely be telling Grey at any moment.

"Yes and no." She took a drink. "I told him I'd hired an investigator but not the rest."

Elsa grabbed my hand on the table.

"I wanted to talk to you first, but I have to tell Gregory the truth--all of it. Just like you need to tell Grey."

"I know," I replied with a sad smile. "I'm just terrified he's going to hate me when he finds out what I really do for a living."

"He's not going to like it, but he'll figure out a way to deal with it. I know Grey. He loves you; that will be enough for him."

Her words reassured me, and I suddenly couldn't wait a moment longer.

"Thank you, Elsa, for everything," I said, standing as I pulled out my wallet.

"Please, lunch is on me. You have places to be." She placed her credit card on the table.

I weaved through the tables out onto the sidewalk, waving at cabs like a madwoman until one finally stopped. I dialed the number for Grey's temporary assistant and sat back, trying to steady my heart as I prepared to reach out and grab a future I never believed I could have.

Chapter 17

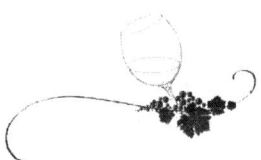

I found myself wishing I stopped at home to change before coming to Grey's house. I'd called G&G and checked with his assistant on his schedule. He'd called in, saying he was taking the day off, so I assumed he was home. I considered texting him to be sure, but I wanted to surprise him. If he wasn't there, I'd figure something else out.

I paid the driver before I jumped out and approached the door. I couldn't seem to wipe the stupid smile off my face. It was hard to believe this was my life. I'd spent so many years fighting my true feelings and the desires buried so deep in my heart I'd almost forgotten them entirely.

All those years I spent saying I would never let a man control me--that'd been exactly what I'd been doing. I let what my father did to me and my mother keep me from living. I let him take my ability to trust--to love.

Not anymore.

Knocking on the door, I took a deep breath, ready to give into love and live life surrounded by it.

It's hard to explain the way I felt when the door finally opened. The pain was so acute I think I went numb.

"Can I help you?" Ashley Slade stood in the doorway, wearing what I could only guess was one of Grey's shirts.

Much like the one I'd worn the morning I spent there.

"Oh, wait, aren't you the girl from dinner the other night? Claire, right?" I wanted to slap the stupid smirk off her face, but I couldn't seem to make my body move.

It was as though I was floating above myself watching some horrible nightmare unfold.

Somehow, words found their way to my lips.

"I'm looking for Grey." I tried to stand straighter, although all I really wanted to do was run and hide.

"Sorry, he just stepped out to get something for lunch. He loves spoiling me," she said smugly. "You're Gregory's assistant, right? Did you need to leave a message or something?" She blatantly played with the buttons of Grey's dress shirt.

Fucking bitch. She'd rattled me, but I wasn't going to give her the satisfaction of seeing me broken.

"I was just stopping by to show him a piece of art the decorator at G&G thought he would be rather excited about. He expressed quite an interest in this particular piece, and since he wasn't in the office, I thought I'd bring it by," I lied through my teeth.

Some of her smugness melted away. I could see the wheels turning behind her eyes. She'd been hoping for a stronger reaction.

Too fucking bad.

"Oh, well you could just leave it with me." She opened the door further and looked around behind me. Shit, might have helped if I hadn't sent my taxi away.

"I'm afraid that won't be possible. I left it in the car parked around front, and it's far too valuable for me to just leave with some, um, friend of Mr. Michaels," I said, looking her up and down. "I'll just see him back at the office."

I turned and walked off around to the front of the house, praying she didn't come after me.

What was I thinking? I knew better. I knew exactly how the story would end. Why did I think Grey was any different from any other man I'd ever met? They were all the same.

Selfish, disloyal, liars.

If my father taught me anything, it was men could only be counted on to do one thing: disappoint.

I was grateful Grey's driveway turned into the trees a short way from the front of the house, hiding me from Ashley's view as I sunk down to the ground and sobbed.

After all those years of being shut off, protecting my heart, I finally let someone in and this was what I got. Tears and grass stains. I could only imagine how pathetic I must have looked huddled down in the grass, crying like a child. I had to get out of there. I couldn't bear the thought of Grey coming home and seeing me like that. Seeing how he'd hurt me. Or worse, of Ashley coming out and getting the satisfaction of knowing she'd broken me.

Fuck them, I thought, standing and dusting myself off. I pulled my phone out and called for a car as I started walking.

"Are you all right, miss?" the driver asked when I slid into the backseat.

I must have looked as bad as I felt. Being hidden in the safety of the vehicle made me feel a little better. There wasn't much traffic out that way, but even the distant sound of cars made me cringe with the worry Grey would pass me before I could get away.

"I'm great," I replied, which was an obvious lie, but he didn't really want to know.

He asked the question to be polite, not because he cared. No one ever really cared.

"Just head back into the city, please," I said, not entirely sure where I was going to go or what I was going to do.

I couldn't face anyone, especially not my friends who would all be waiting to hear how my meeting with Elsa went. I just needed to be alone, to clear my head, and try to forget it all, even if just for a little while.

Times like that, I would normally go for a run, but that would mean going home and I couldn't risk running into Grace or one of the girls. I pulled out my phone and searched what movies were playing at my favorite theater. There were three I'd been wanting to see, but the romantic comedy and the drama were out. Instead I opted for the action-adventure movie with lots of explosions and special effects to distract me from the ache in my heart. I gave the destination to the driver and shut off my phone.

I completely lost myself in the movie as I intended. It was only to mask the pain simmering just below the surface, threatening to explode out of me at any moment. I ended up staying for a second movie, a thriller that made me jump more than once and had me a little on edge by the time I walked out into the fading light of the early evening. Feeling a little on edge was far better than how I'd been feeling, although I knew it wouldn't be long before the distracting effects of the cinema wore off and I would be right back where I started.

The theater was only a few blocks from home, so I decided to walk back and buy myself at least a few more minutes before I had to talk to anyone. I managed to get up to my front door unnoticed, even by John who was busy helping another resident with some packages from what looked like one hell of a shopping spree when I walked past. I turned on my phone as I rifled around the bottom of my purse for my keys. The device chimed multiple times showing twelve missed calls and a variety of messages and voice mails.

I played the first voice mail, it was from Grey. The sound of his voice saying my name was like a knife to the heart, so I deleted it without hearing another word. I pressed play for the next message as I stepped into the apartment and closed the door.

"Claudia, where are you?" Bridget's voice played, her tone panicked. Please call me, Eric--"

Chapter 18

I'd always fancied myself somewhat of a movie buff. The theater had always provided as reliable a means of escape as running or a nice shopping spree. I liked all kinds of stories, but action films have always been one of my favorite types. I'd even venture to say I loved them almost as much as I loved designer shoes. Especially those involving espionage and some plot to destroy the world. I mean, really, what woman can resist a gorgeous hero who puts it all on the line to save his country and some pathetic damsel in distress?

Every time I watched a scene with the helpless woman in danger waiting for the man to come along and save her, I rolled my eyes and laughed at her weakness, knowing if it was me I'd be kicking some ass and pulling my own weight.

Sitting strapped to a chair in my own living room with a gun pressed to my temple gave me a whole new perspective. Other than the involuntary trembling, I was frozen with fear. I could barely think, let alone act in any form of self-defense.

Eric Bennett was beyond reason as he rambled about something while standing next to me in my apartment. It seemed, based on what I could decipher from his ranting, due to some severe gambling issues, which extended to the way he handled his investment portfolio, and the settlement he paid to Mrs. Bennett in their divorce, he was wiped out.

He pulled the gun away and paced the room, still talking, although he didn't notice I'd regained consciousness. I kept my eyes closed and tried not to move as I carefully looked around for any means of escape. My wrists were bound to the arms of the chair so tightly my fingers tingled.

Despite my best efforts a tear streaked down my face. Eric grabbed my chin roughly, tilting my face up to him. My eyes flung wide in fear.

"So you're finally awake, then," he said, pushing my face away.

He ran the cold barrel of the gun over my collarbone and down between my breasts before dipping it inside the fabric of my shirt.

"You know, I thought I was falling in love with you, *Cynthia*. You took your punishment so well when we were together. It's making me hard just thinking about it."

He grabbed my face again, forcing it up as he crushed his lips against mine. Bile rose in my throat, but I didn't fight it when his tongue forced its way into my mouth. He withdrew it quickly and bit down hard on my lip. The tinge of copper covered my tongue as I tried to contain my whimper.

"But you had to fucking ruin it! Imagine my surprise when I came here looking for that other bitch and I found you instead, *Claudia*. I should have known when you never called me back.

Working for that dumb bitch I was stupid enough to marry," he seethed. "My father warned me, told me the fucking infidelity clause was a mistake. Maybe you two were in on it with her from day one. Trick me into signing that bullshit contract and then lure me into cheating so you could run off with all of my money?"

My head snapped to the side when his palm connected with my cheek, a blow I didn't see coming through the tears.

"I never would have cheated if it wasn't for you," he spat, pacing the floor again.

He was full of shit, but I wasn't really in the position to be splitting hairs about the accuracy of a sociopath's perception of the facts. Our surveillance indicated he'd enjoyed the company of more than one escort in the short time we were following him, but we couldn't get the proof Alaina needed from them without risking Eric finding out.

"You're worse than that stupid cunt!"

He flopped down onto the couch, setting the gun down on the cushion beside him.

"I took care of her; now it's your turn," he sneered, pulling a blade from a bag sitting on the table in front of him. I struggled against my bonds, my heart pounding. "And when I'm done with you, I'm going to wait for that other slut who helped you, Grace. She's got a nice voice. I was waiting here for her to come home, but this is even better. I can't wait to hear you beg, just like I'm going to make her beg."

He smirked at me before I squeezed my eyes shut and waited for the inevitable horror to start.

"Let's move this party somewhere where we can get a little more comfortable, shall we?" Eric whispered, pressing his face against my throbbing cheek before he grabbed the back of the chair and dragged me across the hardwood floor down the hallway toward the bedrooms.

He pushed open the door and shoved me through, the chair and me falling over. I groaned when my knee and shoulder smacked against the hard floor. There was a sharp pinch in my neck.

"A little something to make you a bit easier to deal with," Eric said before setting the chair up and using his blade to cut the ropes from around my waist.

Each piece gave way with a slight snap as the knife sliced through them, the sounds bringing me closer to whatever awful ideas Eric Bennett had bouncing around in his sick head. My vision swam as he moved on to the ropes at my feet.

When my first leg was free, I willed it to kick him in the face, but I barely managed to move it a few inches as he moved on to the other leg and then my arms. Without the support of the ropes, and thanks to whatever he'd injected in my neck, I slumped forward into his arms. The only protest I could muster was a low groan as he carried me to my bed.

I stared up at the ceiling, barely able to turn my head. I could hear Eric's footsteps as he left the room, and I prayed his drugs would pull me under further, allowing me the ignorance of unconsciousness for whatever came next. There was no such reprieve. His steps pierced the silence again, this time growing louder. The black bag from the living room thudded down beside my head.

"I thought you might like to see all of the lovely toys I brought for you." He sounded eerily cheerful.

I closed my eyes, not wanting to give him the satisfaction of seeing the fear in my eyes.

For the briefest of moments, I thought I heard footsteps, but Eric was on the bed with me. I was racked with panic; my first thought was Grace had come home. I tried to cry out, but only managed a strangled moan.

Eric propped my head up with pillows.

"There now, so you can see better," he said, pulling some whiplike contraptions made of leather and metal from the bag.

Then I saw him. Grey peered around the side of the door and my heart soared. I didn't know how he'd found me, he'd only ever been to my other apartment, but I wasn't in a position to worry about that. My eyes darted around, looking for the gun and finding it lying on the end of the bed by my feet. Eric was focused on his bag, taking his time choosing the next implement to show me.

Grey crept into the room, spying the gun, and lunged for it, but that fucking squeaky floorboard gave him away a second too soon.

Eric sprung from the bed and crashed into Grey, sending them both thudding to the floor. I saw a hand reach up for the gun. Whose I couldn't tell from my position but somehow in the struggle, it went flying over the side of the bed and clanged down on the hardwood.

Grey cried out and rolled into view on the floor beside the bed. Our eyes met before I saw the blood on his hand as he reached for the gun. Eric stood at the end of the bed, the knife in his hand covered with blood--Grey's blood.

"Guess playtime will have to be cut short." Eric grabbed my leg and yanked me off the bed.

My ass smacked down on the floor, sending a rattle through my spine. I was still virtually paralyzed, my head falling back to the floor as Eric dragged me toward the door. Darkness crept into the corners of my vision, threatening to overtake me. Just before the light disappeared entirely, I heard it.

Chapter 19

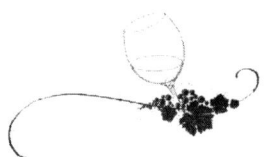

The beeping of my alarm pulled me from my nightmare. Except when I pried my eyes open, I wasn't in my room and the sound wasn't my alarm. I struggled to focus my vision as a figure appeared above me.

"Oh my God, Claudia!" Jessica yelled. "Nurse!"

"W-wa-water." My throat felt like sandpaper.

Jessica held a cup to my lips. Most of the water dripped down around my neck, but I was able to get a few sips of relief.

"Ms. Mason," the nurse said, appearing next to Jessica. "Do you know where you are?" She shone a light in one eye and then the other.

"Not specifically, but I'm going to make an educated guess and say this is a hospital," I replied sarcastically, my voice gravelly.

"Sarcasm is a good sign, Ms. Mason." The stout woman smiled. "You've suffered a pretty severe head injury, and you've had a lot of people worried sick, especially those friends of yours. They've been quite impatient."

I lifted my head, scanning the room while the nurse checked my vitals. "Where are they?" I asked, looking to Jessica.

"I'm afraid only immediate family is allowed back here. I'm going to fetch the doctor and have him give you a once-over. Now you're stable and awake, we can get you moved out of the ICU and your friends can visit you." The nurse patted my hand before she walked out.

Jessica took my hand, lifting it to her face, and pressed it against her cheek. "I was so scared," she whispered, a tear slipping down her cheek and over my hand. "I don't understand any of this. Why would that man attack you? If it wasn't for your friend, who knows what could have happened."

"I-I don't know," I lied, not knowing how to explain any of it to my sister who'd always been in the dark about the true nature of my business.

The image of Eric standing, his knife covered in blood flashed in my mind.

Grey.

I fought back the sobs that threatened to burst free.

"How long have I been here? Where is Izzy?" I asked, afraid to ask the one question that had been pressing on my mind since I opened my eyes.

"You've been here a few hours. She's with Shawn in the waiting area. Kids under twelve aren't allowed back here, and thank goodness for that."

"Ms. Mason, I'm glad to see you're awake," the doctor said, walking in as he flipped through what I presumed was my chart.

"I'm going to go check on Izzy and Shawn and let everyone know you're awake." Jessica squeezed my forearm before she walked out.

"The good news is your scans don't show any significant swelling or bleeding." The doctor continued, "But you did need a few stitches and you have a concussion, so we'd like to keep you overnight for observation, but I'm going to go ahead and move you downstairs to the general ward."

"What about my, um, what about Mr. Michaels?" I asked, my voice shaking despite my best efforts.

"I believe the young man you were brought in with is still in surgery, but I'll have the nurse check for you." He stopped scribbling on my chart to give me a sympathetic smile. "You were very lucky, Ms. Mason."

"I know," I whispered as he walked out.

"Have you heard anything about Grey?" I asked as soon as Grace walked into my new room. "They just keep telling me he's still in surgery!" I couldn't fight the tears any longer.

She rushed over and wrapped her arms around me.

"Nothing yet. His family is out in the waiting area, too. His parents, Elsa, Gregory, Chad..." she replied, holding me tight as I sobbed. "Just let it out, girl. No one else is coming back here until you're ready."

"This is all my fault." My words were muffled in Grace's chest. "He's going to die because of me."

"It's not your fault, Claud. Eric Bennett was a fucking psycho, and he was going to snap eventually no matter what we did or didn't do."

I looked up at her.

"Was?"

"He died on the way to the hospital. The detective John talked to said Grey managed to get a shot off before he passed out. John and Gina are waiting out there. He feels awful Eric slipped by him somehow."

"John is here?"

"Claudia, everyone's here. The girls, Bobby, Jason, even--"

"Even who?"

"Your dad."

"Fucking Jessica. She just won't give up," I said, wiping my eyes.

"Actually, I called him," Grace said softly.

My eyes widened. "Why the fuck would you call him?" I said, my voice getting louder with each word.

"Because I love you, Claud, and you need to let go of the past if you want any chance at a future," she said, her eyes full of love I didn't want to see in that moment.

"You just don't understand," I whispered.

"I do understand. I know what your father did, and I know what it's like to be abandoned by someone who's supposed to be there for you no matter what. I hated my mother for a long time, but one day I realized hating her was hurting me more than anyone else."

I didn't have any words. Of course she understood how I felt, but I'd always been so consumed with my own hatred and fear I didn't really recognize how similar her pain must have been. Maybe it was because I knew if she'd found a way to move past it, I needed to as well.

"I'm not saying you have to talk to him yet, but letting him be here is a step. Do it for your sister and your niece. He's an important part of their lives and they're a part of yours. He's sick and I don't know what's going to happen, but I do know it's time to move on--for all of you. Life is too short for anything else."

Grace wiped away a tear, and something that'd been gnawing at me just under the surface sprang forward.

"Oh God, Alaina. Is she...?"

"She's alive, but it's been touch and go since they found her. They're not sure how she survived everything Eric did to her, but she managed to hold on. It was a miracle really, after being in a coma for over a week, she woke up long enough to tell the officer guarding her hospital room Eric was coming to Chicago for us before she passed out again."

I squeezed my eyes tight. Poor Alaina. I'd known something was off about Eric; I should have done something.

"I know what you're thinking, Claud." Grace gripped my hand. "You couldn't have known and there wasn't anything you could have done legally. I spoke to Patty and it sounds as if Eric must have tortured information about the agency out of Alaina before he broke into the car of one of Patty's employees and stole a laptop. He must have gotten my name and phone numbers from the files."

"Jesus, Grace, he told me you had a nice voice," I said, careful not to mention the rest of what he said. Grace didn't need to share in the nightmares I was sure to have for a long while.

"We can talk about all that later. Right now, there's something else I need to tell you." She sucked in her bottom lip and squeezed my hand. "About Jared, about why I didn't bring him around much before. I was nervous about him finding about what we do but more than that, I was worried about you all finding out what he does."

"You told me he works security," I said, feeling lines form on my forehead.

"He does, but that's just a part-time gig. He's a cop. A detective, actually. I'm sorry I hid it from you, but I really liked him and I thought you'd be pissed I was risking exposing us for a man," she blurted in one breath.

"What right do I have to be pissed at you for following your heart? I was basically doing the same thing, probably worse." Thinking over the risks I'd taken for Grey, my heart tightened as I fought the urge to cry again.

"I'm glad you feel that way because it turns out we're really lucky he's a detective. I called him when we were trying to get ahold of you and he was the first on scene at our apartment, so he's the lead detective on this case."

"Jesus."

"Yeah, he's going to do everything he can to keep our business out of all of this. You'll need to give him a statement, but he's going to talk to you *off the record* first," she said, inclining her head toward me and widening her eyes. I nodded in understanding. "I know everyone's eager to see you. Do you feel up to talking to him now?"

"Actually, I'm really tired. Do you think we can hold off for a couple of hours so I can rest?" I asked, leaning back onto the bed.

"Sure, whatever you want. Just let the nurse know when you're ready," she said, touching my hand before she left.

While I was exhausted, my need for alone time had more to do with my inability to control the hurricane of emotions blowing around my mind. It was all too much and the only escape was sleep.

❖

"I'll give him five minutes," I told Jessica. "Don't ask for more than that. It's all I can promise."

She nodded and shot out of the room; no doubt worried I would change my mind. Hearing Grey was out of surgery and stable put me in a generous mood. He might have turned out to be like all the rest, but I had the unfortunate experience of learning firsthand why so many wives gave their cheating husband's chance after chance. Despite how Grey hurt me--how part of my heart burned with hatred for what he'd done--I still loved him.

And there was the little matter of him saving my life and getting himself stabbed in the process.

I could barely breathe. After all those years, I was going to face my father. Although looking around my hospital room, the scenario wasn't anything like I'd imagined it would be.

I supposed that was a step: acknowledging there'd been times over the years when I thought about him, wondering if and when I would see my father again.

I didn't notice it when I saw him in Jessica's yard just a few weeks before. I was too angry to really look at him, but when he walked into my hospital room, it was obvious. He was still handsome, very much the man I remembered from when I was a girl, but his face was drawn, his skin paler, and his walk was slow and deliberate, like a person in pain.

"Hello, sweetheart," he said quietly as he pulled a chair close to my bed. "I'm so glad you're all right and you agreed to see me. It's been far too long."

He reached for my hand, which I snatched away as if his was on fire.

"Sorry," he whispered, reaching inside his jacket and pulling out a plain white envelope.

"I know I made a lot of mistakes all those years ago, unforgivable mistakes, Claudia, but I was so hurt the pain of what happened made me blind."

My eyebrows furrowed. He was hurt? He drove my mother to kill herself and he was hurt? I wanted to scream, to slap him again, but I remembered what Grace said. I needed to let go, but it seemed like an impossible feat.

"I know you don't understand. I should have told you back then, but I--" He put his fist to his lip, fighting back the tears welling in his eyes.

"You should have told me what?"

"Teresa was gone and you two were so close. I didn't want to take any of that away from you, so I kept her secrets."

What the hell was he talking about? We were close and Mom told me everything. She didn't have secrets from me.

"This was a mistake," I said, searching around my bed for the call button.

"Claudia, please, just a few more minutes."

Even after fifteen years of hating him, I couldn't help feeling the pain in his voice. He seemed so fragile compared to the man who'd been a superhero in my eyes for so long. I let out a heavy sigh and folded my hands on my legs.

"Fine."

His expression washed over with relief before he continued.

"In the years before you were born, Teresa would have these mood swings, which were fairly mild as far as I could tell, but I was gone a lot for work. I knew she was lonely, but I was an ambitious young man, and I thought all the money I was making would soothe her in my absence.

I had no idea what she was really going through. When you were a few months old, your mother's mood swings got worse. She would stay in bed for days at a time and then suddenly be on top of the world, taking you all over the city and showing you off to our friends and family. It was easy for her to hide it from me those first couple of years with me traveling so much but when I was promoted, I stayed home a lot more and I could see something was wrong."

I found myself remembering the unpredictable mood swings Mom would have, which were part of Jessica's reasoning in living with Dad after the divorce.

"You were almost three when she was diagnosed with bipolar disorder. She wanted to get better for you. She got treatment, took her medication religiously. You were the center of her life, of our lives. Things got so much easier it was easy for me to forget Teresa's condition. She managed it so well up until she got pregnant with Jessica. The doctors recommend she stay on her medication. That the risks of going off it were greater than the risks to the baby, but your mother wasn't having it. Those months were hard and her symptoms were worse than I'd ever seen, but we got through it.

Jessica came and she started taking her meds again. Things went back to normal; we were happy."

"How could I not have known?" I swiped at my tears.

"She didn't want anyone to know. I don't think I wanted anyone to know. It was easier for me to be able to ignore it. I was selfish. I wanted my perfect family and my perfect life. So much so, I failed to realize just how alone she'd been when we were first married."

He placed the envelope he'd been holding next to me on the bed. My name was on it. I recognized the handwriting and broke down again.

"This came a week after your mother passed away," he said quietly, a single tear falling from his eye. "She wrote me as well, saying it was my decision if and when to give this to you. I think it was her way of trying to make amends with me."

"Why, why would she want to make amends with you? You left us; you cheated on her even though you knew she was sick!"

"I did leave, but I never cheated on your mother."

He ran a weathered hand through his mostly silver head of hair. "I'm sure you remember the summer you tore your ACL right after we got back from Italy and had to have surgery."

I nodded. How could I forget? The trip was amazing, but my injury kicked off what turned into the worst year of my life.

"A few days after, I was filing your paperwork and saw your blood-type. You're A positive."

"So what," I said, not knowing why he was bringing up my blood-type of all things.

"I'm O positive, and so was your mother," he continued as if that was supposed to mean something to me. "And so is your sister."

"What are you saying?" I said as understanding started settling in.

"I'm not your biological father."

It wasn't possible. She would have told me, and my mother never would have cheated on my father. She was so in love with him. She would have followed him over a cliff if he asked her to.

That's why I hated him so much for leaving. She wouldn't live without him. She couldn't.

I shook my head. It couldn't be true. There had to be another explanation. As if he'd read my thoughts, Robert pulled something else out from the inside pocket of his jacket. The piece of paper was worn, as if it'd been handled a million times. He opened it and laid it next to the envelope.

Paternity results.

It was true.

"Walking away was the biggest mistake I've ever made, but my heart was shattered. At the time, I didn't think I could forgive her. I didn't even consider her illness was a factor. The day you were born changed me, made me a father and seeing these results, I felt as though your mother had stolen that from me. It wasn't until later, when it was too late, I realized how wrong I was."

I'd been so blind, so angry at him for so many years when it was Mom who'd betrayed our family.

"Being a father isn't about blood; it's about showing up, about being there. I will never forgive myself for walking away from you and your mother. She was sick and she was lonely, which was my fault. I failed to see how much she needed me. Her mistake was mine as well, but I let my pride push me away from you both. I will take that regret to my grave, very likely sooner rather than later."

"Why, why didn't you tell me right away?" I asked, my voice shook.

"You loved your mother so much. You'd already lost her and I didn't want to take anything else from you."

"You took yourself from me! I loved you, too, and you left me," I whimpered, my sobs starting anew.

My mother's behavior in the months after he left made so much more sense once I knew the truth.

"Oh, sweetheart," he said, standing and taking my hand. "I'm so sorry. I will never forgive myself for walking away from you. I felt so guilty after your mother was gone, and I knew you blamed me. I just couldn't face you at first. You were so angry and it...it was my fault. I should have known what my leaving would do to her, I just didn't, I--"

I pulled him to me and wrapped my arms around my father for the first time in fifteen years. We both cried for all we'd lost.

Chapter 20

When my father left, we promised to see each other the following week. Fifteen years was a long time, and there was a lot of pain between us, but we both needed to let go of the past and move forward. I slipped the envelope he gave me into my bag. The final letter from my mother apparently revealed the identity of my biological father and I imagined a lot more my mom wanted to say to me in her final hours.

I didn't know how to feel about any of it. It was all so complicated and I needed time to process it all. I knew I would open it someday, but I just wasn't ready yet.

The one thing I did feel was shame. After so many years never trusting men, I'd become as untrustworthy as I believed they were. I deserved the pain I felt when Ashley opened that door.

The next morning, after a scan, the doctor cleared me for discharge.

"Knock, knock," Elsa said from the doorway as I slipped on my shoes. Grace had brought me some fresh clothes from home. I was happy to be leaving the hospital, although I wasn't quite sure how I felt going home after what happened there. I found myself wondering if Grey's blood was still on my floor or if there would be police tape across my bedroom door. I shivered and shoved those thoughts to the back of my mind.

"How are you feeling?" she said with a small smile.

"I've been better, but I'm happy to finally be getting out of here. How's Grey?" I said, sitting down on the bed.

"Getting stronger, eager to see you. The doctors practically had to strap him down to keep him from trying to get down here to see you were okay with his own eyes."

"He may not be so concerned when I tell him the truth about everything," I said with a sigh.

Elsa glanced at me sheepishly. "Actually, I kind of already told him, accidentally," she said softly.

"Oh," I said surprised but relieved.

Him already knowing the truth made things simpler for me. I could thank him for saving my life and be on my way. Don't get me wrong, I was grateful. Hell, I even knew I was still in love with him, but the image of Ashley opening his door half naked was in the loop of nightmares that plagued me every time I closed my eyes. Maybe he'd just made a mistake, or maybe he'd decided to work things out with her. Both possibilities were devastating and with everything that happened and what I learned about my parents, I just didn't have the strength to deal with Grey yet.

"He wasn't mad." She leaned down to meet my eyes. "At least not at you. He was a little pissed at me for being so gullible."

She laughed. "Gregory and I had been with the family in the waiting room until they let us go back to see Grey, and I couldn't really tell him about everything in front of his parents.

When Grey was out of surgery and they finally let us see him, I thought he was still unconscious so I took the opportunity to confess everything to Gregory. Turns out Grey was awake, sneaky bastard."

I didn't want to smile, but I couldn't help it. That seemed like something he would do.

"You are going to go see him before you leave, aren't you?" Elsa said, looking at me curiously.

"Yes, the least I can do is thank him for saving my life," I replied seriously.

"That's all you have to say to him?" she asked, sounding irritated. "What's going on, Claudia?" She crossed her arms over her chest.

"I'd rather not talk about it right now." I grabbed my bag to leave.

I'd insisted Jessica and all my friends go home and I would call them when I was ready to be discharged, but I had no intention of doing that. I would stop to see Grey, very briefly, and then take a taxi home, or wherever the hell I was going.

"Claudia, don't do this," she pleaded. "Grey told me how hard you've fought what's between you, and I don't believe for a minute it was just because of your responsibility to me. He loves you. He was willing to die to save you. Don't walk away from that."

Clutching my bag to me, I took a step toward the door. Elsa stepped in front of me.

"Look, I'm sorry, Elsa, but you're wrong about how he feels. If he loves me so much, why did he fuck Ashley just a few hours after he crawled out of my bed?"

"What?" Elsa winced, her forehead tight. "He would never. He can barely stand to look at her when you're not around."

"After I left our lunch, I went straight to his house to tell him everything. I was so fucking excited. Until Ashley greeted me at the door wearing his shirt and nothing else."

"I can't believe it," Elsa said quietly.

"She's here, isn't she?" I asked, knowing she had to be.

"Yes, but the whole family has been here on and off."

"That's just it, Elsa. She's already a part of his family. She fits, and it was so easy for her to slip right back into her place in his life. I will always be the woman who was being paid to try and ruin his brother. It's as simple as that."

"I just don't understand." She sat down on the chair by the door.

"I do. Finally, I understand it all too clearly," I said and walked out the door.

With the way Grey's face lit up when I stepped through the door, for a second, I almost forgot about Ashley. Almost.

"Claudia, thank God. I've been trying to get them to let me come see you all day," he said, grimacing as he struggled to sit up.

"Please, don't try to get up, Grey. I just wanted to stop by to let you know I'm fine and I'm being discharged. And to say thank you for what you did for me. I don't know what would have happened if you didn't show up when you did."

"I'd do anything for you." He patted his bed for me to sit. I took a few steps toward him but stopped short. He looked confused at first.

"About all of that other stuff with Elsa and my brother, I don't care about any of it. It was actually a relief to hear. It explained so much about the way you were. I'm not going to pretend I like or understand the choices you made before, but I love you. I see *you,* not your past."

He smiled up at me, even pale and lying in an unflattering hospital gown, he was still sexy. I was so tempted to take the next step and sit with him, just to feel his warmth one more time. I knew if I did, I'd only end up shattering my heart even more.

"I'm sorry I lied to you, but I didn't have a choice," I said, looking out the window on the side of the room. I couldn't look at him for the next part.

"It doesn't matter now. Just come sit with me," he commanded, but I didn't move.

"I can't stay. I just came to thank you and say good-bye," I said, keeping my gaze on the window as I crossed my arms.

"What the hell is going on, Claudia? Why are you acting like this? Everything has changed: there are no more lies, no secrets. We can be together, really together."

"There will always be lies and secrets, Grey," I responded, sounding a little bitchier than I intended. "Secrets are my job."

"What are you saying?"

"You know what I do for a living, what my real business is?" I said, pushing him.

"But you don't have to keep doing that. You could do anything you want. I can take care of you." He shook his head, his eyebrows furrowed as he tried to understand what I was saying.

"I like my work just the way it is, and I'm not willing to give it up. I have partners who depend on me, I have dreams I need to fulfill, and I need to do that on my own."

"Claudia--"

"I'm sorry, Grey, but a relationship with you or anyone else just isn't what I want or need. Besides, you have enough relationship issues to deal with without me. Work things out with Ashley and forget about me," I said, rushing out, knowing he couldn't follow me. I knew it was irrational and childish to run away without telling him I knew about Ashley, without giving him a chance to explain what happened, but I couldn't see past my pain and I had to get away.

"Claudia! Don't do this!" he yelled after me. I sped down the hallway toward the elevator. When the doors closed, I slumped against the wall and let the tears fall.

Chapter 21

"Has there been any news on Alaina Bennett, Detective Anderson?" I asked, sitting down across from Grace's new boyfriend at the precinct.

"Please, call me Jared. As for Mrs. Bennett, she's still unconscious, but it's looking like she'll pull through. They're keeping her in a chemical coma until the swelling in her brain goes down."

"That bastard," I spat.

"Eric Bennett got what was coming to him thanks to that boyfriend of yours. I hear Mr. Michaels is doing well and will make a full recovery. That's good news."

"It is good news," I replied, not bothering to correct his title usage.

I wasn't going to discuss my love life, or lack thereof, with a virtual stranger even if he was in love with my best friend. I still hadn't shared any of it with my actual friends, something I was dreading.

"You know you didn't need to come all the way down here. We got everything we needed from you in your original statement at the hospital." He leaned back in his chair. "And my contacts in L.A. came through on that end of things," he continued, his voice lower. "As far as LAPD is concerned, you met Eric Bennett when you were working as an investigator for his wife. After the divorce he snapped and went after her and then you. There's no evidence of anything else, at least nothing they can legally get their hands on, and it sounds like Bennett's father wants to keep things as quiet as possible, and he's got some pull, so I suspect they'll be closing the case quickly."

"What about everything here?"

"Given the circumstances, it's a pretty clear case of justifiable homicide. I talked to a friend in the DA's office. They aren't looking to pursue anything against Mr. Michaels. They're backlogged enough as it is. We couldn't keep the press out of it, but so far they're calling him a hero."

"And me?"

"You're the girlfriend he rescued. You met while you were working as his brother's assistant and personal security consultant at G&G. That story lines up with what all the employees witnessed and covers you if any reporters dig into your work as a PI."

I let out a heavy sigh.

"Thank you, Jared, for everything," I said, standing to leave as a cloud of dread hung over me.

I'd gone down to the police station to avoid going home. Grace promised to keep everyone away to give me some time, with the exception of my sister, who'd insisted on helping clean up and get the apartment ready for me to come home. I was more afraid of being in that space than of dealing with questions.

Stepping out into the sunlight outside of the precinct, I slid my shades down over my eyes. It wouldn't be long before Grace's boyfriend let her and my sister know I'd left the hospital. The last thing I wanted was to make them worry about me any more than they already had, so I hailed a cab and hopped in.

"You didn't have to stay, Jess. I'm sure Izzy is driving Shawn crazy by now." I dropped my bag on the bed in the guest room, which would likely become my permanent room.

There was no way I would be able to sleep in my old room. I wasn't even sure if I'd be able to sleep anywhere in the apartment yet. Just walking through the front door made my heart pound in my ears.

Jessica followed me into the room. She'd been watching me closely since I walked into the apartment. Grace had the good sense to give me some space.

"I just needed to make sure you were okay. Seeing you in the hospital like that brought back some bad memories," she said, unzipping my bag.

I couldn't even imagine how hard all of this had been on her. I'd been crushed by losing Mom but Jessica, who was only fourteen at the time, had been the one to find her and ride with her to the hospital when she died.

"I'm okay, Jess, really." I sat down on the bed, patting the spot next to me. She sat and leaned her head on my shoulder like she used to when we were kids.

"How was your talk with Dad? He seemed pretty optimistic after he saw you."

I swallowed hard. "It was okay, a lot of stuff to take in."

"Yeah, I had no idea Mom was sick when I was a kid. Dad only told me a few years ago."

"Why didn't you tell me?" I asked, stroking her hair.

"Like I said, it wasn't my secret to tell."

Tears welled up in my eyes. Before my father left my room, he let me know he'd only told Jessica about Mom's illness and her affair. She didn't know we were half sisters.

"There's something I need to tell you."

She sat up so she could look at me, a hint of fear in her eyes.

"Mom's affair, it was more than that. Dad isn't my biological father."

Her eyes went wide, but she stayed quiet for a minute.

"That's not as bad as I was expecting," she said finally, looking relieved. "You're my sister. Nothing can change that. How do you feel about it?"

"I don't feel about it, not yet at least. I don't think I've really had a chance to process it with everything else that's been happening."

I reached into my bag and pulled out the envelope my father gave me in the hospital.

"Mom sent this to Dad before she died. He never opened it, but she told him it identifies my biological father."

"You haven't opened it yet?" she asked, likely surprised I hadn't jumped on the chance to feel that connection to our mother, even if just for a moment.

"No, I'm not ready to know yet. I think I need to take some time to work on things with the father I have first."

She smiled.

"How sick is he?" He didn't bring it up when we talked and I didn't asked, but I had a feeling it was bad.

"It's pancreatic cancer. We only found out a few weeks ago. That's why he was at the house that day you came by."

"What are his options?" I asked, my eyes stinging with tears that had yet to fall. I didn't know much about cancer, but I'd heard enough to know cancer of the pancreas was tough to beat.

"It's too advanced for surgery, but he's going in for his second round of chemotherapy next week."

The chemo explained why he looked so different in such a short time.

"Have the doctor's given him a prognosis?"

"He had a scan three days ago, the doctor said he...he--"

Seeing the grief well up in my sister refreshed my own tears. I pulled her against my chest, holding her tight as she tried to find her words again.

"Ugh," she said, sitting up and swiping at her face with a tissue she'd pulled from her purse. "I've already cried so much. I really thought I was done for a while. It seems you never run out."

She blew her nose, making a rather unflattering sound. I giggled. She responded by tossing her wet tissue on my lap.

"Gross!" I yelled dramatically and then leaned in and wiped my face on her shirt.

She jumped back, wide-eyed, before we burst out laughing. It felt good to laugh. It was the first time I'd laughed in what felt like a lifetime, although in reality it had only been days. Days in which I'd experienced a lifetime of changes and emotions.

"They estimate he has between twelve and eighteen months," she finally said after we'd settled down. My hand shot up to my mouth. I'd known it was bad, but to hear it quantified was something else altogether.

"Jesus, why am I so fucking stubborn!" I stood and paced the floor. "If I'd just talked to him sooner. God, all those years I wasted."

"Claudia, you did the best you could with what you had. It wasn't his fault, it wasn't your fault, and it wasn't Mom's fault. We're all human, we all make mistakes, and some just take a lot longer to learn from than others. And sometimes it takes a tragedy to open our eyes and our hearts."

"How'd you get so wise, baby sister?"

She smiled up at me. "I just learned how to forgive and that sometimes, no matter how bad things may look, they're not always what they seem."

I nodded. She was right; my dad was proof of that. Gregory Michaels was proof of that. The pictures Elsa received were damning at best, but they proved to be misleading, cards of deception played deliberately. The pictures had been nagging at me since I'd last spoken to Elsa. Suddenly things started making sense.

"I'll be right back, Jess." I grabbed my phone and dialed as I made my way out to the balcony. I closed the door behind me just as my call was answered.

"Hey, Lydia, I need you and Bridget to do me a favor."

Chapter 22

"I'll get a cold towel." I jumped up while Jessica held the trash can for Dad to throw up in.

It'd been two days since his second round of chemo, and the side effects had taken a couple of days to kick in. Jessica insisted he move in with her and Shawn so she could take care of him because he'd divorced Betty, the woman I'd wrongly accused of being his mistress, the year before and was living alone.

I was glad he was getting some extra time with family, especially Izzy, whom Shawn was occupying in the tree house until her grandpa was feeling better.

I'd been staying there since I got out of the hospital, as well.

I'd tried to stay in the apartment but after Jessica left that first day, I had my first panic attack when it started to get dark. I'd completely freaked Grace out, and I didn't want her hanging around worried about me all the time when she had her own shit going on--namely a new man and running our business without me. The time at Jessica's gave me a chance to make up for lost time with my father and was the perfect way to avoid Grey, who'd been discharged. He'd called and texted so often I'd shut off my burner phone, which I'd handed off to Bridget as soon as I was home again. I gave her strict instructions to not give Grey, or any of his family, my other number or my sister's address, which probably wasn't necessary because she and the other girls were beyond pissed when I finally told them what went down with Ashley.

In happier news, according to Elsa, Janet was looking for a real assistant to replace her after everything that had happened. I was relieved she still had time to find a replacement without pushing back her retirement and I wouldn't have to go back to G&G and risk running into Grey. I knew I couldn't avoid him forever, but I needed time to sort out my feelings before I talked to him again.

"Do you want some water, Dad?" I asked, dabbing the towel over his forehead.

"I don't think anything soothes me more than having you call me that again." He patted my free hand.

"I'm sorry it took so long." Tears welled in my eyes. "Besides, I think medical marijuana is probably more effective."

I laughed as the tears broke free.

"Don't think I'm not keeping tabs on his supply," Jessica teased from the bathroom.

"I haven't done that since college," I shot back.

"Don't let her fool you," Dad whispered so she wouldn't hear. "Jessica's the one we need to be watching."

My laughter kicked up another gear. I guessed there were some details of her late teenage years she'd neglected to share with her big sister.

When Dad finally fell asleep, I snuck out my phone to check for news from Lydia on the special assignment I'd given her.

"I think he'll be out for at least a few hours," Jessica said quietly, closing the door to Dad's room. She looked over at me and sighed. "When are you leaving?"

"Something came up at work. I need to head back into the city for the afternoon."

"I thought you were taking a couple of weeks off?"

"I am. It's just one thing I need to take care of, and I want to see Grace and everyone else. You're not the only one who worries about me." I nudged her with my arm.

"I know and I'm glad for it. Speaking of worrying about you, what's going on with you and your personal hero? Are you going to see him, too?"

"I don't know."

"I know you're a private person so I won't push, but I will say this: If the last couple of weeks have taught you anything, let it be to remember how short life is and to grab joy wherever you find it. It might be messy, it might be inconvenient--grab it anyway, and hold on with everything you have."

"Nothing seemed out of the ordinary until I followed her here." Lydia pulled up a photo on her laptop. "I suppose there's a chance she was there to see another resident, but I couldn't find connections to anyone else."

"Holy shit." I scrolled through the photos Lydia had taken. "Why the hell would she be meeting with her?"

"Your guess is as good as mine."

"Is Bridget here?" I asked, grabbing Elsa Michaels's file from the cabinet on the back wall of my office.

"I think so. You want me to get her?"

"Please, I need her to work some of that technological magic of hers to help me figure out if my theory is correct. I think there's more to those pictures Elsa received than a little blackmail."

"Jesus, that is fucked up," Grace said when I filled her in and asked her to come to G&G Components with me.

Bridget found the information I needed in a matter of minutes. My theory was correct; I just didn't know how Gregory and the rest of his family were going to handle the news.

"I know. I already called Janet. She said Gregory is free for the next hour or so, so we need to get down there. I have a feeling it isn't over yet."

Grace scooped up the file, which included Elsa's prenup, G&G financials, and some stock information Bridget printed.

"Let's go. Elsa is meeting us," she said, reading Elsa's confirmation on her phone.

"Good, I'll drive." I pressed the button that would take us down to the garage level.

"Claudia, I didn't think we'd be seeing you so soon. Are you here for work?" Chad Michaels looked me up and down like he always did.

"Some of us have to make a living the old-fashioned way," I replied, walking by him.

"Guess you're in a hurry," he said with a frown, his tone annoyed.

"Something like that." I tossed my hair back over my shoulder as I approached the security desk.

"Way to hide your feelings," Grace teased as soon as we were on the elevator.

"I'm pretty sure he deserves it," I replied when the door closed.

The ride up seemed faster than I remembered. My pulse quickened at the ding signaling our arrival on the executive floor. The floor Grey worked on. I didn't include him when I requested the meeting, but he always had a way of finding me, so I tried to prepare myself for the possibility of seeing him while we were there.

Chapter 23

Walking into Gregory's office, I thought I'd sufficiently prepared myself to see Grey. I was wrong. He looked better than I remembered, which seemed impossible, especially considering he'd couldn't have been out of the hospital for more than a day or two.

"Claudia, it's so good to see you." Gregory pulled me into a hug.

Elsa followed in kind. "You were wrong about Ashley," she whispered before pulling away. She winked at me then turned her gaze to Grey.

I felt as if I might faint with how fast my heart pounded as I turned to him. I was scared of what I would find, but I steeled my nerves and looked into his eyes. The emotions I saw there weren't the anger and hurt I expected. He looked down at me with love and maybe a hint of hope. Elsa obviously told him about Ashley. I'd been wrong. My heart soared and my breath caught as he took my hand, his touch sending a surge through me like a jolt of electricity.

"I've missed you," he whispered, bringing my hand up to his lips.

He placed a soft kiss on the back of my hand and flashed me that sexy smile of his. Suddenly the betrayal I'd felt before seemed like an utter impossibility. How could he look at me like that if he really wanted someone else?

"We know you're busy Gregory," Grace said, interrupting my moment with Grey, which I imagined was fairly awkward for everyone else in the room.

I'd nearly forgotten they were there or why I was even there for those moments when I looked into his eyes. Grace gave me a knowing smile as she passed me a few papers.

"Sorry, you're probably wondering why we called this meeting." I smiled at Grey and took a step away from him. As much as I yearned to ask him what really happened, it would have to wait, at least a little while.

"It was certainly a surprise to get your message," Elsa said. "I'd been trying to get in touch with you."

"Sorry about that. I just needed some time to process everything. Taking it helped me to see what we'd been missing on your case. Gregory, Elsa, what happens if the infidelity clause of your prenup is broken and you get divorced?"

They looked at each other and then me, their expressions confused.

"I'd owe Elsa half of my individual net worth, but I've never cheated on her and we're certainly not getting divorced. Not for your lack of trying," he said with a smirk.

I glanced sideways at Grey; he wasn't amused.

"Sorry," Gregory said, noticing the drop in temperature. "Too soon?"

"Definitely too soon," Grace replied and we all laughed, except Grey, who just smiled.

I supposed the fact I'd told him I wouldn't be giving up the business of Homewrecker Incorporated made Gregory's joke less than amusing, but Elsa talked to him so he knew why I said it.

"So, hypothetically, if that happened would you have enough liquid assets to pay her?"

"Of course not, my net worth includes our home here, a vacation home in Florida and my stake in the company."

"Meaning the only way you could meet the obligation would be to sell nearly half of your shares in G&G, correct?"

He nodded.

"I think Kristen Page was trying to force that outcome for the benefit of her employer, Arrow Components, by seducing you into, or at least convincing Elsa, you were cheating."

"Even if she'd been successful, that wouldn't give Arrow a controlling interest, not with the number of shares Grey, Chad and our parents own."

I gave the papers in my hand to Gregory. His jaw clenched when he realized what he was looking at.

"How did you get this?" he asked, passing the information to Grey.

"My friend Bridget has a talent for digging up things people don't want found."

"Shit, Chad sold his stock to Arrow Components," Grey said.

"Not yet, but it looks as though he's about to," Grace added.

"So my little brother's an idiot and agreed to an offer for his shares without telling us." Gregory sat down. "That still doesn't explain how they knew about our prenup and infidelity clause."

"Yes, it does," Elsa piped in. "Someone told them and it doesn't take much to figure out who."

"Did I miss the memo for a family meeting?" Chad opened the door to Gregory's office without knocking. It was rather fortuitous he'd shown up just then because I was pretty confident he had the answer to his brother's question.

"Chad, your timing couldn't be better," I said, crossing my arms over my chest.

"What the fuck is going on, Chad?" Gregory stalked toward his brother, his brow furrowed. "Why are you selling you shares to Arrow?"

"I-I," Chad stammered, running a hand through his hair before he sighed and slumped down onto the couch at the side of Gregory's office. "I wasn't given much of a choice."

"What does that mean?"

"Someone's blackmailing me."

That wasn't the answer I expected, but it made more sense than my original theory.

"Who's blackmailing you?" Grey asked, regarding his brother carefully.

Chad buried his face in his hands. "Ashley," he whispered.

Gregory and Grey glanced at each other before I handed the photographs Lydia had taken to Gregory.

"She's working with Kristen Page?" Gregory said, seeing the picture of the two women together.

"Yes." Chad finally raised his head. "She knows about something awful I did a long time ago, and she threatened to tell the family if I didn't agree to sell my shares to Arrow once Gregory sold his."

"What did you do?" Gregory sat next to his younger brother, his expression a bit softer than before.

Chad looked at Grey, the look in his eyes nothing short of pained.

"It was a few weeks before Grey and Ashley's wedding. I relapsed and took a cab out to Grey's place looking for him to help me get straightened out, to get sober again before Mom or Dad found out. Grey wasn't home but Ashley was there."

"So it was you. You're the guy she cheated with?" Grey said calmly.

Gregory snapped his head toward his twin, his expression shocked. Elsa, who'd kept the knowledge of Ashley's infidelity to herself at Grey's request, put her hand on Chad's shoulder as she sat on the other side of him.

A tear slid down Chad's cheek.

"I'm so sorry, Grey. I was so fucked up; I don't know how it happened. When I realized what I'd done, I took off and checked myself into rehab. I never told anyone about it, and Ashley swore she wouldn't say anything." Chad's face was wet with tears. "We never talked about it again until a few months ago when she threatened me."

Grey kneeled down in front of Chad. "I don't blame you, bro. Ashley took advantage of you. That girl is a manipulator and your mistake probably saved me from a lifetime of misery."

Grey grabbed Chad's hands as he stood and pulled him into a hug.

"That's why they sent me those pictures of Gregory and Kristen. Ashley knew the details of the prenup since she signed one before," Elsa said, looking to Grace and me.

"And Kristen used threats of releasing those other stories to keep Gregory quiet and feed the suspicion," I added.

"I can't believe I almost married her," Grey said, his voice full of relief.

I couldn't hold it in any longer. I was confident there was a reasonable explanation, but the pain of what I'd believed lingered and I needed to hear from him what really happened.

"Maybe now you can tell me why Ashley was at your house wearing one of your shirts the morning after you stayed with me at my apartment."

"I'd been wondering the same thing myself since Elsa told me what happened," Grey said, stepping closer to me. "I never saw Ashley after the gala until she showed up at dinner at my parents' house. Right before I left there and went to your apartment, she came back and cornered me, begging for a chance to work things out. I told her to go to hell. I had no idea she was ever at my place until right after you ran out of my hospital room. As soon as I knew, I confronted her and she admitted she'd hung on to my spare key all these years. She went over to my house that morning to try talking to me again. When she saw you get out of the car, she staged that little scene to scare you off."

He gripped both of my hands in his. "I would never hurt you like that," he whispered, staring into my eyes.

I didn't bother trying to stop the tears. I didn't want to hide from him or the way I felt about him anymore. My sister was right. He was my joy and I needed to hold on to him with all I had.

"Not to impose on this moment for you two"--Gregory clapped Grey's shoulder--"but Claudia, do you think your friend could help us dig up something to keep Kristen and Arrow from releasing those stories and enforcing the contract Chad signed?"

"If anyone can, it's Bridget, but you should probably ask her yourself. She does work for you after all." I laughed.

"That's who you were talking about? The girl Josh is in love with?" Gregory said, his expression shocked.

"The one and only," I replied with a smile.

"Well shit, I'll have to give Ben a bonus for hiring her, or maybe I should fire him since she was only here to spy on me," he said with a laugh.

Grey inclined his head toward the door and held out his hand for me. I took it and walked out with him.

"I don't want to let you out of my sight. I know we need to talk more, but I need to stay and help Gregory and Chad deal with all this shit," he said as he walked Grace and me to the elevator.

"I can stay and wait for you," I said, smiling up at him. My gaze drifted to his lips.

"I have a feeling it's going to be a while. Can I meet you at your place?"

"I can find somewhere else to be tonight," Grace said with a smile.

"I think he's talking about my other place," I reminded Grace. "But I'd rather go to your place instead?"

"Of course, you can take my key and Vince can drive you."

"I can drive myself, I have my car here, but maybe Vince can take Grace home instead?"

"I can just take a cab," Grace interjected.

"No, take the car. Vince is probably bored of shooting the shit with Bruce downstairs by now," Grey said.

"Okay." Grace nodded.

"Guess it's settled, then." Grey wrapped his arms around my waist. "I'll see you at home later."

I really liked the sound of that.

Chapter 24

I smiled wide when Grey walked through the door into his kitchen where I was waiting with the remnants of my sad attempt at cooking dinner.

"We should probably order some takeout," I said, scrunching my nose as I shrugged.

He laughed, the deep timbre resonating through me as he eyed the plates of slightly burnt pasta.

"Let's talk first," he said, taking my hands and pulling me to him. He cupped the side of my face as I looked up at him. "Why is it so hard for you to trust me? It doesn't matter what either of us do, how much we love each other, if we don't have trust, we'll never truly move forward." He searched my eyes as I considered his question.

"Isn't it hard for you? After what Ashley did?"

"Yes, but I'm not going to let her bullshit keep me from finding my happiness. I won't let it keep me from you. It took me years to move past it, but I have moved past it. Part of what helped me to do that was sharing my pain with you."

I took a deep breath. He was right. I had to let go, to share my past, my pain with the only man who'd even come close to my heart in fifteen years.

"You remember what I told you about my mom?"

"Of course," he replied, stroking my cheek with his thumb.

"When she died, I blamed my father. I thought he left my mom for another woman, a woman he'd been cheating on her with. I spent months trying to console her. She fell into a deep depression for weeks at a time. I was always worried about her, so much so I almost didn't go to college because I was afraid to leave her alone, but as time went on, she seemed to get better and she insisted I go to school. She didn't want me to put my life on hold."

Grey continued to hold me, wiping away the tears that were streaming down my face as I talked. I didn't try to turn away or hide them. I felt safe for the first time in as long as I could remember.

"A month or so after I left for school, my sister found my mom's body. I was so angry. When I finally saw my father again, I attacked him. I called him a killer because he was the reason she wanted to die. He was the reason she left me." A sob escaped me but I kept going. "But that wasn't it, not really. I've never said it out loud before, but I blamed myself. I left her, just like he did." I buried my face in Grey's chest. He held me tight as I cried.

"It wasn't your fault, sweetheart," he whispered against my hair. "None of that was your fault."

"I know," I said when my tears slowed. "And now I know I was wrong about my father, about what happened between them."

Standing in the kitchen with Grey's arms around me, I recounted everything my father shared with me in my hospital room. My mom's affair, the paternity test, the letter, and my father's cancer.

He listened in silence until I'd told him all of it.

"How do you feel now?" He looked down at me and my heart melted when I saw the redness in his eyes. He'd cried with me, truly shared my pain.

"Better than I have in a really, really long time."

He placed a gentle kiss on my lips. "Me, too."

"I don't want to ruin this moment," I said, taking a step back as I wrung my hands together. "But I want everything out on the table."

Grey's lips tightened.

"Do you want to know about my work, about Homewrecker Incorporated? I'll tell you anything you want to know."

He laughed and I felt a wash of relief. "You guys seriously called it that?"

"It started out as a joke but somehow it stuck. Officially, the business was Mason, Dawson, & Associates, LLP Private Investigators, but that isn't exactly sexy."

"All I need to know is you're done with it, at least the part about seducing other men," he said, stalking toward me. He put his hands on the wall behind me, boxing me in as he stared down at me, his eyes dark with lust. It was quite a shift in mood, but I was more than ready to roll with it.

"Because while I'm a pretty understanding and supportive guy," he whispered against my ear before I could respond. "If you're mine, if this"--he slipped one hand between my thighs--"is mine, I won't share."

I melted under his touch, my body liquid against the wall while he moved his hand back and forth between my legs.

"Yes, I'm done with it," I breathed out, desperate for more.

"Then say it," he commanded.

I pried my eyes open to look at him. "Say what?"

"Say you're mine."

He pressed his hand harder against my jeans and I let out a breathy moan.

"I'm yours, Grey. Only yours," I whispered.

Those simple words snapped the tether of his restraint. He crushed his full lips against mine and gripped the underside of my thighs, hoisting me up. He groaned but didn't stop. We spun around and my ass connected with the cold marble of the countertop.

His kiss was rough--possessive. I'd never been a woman who could be possessed. I could never give up the control, but with him it was as easy as breathing.

Grey broke the kiss long enough to pull my tank top up over my head, and then his lips were back on mine as his soft tongue dipped into my mouth and he fumbled with the clasp of my bra. When the red satiny material fell away, Grey moved back, his eyes hooded as he admired my ample curves. He dipped his head, his large hands cupping my breasts as he sucked my nipple between his teeth. I threw my head back as he rolled his skillful tongue around the sensitive flesh. The sensation traveled straight down between my thighs. He worked the same magic on the other nipple before our lips met again.

I pulled his shirt free from the waist of his pants and slowly undid the first couple of buttons while he unzipped my pants. He started to lift me to pull my pants off.

"Let me." I pushed him back gently.

I'd gotten lost in the moment when he lifted me earlier, forgetting his body was still healing. I slipped down off the counter and slid my jeans down to the floor. Stepping out of them, I grabbed his shirt and pulled him toward me. I stared up into his golden hazel eyes as I finished with the buttons and pushed the shirt off his shoulders. Grabbing the hem of his undershirt, I lifted it up as he raised his arms.

Seeing his wound for the first time, I cringed. The laceration on the side of his abdomen wasn't wide. There were probably ten stitches, but I knew it was deep. I traced my fingertips around the area, which was purple and yellow with bruising.

"When do these come out?" I looked up at his face.

"They were supposed to come out today," he replied. "But I got busy and had to cancel my appointment," he said with a smirk.

I leaned down and pressed a gentle kiss over the injury. Standing up straight again, I felt as if I might burst. I placed my palms on the side of his face, gazing into his eyes as they swam with emotions matching my own.

"I love you, Grey," I whispered, pulling him to me.

His pupils dilated and a slow smile spread across his face.

This time our kiss was sweet and full of love.

"I've loved you since I watched you run and hide from me in the lobby bathroom," he announced, trying to contain his laughter.

"Oh my God, you saw me!" I said, my face flushing and my eyes widening at the revelation.

"I can't believe you didn't say anything!"

"It would have scared you away. I did a pretty good job of that without telling you," he said, his tone grew more serious as his gaze drifted to my mouth.

I bit my lip and one corner of his mouth turned up as he leaned down and took my bottom lip between his teeth. I ran my tongue along his top lip. He moaned deep in his throat and released my bottom lip before his tongue met mine.

He hooked his thumbs inside the waist of my red panties and dropped to his knees, slipping them down as he peppered my torso with kisses. When I stepped out of them, he ran his tongue up from the inside of my knee, stopping just centimeters from where my body ached for him.

"I love the way you taste," he whispered, looking up at me with those beautiful eyes.

I moaned in anticipation and he flashed a crooked grin, obviously pleased with the way his words affected me. Using his fingertips, he spread my swollen lips and licked slow circles around my clit.

I cried out as my legs trembled beneath me. He slid his tongue down between my wet lips and then moved away to stand. The loss of his mouth was acute.

"Can you taste how sweet you are?" he asked, kissing me and slipping his tongue into my mouth.

I sucked on it and smiled lazily.

"Yes, I like tasting myself on your lips," I whispered before he kissed me again.

He ran his hands through my long waves, fisting it, before he tilted my head back to gain access to the sensitive skin on my neck. I moaned as he nipped and sucked his way up to my ear before he released my hair and kissed my mouth again. He stepped away, gazing into my eyes as he undid his pants. The look he gave me was intense, full of need. My gaze drifted down to his hands as they moved the zipper down. His erection strained against the charcoal material. I licked my lips in anticipation as he moved his pants and underwear down, releasing his hard cock from its confinement.

Swallowing hard, I put my hands over his, dropping to my knees as I took over the task of undressing him completely. I flicked my tongue over the swollen crown, tasting the salty sweetness of his arousal. He growled, stepping out of his pants before I took the head of his cock into my mouth. I rolled my tongue around the silky hard skin and then flicked it along the underside as I took in as much of his length as I could handle.

"I need to be inside you." He grabbed my biceps to pull me upward.

"I wasn't done." I pouted.

He huffed and picked up his pants, rifling through the pockets for the condom he ripped open. I watched with rapt attention as he slid the material over his impressive length before he grabbed my face and kissed me hard, backing me up against the counter.

"Turn around," he commanded, his eyes hooded.

Obeying the command, I leaned over the counter. My hard nipples brushed against the cold surface as Grey gripped my hips. His erection pressed against my wet lips, spreading them apart as Grey slowly pushed inside me.

"Oh. My. God." I moaned as he filled me completely, his cock seeming to touch places inside me I'd never felt.

He planted wet kisses all over my back as he thrust back and forth, slowly at first, but gaining momentum with each motion. My orgasm barreled down on me like a freight train. My legs shook as the fire exploded low in my belly and spread like lava through my veins.

"I can't stop, you feel so--aah fuck, Claudia, you're going to make me come," Grey growled with one last hard thrust as my pussy clenched around his cock.

He collapsed against my back, both of us heaving with each breath. When my heart finally slowed a little, he lifted up, slipping his still erect cock from inside me. He gripped my arm and pulled me toward him, kissing my lips slowly and thoroughly.

"I'm not finished with you yet," he whispered definitively, gripping my hand and leading me toward his bedroom on my still trembling legs.

Chapter 25

Six months later

"I still can't fucking believe this." Lydia gripped my hand to look at the ring again. "It's the end of an era, but who can blame you with that sexy husband of yours? Too bad he's not a triplet," she teased.

"Right, like you're going to settle down?"

"Good point, although I would have said the same thing about you six months ago," she replied.

Touché.

I smiled at Grey across the room where he was talking to his mother. It seemed as though I'd known him my whole life, not just a few months. She noticed the change in his expression and turned my way giving me a little wave and a smile. It was amazing how easily his entire family welcomed me. It was as if I'd always belonged there.

In the short time since my father revealed the truth about my mother and me, we'd managed to become close again. So much so I wanted to be sure he had the opportunity to walk me down the aisle. Grey certainly didn't have any objections to the speedy wedding. He'd proposed to me on the two month anniversary of the day we met.

"I just got confirmation the anonymous endowment to the Adam Dawson Foundation was just received," Elsa announced, drawing the attention of everyone in Carter and Bethany's family room, before giving Grace, who had tears running down her face, a warm hug.

"That's all thanks to you and Bridget," I said, nudging Lydia proudly. "That *anonymous* donor wouldn't have felt nearly as generous without the information you and Bridget found for Gregory."

Not only had they found enough dirt to make Kristen Page and Arrow cease their attempts to takeover G&G and prevent them from releasing stories about Elsa and Gregory to the media, they'd acquired enough to make them realize a few years of generous philanthropic ventures were in their best interests.

I noticed Grace talking to Gina, no doubt about the formal event they were planning to roll out the new charity. Jared was behind her, beaming with pride. The two of them were virtually inseparable since the gala all those months ago. I was thrilled for her, standing there with everything she'd always dreamed of and worked so hard for. I didn't know anyone more deserving of happiness than my best friend.

"We can't take all the credit. It was Elsa's idea to funnel most of those donations to Grace's foundation, and you're the one who told her about Grace's dream," Lydia said, sounding a little sad. "Work just isn't going to be the same without you two."

"But Davis, Hall & Associates has a nice ring to it," I replied, reciting one of the possibilities for the business's new name now Lydia and Bridget were the sole owners. Grace would be running the foundation named for her brother full-time with a little guidance from Elsa.

"This little impromptu celebration of yours really came together." Gregory came up and put a brotherly arm around my shoulder.

"I was just talking with Scott and Paula." He nodded in the direction of Ashley Slade's parents.

"It seems Ashley left for an ashram in India two days ago. She claims to be on a path of self-discovery."

He shook his head, laughing at the thought. I couldn't help joining in as I pictured Ashley giving up her designer shoes and couture for bare feet and baggy clothes. We'd only seen her occasionally over the months, but as was the way of my new family, she was still welcome at most family gatherings. I suspected mainly for the benefit of her parents whom I was told apologized profusely for their oldest child's poor judgment. I wasn't entirely sure they'd truly forgiven her, but everyone put on a good show anyway.

Elsa caught Gregory's eye, a hand resting gently on her barely noticeable new belly. He strode over to her, placing his hand over hers as he kissed her forehead. They looked happier than ever. A few months before I would have never considered having children, but seeing the contentment in Elsa, the joyful little smiles, the subconscious touching of her belly, I started to wonder.

As if he'd been reading my mind, Grey appeared behind me, wrapping his strong arms around my waist.

"I wouldn't mind seeing you like that, Mrs. Michaels."

I turned my head back and placed a small peck on his lips.

"We'll see," I replied with a sly smile.

Epilogue

Eighteen months later

"Are you ready?" Grey took my hand to help me out of the car.

I'd gotten far less graceful once I hit the second trimester, but he still looked down at me as though I was the most elegant woman on the planet.

"I think so." I rested my other hand on my belly as I looked up the walkway to the house. "Oh."

I stopped, bending over a little.

"What's wrong? Are you in pain?" Grey kneeled down to see my face.

I laughed, seeing the fear in him. With each passing day, he grew more and more anxious.

"No, Grey. Your daughter just kicked me in the bladder, that's all."

It seems our little vacation to Tuscany, and the copious amounts of wine and good food, helped Grey to finally persuade me to have a baby. Although, I think my mind was made up long before we left.

Relief washed over him.

"She's going to give her cousin Liam a run for his money," he said, rubbing my tummy.

Elsa sent us a video of Liam that morning taking his first steps toward the stuffed soccer ball we'd given him for his birthday. Because Gregory and Grey both played, it seemed an appropriate gift.

"I'm guessing both of them will," I said as baby girl number two joined in the fun with a jab to my ribs.

It was still hard to fathom there were two of them in there, except for the fact I was already huge at just six months.

My dad hung on just long enough to hear the good news, but he would never meet his two new granddaughters--a thought that brought tears to my eyes. It'd been nearly three months since he passed, and I finally felt ready to open Mom's letter.

I'd read it every day since, those last precious words meant just for me from the woman I loved more than anyone in the world. Those words are private, a little piece of her I keep all to myself, even from the man who owns my heart, but he doesn't seem to mind.

They'd found their way to me when I needed them most, and although I wasn't particularly religious, I'd known deep in my soul she'd made sure of that somehow. She hadn't been perfect, she had her secrets and had made a lot of mistakes, but she did the best she could with what she had. Despite her shortcomings, she got one thing exceptionally right, one thing I hoped I did as well for my daughters. Not a single day went by with her that I didn't know with absolute certainty I was loved.

"Do I look all right?" I asked Grey, standing on the front porch, my heart pounding as I prepared to meet my biological father for the first time.

I didn't know what to expect, if he would be happy to meet me or throw us off his porch, but I needed to know, to see him at least once.

"You look beautiful," he said, tipping up my chin and planting a soft kiss on my lips.

The anxiety I felt suddenly melted away. I smiled up at him, wondering how I could have possibly gotten so lucky. After all those years of me believing love wasn't possible, that men couldn't be trusted, Grey had shown me a love that changed my opinion, that changed me, forever.

No matter what was waiting on the other side of that door, I knew it would be okay because Grey was, and always would be, by my side.

The End

Join my mailing list to stay up to date on new releases, sales, giveaways, and more at http://eepurl.com/7Ydin

Titles from S. Simone Chavous

Contemporary Romance

Homewrecker Incorporated

Paranormal Romance

The Fate Series:
Choices of Fate - Book 1
Redemption of Fate - Book 2
Absolution of Fate - Book 3
The Complete Fate Series Box Set

For more information on titles by S. Simone Chavous please visit

www.ssimonechavous.com

Acknowledgements

Where to even start, there are so many people I want to thank for helping me along this crazy journey!

Brian, none of this would be possible without your love and support. Thank you for letting me follow my dreams. I love you more than words can say.

Cami and Izzy, you aren't old enough to read this book, but you are what motivates me everyday.

Danielle Allen and Kendall Grey, the amazing writing retreat you put together helped me find my passion again. I can't thank you both enough for that gift. You embody the concept of paying it forward.

Danielle, again, you have become one of my dearest friends and I'm so grateful to have met you. Your support and encouragement mean the world to me.

Amy, Danielle (yet again ;)), Josie, Melissa, Niquel, and Zolie....twerk on my friends!

Lindee Robinson, thank you for the beautiful photographs and cover. Michael Door and Denise Emilia, it wouldn't be beautiful without the two of you on it.

Lauren Schmelz, you're the best and you helped me find the best in my story. I look forward to working with you for years to come.

And finally, all my author friends from Author BFFs, you've been a shoulder to cry on, a sounding board, pretty much anything I needed when I needed it. I'm so happy to be a part of such an awesome group.

About the Author

S. Simone Chavous is contemporary and paranormal romance author. Her debut trilogy, The Fate Series, has been a best seller in the paranormal romance category. When she isn't writing, she enjoys reading, sketching, cooking, and spending time with family. She lives in northern Indiana with her boyfriend, two beautiful daughters, and their rambunctious vizsla.

To learn more about S. Simone, please visit: www.ssimonechavous.com

or connect with her on Facebook at
www.facebook.com/ssimonechavous